"You're not very modest, are you?"

She drew her silver cigarette case from her shoulder bag and plucked out a Gitanes. "Why should I be a hypocrite about the obvious?" Her cool fabricated smile chastised them both. "If you think looks don't matter in men as well as women, then you've been out of touch with the real world, messieurs."

When David leaned over to light her cigarette, she saw a faint tic of barely restrained amusement at the corners of his mouth. What did he think about her? Did he find her beautiful?

Henri hunched forward over his tankard of stout, absorbed by her statement. "Then will you also admit candidly that beauty bestows power to women— n'est-ce pas?"

Slowly, she exhaled. "Most certainly, but most women haven't the foggiest notion of what to do with it."

"But you do?" David asked, more as a statement than a question.

"Certainly, because I manipulate the manipulators."

Also by Parris Afton Bonds
Published by Fawcett Books:

BLUE BAYOU
LAVENDER BLUE
MOOD INDIGO
DEEP PURPLE

SNOW
AND
ICE

Parris Afton Bonds

FAWCETT GOLD MEDAL • NEW YORK

Library of Congress Catalog Card Number: 86-91067

ISBN 9780345465771

The author gratefully acknowledges use of *Great Cases
of Interpol*, selected by the editors of *Reader's Digest*
and published by Reader's Digest Association, copyright
© 1982.

146689836

FOR CHUCK AND MAGGIE NEIGHBORS
With gratitude to a great agent team

*WITH SPECIAL THANKS TO
DEPUTY CHIEF STEVE LASATER
AND LIEUTENANT JIM MURPHY*
*Your law enforcement classes were
worth their weight in looted gold.*

1

In his long black ghetto frock coat, curly *payiss* earlocks springing out from beneath a broadbrim black beaver hat, he could have been the wizard of an arcane cult. Perhaps he was.

On this particularly blustery, gray morning, the Hasid was striding briskly toward the five acres of city blocks that made up the diamond capital of the world. Some distance from Antwerp's Renaissance cultural center, gothic mansions, and majestic palaces, Beurs voor Diamanthandel was little more than just another gloomy inner-city train stop.

With a pleased expression despite the weather, the Jew bowed forward and braced himself against the wind as he moved along the sidewalks. His Hasidic sect, the largest community of Orthodox Jews in Europe, had kept alive in Antwerp the mysticism and ecstatic worship that had embellished their observance of rigidly orthodox ritual law since the eighteenth century *shtetls* of their native Poland and Russia.

The man in the black coat strolled now as he entered Lange Leemstraat, where most of the diamond dealers were congregated. In that one tiny district of Antwerp worked diamond cutters, polishers, and dealers whose reputations were rooted in more than five hundred years of diamond history. They handled some seventy percent of the world's cut stones, a market controlled almost entirely by Orthodox Jews. For them, loose diamonds were as common a currency as folding money. Their diamonds voyaged in vest pockets.

The Hasid surveyed the north-facing shops and cleaving rooms, which belonged to the better dealers who had discovered that the wan Flemish light heightened the brilliance of their stones. The same incandescent glow was found in the paintings of Peter Paul Rubens and Vermeer. There was nothing about the old shops, darkened with centuries of soot, to indicate the fabulous wealth that was stored within.

The Hasid did not enter any of the select shops. Instead, he walked past the stone maidens on the facades of the Diamond Club and Diamond Bourse, the inner sanctums of global diamond trading. He crossed the railroad track to the large synagogue, busy at that hour of the morning.

An involved, esoteric Talmudic discussion was taking place in Yiddish in a corner of the synagogue. Unobtrusively, he introduced himself to those present as Judah Shapiro and was welcomed by the group. For a while, he sat quietly, listening as the various positions were argued.

Then, with humility and courtesy, he expressed a few of his own opinions, and soon others began to listen intently to what he had to say. The leaders of the discussion were impressed. Here was a man of erudition, a religious man and a true scholar of the Talmud. By tea time, he had met with Josef Tabinowitz, the synagogue cantor, who discovered to his delight that Judah Shapiro was also from Poland.

Over steaming glasses of tea, Judah Shapiro said in Polish, "Incidentally, I happen to have a few diamonds with me I'd like to sell. Can you introduce me to a reputable dealer?"

"It would be my pleasure," the cantor replied readily. He mentioned several names, describing where the experts could be located, and even proffered his own card to be shown as an introduction.

Judah Shapiro returned to one of the shops he had surveyed earlier, that of one of the recommended diamond dealers, Sol Faberstein, who was a corpulent man with a sly look. Now in fluent Flemish, the language of northern Belgium, Judah began politely, "My friend, Josef Tabinowitz, gave me your name over tea today. I have two diamonds I would like to sell—and, if possible, I would like to purchase a bracelet for my daughter, if I can find the right one."

"We will find you the perfect bracelet, I assure you, my friend."

Almost reverently, the dealer placed Judah's diamonds on a double sheet of slightly waxed and shiny paper that heightened the sparkle of the stones. Faberstein screwed in his loupe to inspect the crystalline hearts of the two diamonds. His hand revealed the stock-in-trade jeweler's tremor.

"This brilliant is about, I would say, two-point-seven-five carats. That one less, perhaps two-point-three-four carats."

"I know little about diamonds," Judah said. "What do you think they are worth?"

Faberstein had a keen eye for precious gems. The cut stones, he saw, were of the highest color "D" quality and were an Antwerp cut, the standard of highest craftsmanship. Furthermore, they were loupe-clean, or flawless, representing the best grade for quality.

The diamonds themselves, however, had no fixed value. With gold, a dealer simply weighed the metal and checked the current fixed price. But, ahh, a diamond could be valued differently by different dealers. Its beauty really was in the eye of the beholder.

"For the two of them—roughly a quarter of a million Belgian francs." The sum was far below market value, but in every community there were always the unscrupulous. The underworld of diamonds was populated by men conducting shady transactions.

"That seems fair enough," Judah said.

"That is more cash, though, than I have with me," the dealer admitted reluctantly. "Would you be able to return tomorrow?"

"I will leave the diamonds with you until tomorrow and take whatever you wish to give me as a deposit," Judah said. "After all, as men of God, we can trust each other, eh?"

In this market there were no legally binding contracts, no receipts. Trust was the only currency. Millions were exchanged between dealers on simple handshakes and the benediction *Mazel und Baruch*— luck and blessing—a Yiddish phrase that was standard whether you were Jewish or Japanese. It signified a contract that would stand up in Belgian court, if necessary.

"Exactly, my friend," Faberstein said, avidly folding the paper in a special way several times, the customary practice. "You should buy a diamond from someone you can trust and live with it and enjoy it and grow old with it, as if it were a woman you loved."

He withdrew a ballpoint from a cannister of pens and pencils and carefully marked the weight of the stones, in carats, on one corner and slid the folded package inside an envelope and folded it again. The diamond business was a secret world, its deals conducted in cash or exchanges of one kind or another, often hidden from tax collectors and law enforcement agencies.

Before Faberstein could mark the sum that had been agreed upon on the envelope, Judah's elbow brushed the cannister of pens, knocking it over. In the twinkling of a moment it took for the jeweler to collect the pens scattered on the floor at his feet, a duplicate of the envelope was substituted.

The new envelope was then initialed by both Judah and the unsuspecting dealer and thereupon sealed with wax. A straightforward and foolproof method.

Judah accepted the 125,000 Belgian francs the dealer pressed on him. "I will return tomorrow," Judah said and added benignly, *"Mazel und Baruch."*

After the customary twenty-four hours passed, Faberstein became suspicious and had the temerity to open the envelope left by Judah, only to discover the paste stones.

2

City of Gold.

Shrewd-eyed representatives of illustrious jewelry firms in Beverly Hills, Tokyo, and London made yearly trips to scrutinize, deliberate over, and finally order fine pieces of goldsmithing from this tiny terraced town.

Trusted ambassadors of Bolivian tin, cocaine kings, Saudi sheikhs, and Greek shipping magnates cruised along its narrow streets in bulletproof limousines, bearing well-protected pouches of rare gems that goldsmiths in that ultrarich village would handcraft into fabulous million-dollar sets.

Tucked away in the northwestern corner of Italy, a hundred kilometers south of Milano, Valenza Po was home not only to 7,000 jewelers, accounting for ninety percent of its work force, but also to millions of dollars worth of precious metals and gems—all safely protected by invisible security systems that rebuffed burglars and terrorists alike.

Beating the complex security systems was a challenge to the Austrian, who had scouted Valenza for three days as a tourist—enjoying its sienna mountains, blue skies, mild late winter air, and its ancient piazza with darting compact cars.

6

His peripheral attention, however, was riveted on the factories and shops that crowded the winding cobblestone alleys. The factories ranged in size from a new industrial complex on Valenza's outskirts that accommodated thirty-four jewelry companies to the basements of private homes. Each home was a tiny laboratory, where goldworking was done entirely by hand, as an art form, relying on inspired individuality rather than the machine.

The Austrian settled on the renowned firm of Pierluigi. A company that made everything from jewel-encrusted cufflinks to million-dollar necklaces. In reality, the firm was a stronghold situated behind iron-studded gates as thick as an oak tree and covered by a series of alarm-rigged doors in the spacious neoclassical building.

Over cups of steaming cappuccino in one of the piazza's *trattorias*, a Pierluigi salesmen bragged innocently to the thief, "Would you believe, our master craftsman is currently fashioning a purse for a Saudi Arabian woman. Its embryo of gold, *mio amico*, is covered with rubies, diamonds, and emeralds, no less!"

Perhaps the image of the purse captured the Austrian's fancy and caused him finally to select the firm of Pierluigi as his target. Pierluigi himself was a revered citizen of Valenza, having moved there more than forty years earlier from Milano, after Mussolini's government, of which he had been a supporter, had been toppled.

For an entire afternoon, the Austrian sat in the *trattoria*—devising and discarding various means of accomplishing his goal. At last, lingering over his fourth cup of cappuccino, he put into action the plan he had settled on. A simple stroll around the block-square building revealed a plaque on one iron gate, warning that the firm was protected by the Pozzi Security Company.

The Austrian walked several more blocks to the telephone company. Its gloomy lobby housed directories of the major Italian cities. Operating on logic, he withdrew, first, the directory for Milano, the nearest big city. He was rewarded with the name and address of Pozzi Security Company.

That evening, he caught the train to Milano and checked into a Cigahotel, not far from the Stazione Centrale, a monumental heap that resembled a melting iceberg. By nine the next morning, he was on Via Cordusio, across from Pozzi Security. He observed that the men operating the installation and maintenance trucks wore ordinary khaki uniforms with the company's name monogrammed over one pocket and the wearer's name over the other.

He spent the rest of the afternoon browsing through Milano's shops, hunting for a coverall similar to the Pozzi uniforms. That was the only difficult part. When he found one, he bought it, along with a pair of workman's gloves. He took the coverall to a nearby laundry, which unquestioningly monogrammed the names he requested. Next, he visited a hole-in-the-wall printing firm in a shabby district.

The following morning, he was once again waiting across from Pozzi Security. A chilly wind seeped through the uniform he wore, and he chafed his arms as he paced a few feet in either direction. When an installation truck wheeled away from the company's loading dock into the street, he loped after it, shouting for the driver to wait.

As the truck slowed, he swung through its open passenger-side door. "I am . . ." he panted, ". . . a new hand. They told me to go with you."

During the afternoon, as the truck made the circuit of private homes and companies Pozzi protected, the Austrian joked amiably with the two other men aboard.

The driver discovered that like him, the new hand was from southern Italy. "Naples, I bet," the driver said.

"How did you know?" the new man asked.

"Your accent gives you away."

By the end of the work day, the three employees had fallen into a camaraderie that eventually descended into braggadocio, bawdy jokes, sexual reminiscences—and even debates about the always-popular subject of the Roman Catholic Church.

"Whatever it has been doing wrong," the new hand said, with an adherent's smug tone of pride, "it has been doing it successfully for two thousand years."

By the end of the work day, the new hand knew that most of the firms serviced by Pozzi used a silent security alarm—a system that once set off triggered a tape programmed directly into the firm's own telephone trunk. The pretaped calls then went out to both the local police and Pozzi on ninety-second intervals, informing them of a break-in.

When the truck returned to Pozzi's, the new hand simply melted into the flow of other employees leaving work. Next morning, he stopped again at the printer's and then visited a record shop.

By noon, garbed in a brown pin-striped business suit and a dapper beige Borsalino hat, he was on the train back to Valenza. That afternoon, he presented his newly printed Pozzi business card at the offices of Pierluigi.

"I need to perform a follow-up check on our alarm system," he told the young girl behind the reception desk.

"Of course, *signore*," she said, responding to his expression, a smile that was friendly, assured, and not in any way sexually suggestive.

As she led the way, his accomplished glance took in all that he passed—jewelers in white coats hunched over counters, trays of gold inventory stacked at their sides;

depositories below each laboratory where machines re-
trieved as much gold dust as possible; displays and jewelry cases; a vacuumlike device around a doorway that
sucked in any gold dust that clung to clothing.

The telephone trunk equipment was located in a dimly
lit cellar. Exchanging the tapes was simple enough. Less
than five minutes later, he was tipping the brim of his stylish
hat to the receptionist on his way out the door.

At three o'clock in the morning of the fifth day following his first arrival in Valenza, he scaled the iron-
spiked fence, a feat difficult even for a man in his
superb physical condition. A series of toughened steel
picklocks gathered together in a ring escorted him past
the various locked doors into the rooms holding display
cases and inventory trays.

The moment he entered, a heat sensor mounted in a
small box in one corner picked up the warmth of his
body in the invisibly projected grid area, activating a
silent alarm device at once.

He ignored the fabulously handcrafted jewelry,
choosing instead bars of pure gold, which were scheduled to be mixed with alloys to produce either eighteen-
or fourteen-karat gold. The pure gold had been
purchased in gram quantities from *bancos* run by the
government and sold only to bona fide jewelers.

Calmly, he filled a carryall with them and sauntered
out of the building to scale once more the iron-spiked
fence. All the while, the telephone was repeatedly
screaming alarms—the tape programmed to reach nonexistent numbers.

3

March 29th

Money meant you had enemies in power. Money meant shopping on the boutique-lined Via della Spiga. Money meant a post office box number in Luxembourg. In the opulent pink-marbled gambling casino of Campione, Italy, a former woodcarvers' village and smugglers' lair, money meant high tension converted to discreet entertainment.

The *privée* sanctum of the casino was a petite leather-lined chamber where only internationally known high rollers or those with impeccable connections were admitted. Behind the gilded doors of this exclusive domain, the black-tie and fur-clad guests gambled with solid gold and sterling silver *jetons*. Hushed conversations in assorted languages provided a steady undercurrent of tension to the impartial rattle of the roulette ball, the muted click of ivory dice, and the dry riffle of playing cards at the *chemin de fer* table.

"Place your bets," a croupier announced in Italian, Swiss, German, and French.

Beneath the flattering light of a heavy crystal chandelier, Diana Dickinson spread 40,000 francs worth of *jetons* in the form of a cross on the green baize roulette table. Rubies and sapphires on her fingers glittered in the chandelier's prismatic glow.

She was the twenty-nine-year-old daughter of an American financier and a French countess. To the other big-spending *habitués* at the table she was Diana De Revillon, the name she preferred.

Those at the casino that night were the mega-carat people of the world's society gossip columns: an Indian maharajah; a paunchy Swedish film director; the Begum Aga Khan; an Italian marchioness whose beauty had faded ten years earlier; and Lady Anne Spalding-Hyer, the *soignée* wife of a Birmingham small-arms magnate. In this era of petrodollars and supersonic aircraft, business tycoons and Eastern princesses had replaced the once legendary film stars as favored clients of the superluxury casinos.

The Indian, Murad Murarani, never took his enormous dark eyes off Diana. He was fascinated with her tawny lissome beauty and for more than a month had been pursuing her with an unrelenting fervor that threatened to make her life even more complicated.

The grim-faced men, the young lovelies, and the older once-lovelies who nervously tightened mink and satin stoles about their shoulders watched the silver ball bounce capriciously from slot to slot on the wheel. When it settled into one slot, Diana's *jetons* were doubled as if by magic. The other four players sighed or grunted in defeat as they watched the deadpan croupier, dressed in funereal black, rake in their *jetons* like faded autumn leaves.

Anne Spalding-Hyer frowned prettily and said, "Blast it all, I've lost my last frigging chip, Di."

Diana raked her winnings into her silver sequined bag. "Shall we call it a night, then?" Like Anne, Diana's low, modulated voice had a British accent, though it was somewhat less exaggerated and acquired at the knee of her English nanny.

Anne rose gracefully from her chair. "One more late night and I'll have Louis Vuitton trunks under my eyes."

As Diana was crediting her *jetons* against her Diners Club card, Murad Murarani came up behind her. "*Ma chérie*, I'm having an *après ski* for some friends tomorrow at my chalet. A cozy dinner around the fireplace. I think you know some of the guests—Lars Thurston, for one. He seems to remember you from somewhere."

With a meticulously engineered Mona Lisa smile, Diana turned and looked up at the Indian prince. "Switzerland's former ambassador to Denmark? Yes, I spent a holiday with his daughter at their home outside Copenhagen."

Murad's velvet-brown eyes warmed with triumph. "Then he will be delighted to see you." He looked at Anne. "I would be honored if you would come, also."

Anne, her mascaraed eyes glittering vivaciously, glanced at Diana. "It is up to Diana. I am her house guest for the week."

Diana shrugged. "Let me see how I feel tomorrow, Murad."

Above the sweep of mustache, his expressive eyes flashed dejection at her tentative reply, so as compensation, she allowed him to help her into her hooded Russian lynx and Anne into her sable.

Outside the canopied entrance, the incredibly rude and pushy paparazzi jostled for position. Their camera strobes turned night into day for several harassing moments. When Diana's 1957 coral-sand Thunderbird was delivered from a parking lot overflowing with luxury cars, Murad bestowed a chivalrous departing kiss on the backs of both her and Anne's hands.

"Until tomorrow then," he said seductively. "Meanwhile, I shall recite all the prayers in the *Veda* in hope of seeing you both.''

Inside the car, Anne said, ''Not like you at all, Diana, to hedge on a good time—especially considering the prince's delightfully sinful reputation.''

Murad belonged to one of the most decadent groups society had seen since England's Regency period, which made him provocative even to the most righteous of women. He was very well aware that no nice girl ever dreamed of doing the things every nice girl dreamed of doing.

''All this winter partying has left me badly out of shape,'' she told Anne. ''I was planning to take a ballet class tomorrow.''

She steered her classic convertible onto the Lake Lugano causeway that led across the Italian border back into Switzerland and the resort suburb of Paradiso. The heater's welcome warmth quickly filled the Thunderbird. Deny it though she may, she had a preference for American things, like American clothes designers—and, especially, the T-Bird her father had given her. That she never parted with.

''You—out of shape?'' Anne laughed brittlely. ''Between skiing and your stringent ballet workouts, you've developed that body to a fine tone. Disgusting.'' Anne cupped her hands under her fur-clad breasts and jiggled them. ''We're the same age, but all my body has to show for it are implants and the great suck-off.''

Diana chuckled. ''That liposuction worked wonders, Anne. You look great tonight in that white satin sheath.''

''Do I? I'll have to tell Spencer. He caresses his pistols more these days than he does me.''

There were no passport or customs controls at the spot on the road where the Italian tricolor faced the Swiss flag, white cross on its red field. The T-Bird sped on into Switzerland, Anne regaling Diana all the while about English royalty's latest erotic peccadilloes.

From that first spring vacation Diana had spent with Anne at Sheldon Hall, her parents' Georgian manor in Yorkshire, Diana had found a friend. Anne, whose father was both a peer and a member of Parliament, would enthrall Diana with the most outrageous stories about British politics and love affairs—and Diana proved an expert listener. The poor-little-rich-girls shared both their innermost secrets and sybaritic indulgences, and even over the years and the separations, their friendship held fast.

At three in the morning, the lights of subtropical Paradiso, a cobbled and shuttered Swiss Riviera, still sparkled as the fabulous parties continued on its cypress-and-palm-blanketed hillside. Diana parked her T-Bird in the garage/apartment behind her rented *chaumière*, which was hidden by dark clumps of denuded walnut and chestnut trees. Already the little brownstone cottage was becoming as much a home as her Paris garden apartment.

While Anne poured two flutes of Taittinger Blanc de Blanc, Diana stoked a fire. After Anne took a sip of bubbles, she asked, "Don't perchance have any coke tucked away here, do you?"

When Diana shook her head, her tawny hair swished about her shoulders. She curled up on the deep-tufted sofa, opposite Anne. "Would a Gitanes do in its place?" She proffered a scratched silver Fabergé case from the country-plain coffee table.

The crackling fire highlighted two vertical lines where her friend's short nose met her brows. "Those French cigarettes? Too strong for me. I'll take a smooth Mary Jane any day. What happened to those golden years when we used to sneak off from our classes and share

a toke with some down-and-out artist? Remember those
bloody-awful Montparnasse garrets? Filthy and smelly
and cramped, but, oh God, the good times we had!''

Diana lit a Gitanes and, glass in hand, tucked her
long legs under her, settling back into the mound of
brightly colored silk cushions. ''Do you remember,
Anne, that German hunk?'' she asked, recalling their
junior and senior years at the Sorbonne, when she had
come of age. ''Fritz wasn't it?''

''Do I?! He taught us everything we needed to know
about surrealistic art and serious Teutonic sex.''

Diana smiled at the crossfire of memory and recollec-
tion of those bohemian years and purred a blue stream of
smoke. ''I don't think I ever told you, Anne, but my fresh-
man year at Smith, I was supposed to be studying European literature. Instead, I had an Amazonian roommate
all too anxious to teach me all I might want to learn about
the intimate pleasures of Lesbos Island.''

''Well, did you learn anything?'' Anne asked desul-
torily. Nothing shocked or surprised this young woman,
whose dark hair, cut stylishly short, was already beginning to be invaded by occasional silvery strands.

A scene came to mind that Diana had forgotten—a
tiny dormitory room on a wintery Northampton night.
Sandy, her cropped hair mussed from sleep, was sitting
on the bed beside her. It was just before Christmas, and
Diana had been sick for two days with a low-grade fever. It looked like she was going to be sent home early.

Her roommate had stroked her feverish forehead, repeating, ''I'll miss you, Diana.''

Sandy's tender touch and her concern had felt good
to Diana. Her father's Manhattan apartment and her
grandmother's chateau in the south of France were both
a long way off. ''I'll miss you, too,'' she told the Ju-
noesque girl.

Then, Sandy had startled her, leaning forward and kissing her. "When you're away, will you think of me . . . of this?"

Along with the strange sensation the kiss left, Diana had been assaulted by a host of other bewildering emotions. Curiosity, certainly. Guilt over the forbidden, probably. But mostly a feeling that her most private self had been invaded.

She stabbed her cigarette into a ceramic ashtray. "No, I missed that lesson, Anne. I had been taking some wretched medicine and I promptly threw up all over Sandy. When I came back from Christmas hols, I learned my roommate had dropped out."

"What a marvelous story!" Anne said.

"You think so? I don't remember those times as being so marvelous. Always worrying about who we wanted to be tomorrow."

"You know, Diana, you really are a most fortunate female. Most women would give ten years off their lives to be what you've become. Look at yourself. You're not saddled with any bloody responsibility at all! One night you're gambling in Monte Carlo, the next gyrating at a disco opening on St. Thomas. Always a different man in your life. You lead a playgirl's carefree, glamorous existence on both sides of the Atlantic."

Diana's thick brows, arrow straight and no-nonsense over her rich brown eyes, lifted skeptically. "And you don't?"

"Hardly." Anne gulped down the rest of her wine. "Spencer and I have responsibilities. Our parties are neither free nor fun for us. You know how it is, benefits for various charities . . . cough up a fee before attending. We are never alone. Always businessmen and politicans. I envy you."

"Anne, is Spencer having another affair?"

Her friend got up to replenish her glass. "You've always been perceptive."

"You've had your share, too, if I remember correctly. Let's see . . . there was that Italian actor two years ago. Remember—at Amalfi?"

"Please, darling, it's a bit cheeky of you to remind me. I wound up trying to ride that randy goat through the streets like some spaced-out Lady Godiva. Let's not talk about Spencer and my marital existence. That is why I came here. To get away."

Diana rose and stretched. "God, Anne, it's almost four. Those all-night marathon gab sessions we used to have are over for me. I'm ready to crash. I put an extra blanket on your bed."

Anne set down her already half-empty glass. "Have you made up your mind about tomorrow? About that fireside dinner at your maharajah's chalet?"

Diana wrinkled her patrician nose. "He's not my maharajah. But, yes, we can go, if you like."

In her bedroom, Diana stripped down to her panties, letting her discarded clothes fall to the cold tile floor as she moved about. She removed her jewelry and contacts, but lazily left on the little makeup she wore and slid between the frigid sheets.

Hands clasped behind her head, she thought about Murad's dinner. Lars Thurston's presence would be a stroke of luck. In Lugano for less than a week, she had been angling for just such an impromptu meeting with her former schoolmate's father, who was now a key official at one of the local Swiss banks.

In the dark, Diana's teeth were startling white as she grinned like a Cheshire cat.

 4

With his high forehead and rumpled trousers, Richter
looked like a professor. He boarded TWA's 6 P.M. flight
out of Washington Dulles, taking a seat in the last row,
nearest the restroom. "You headed to Denver on business or pleasure?" he asked the man by the window.

"Business." The man, his tie loosened, was staring
out the window.

At what, Richter wondered? Nothing out there but
runway lights and snow boiling over the wings as the
plane boomed down the runway. "With this weather,
the skiing should be great at Winter Park."

"Yeah."

Mentally, Richter shrugged. Okay, so he didn't want
to talk. Well, that made the trip easier. He could drop
his congenial passenger role and relax.

Fifteen minutes before landing at Stapleton, with the
plane thirty-one thousand feet above the midwestern
plains, Richter got up with his briefcase in hand and
went into the lavatory. Richter's seatmate, a middle-
aged man with a Hispanic's hooked nose and hard-
boned, tough-guy features that made him almost
handsome, had been noticing the passengers who made

19

the trip to the john at the rear of the 747. Only five so
far. Now six, counting the guy next to him.

Who carried a briefcase into the john?

Tom Estevez decided nature's call should be heeded
once more and eased into the aisle. The occupied light
was still on in the john. When Richter came out, Tom
entered, snapped the door lock in place, and hunkered
down in the confining space. He groped a long finger
into the narrow slot of the towel-disposal unit.

He was fishing for a paper clip bent into an S hook
and fastened to the inside of the panel. Attached to the
hook would be a string dangling a dozen men's socks
filled with half-kilo plastic bags of heroin. Narcotic sau-
sage, the agents called it.

At four o'clock that afternoon, a Dulles airplane
cleaner, who had been emptying the towel-disposal bin,
had found a plastic bag containing half a kilo of a white
crystalline powder glinting among the crumpled paper
towels. Instantly suspicious, he had notified a customs
agent. One sniff and a taste—sourer than a persimmon
and as bitter as quinine—had confirmed the customs
agent's hunch.

The Drug Enforcement Agency had been called in
immediately. The packet was prudently resealed and
replaced, and Tom Estevez had reserved a strategic seat
at the rear of the Denver flight.

With a quiet grunt of satisfaction, Tom ascertained
that the heroin stash was gone. He had six suspects, but
he'd bet his pension on just one—the dude with the
briefcase.

For a man like Richter, the job was simple, safe. A
courier, or a mule in drug trafficker argot, boarded a
TWA flight in Frankfurt and, naturally, wasn't sub-
jected to any search. The first layover was London
Heathrow. Between Frankfurt and London all the mule

had to do was hide the dozen packages, each bound in a men's sock, behind the towel-disposal receptacle in the lavatory. At London, the mule left the plane. If customs agents searched him, no problem. He was clean.

The jumbo jet then continued on to Washington Dulles, where Richter boarded. The plane was now a domestic flight, with no further customs searches. Once in the air, Richter would simply enter the lavatory, retrieve the merchandise, and get off in Denver.

At the Stapleton Airport arrival gate, Tom nodded surreptitiously to the two regional special agents, fingering the intellectual-looking man ahead of him. The agents tailed the man to a motel near the airport, where they would wait for him to make the exchange.

Tom was used to the waiting. Twenty years in law enforcement—nine with the Miami Police Department first as a street cop, next as a detective, then eleven more as a DEA agent—had taught him patience. He was used to surveillance—camping out in plain-brown-wrapper cars for so many hours his ass was numb, and holing-up in roach palaces for days on end until he was ready to start snorting Black Flag himself.

Partners, he discovered, got in his way. He disliked working with anybody and in Denver held his own vigil from the room across the hall, while the other two agents monitored the suspect from the room next door. The waiting paid off three hours later. Close to midnight, a man in a gray herringbone overcoat and blue silk foulard scarf knocked on Richter's door.

Tom's telephone rang. "The jackal's here," one of the other agents said. "All set?"

The three narcs moved in for the nab, an easy one. One of the Denver agents, obviously inexperienced, backed off and made a running lunge at the metal motel door, John Wayne–style. Tom squinched his eyes closed at the solid impact. As the man clutched his shoulder in pain, Tom pulled from his pocket a master key he had obtained from the hotel manager and opened the door.

Richter, posed next to the open briefcase sitting on the bed, looked at Tom with a mixture of astonishment and chagrin. "You! The seat next to the window!"

Tom stared at him without speaking. He rarely spoke to the bad guys or to anybody else. Most of the time he looked. Always watching for that abnormality on the streets—an expensive car in a shabby neighborhood, an umbrella in sunny weather, broken tiles on a store roof.

The panicky eyes of the expensively clad street jobber flitted from Tom to the other agents like a helpless moth looking for a safe place to light. Richter flung the brief-case at the three agents and dashed for the door.

A vicious chop to the side of the felon's neck by Tom's locked hands brought the man crumpling to his knees. While Tom braced the street jobber against the wall and frisked him—coming up with $40,000 in cash—one of the agents handcuffed the unconscious Richter. In a monotone voice the other read the jobber his Miranda rights.

After he woke up, Richter and his contact were ready to make like songbirds. Later, at the lab, the bifocaled chemist said, "Almost like an Ivory commercial—ninety-eight and seven-tenths pure."

Not until after midnight did Tom get caught up on the mandatory paperwork, a flurry of forms and reports tapped out on the inevitable battered typewriter. This one had no letter "w." Made for interesting reading.

He just made the early flight back to Dulles, with only one thought in mind—crashing at his apartment for twenty-four solid hours. His place was just as brown-wrapper as the surveillance cars. Nothing on the walls, barest essentials for furniture. Why get fancy, when he was rarely there anyway?

As he opened the door to his bedroom, he paused. His old bear instincts told him he had a visitor. By the bedroom mirror's dim reflection Wendy was framed in his bed, propped on her elbows, her breasts winking at him invitingly.

He pushed the door open all the way. "Manager let you in?"

She grinned. "Don't you ever get tired of being called a rogue cop?"

"So, Reynolds called, huh." He stripped off his tie and looped it over the doorknob.

"Your chief called not five minutes ago." She sat up and combed her fingers through her electric hair, all red as holy fire and sticking out all over. He liked her mop, it suited her. She studied him. "You look dog tired."

He tossed his shirt on the dresser. "I am."

"Too tired to get it on?" Her hands cupped her earth-mama breasts and there was a feigned leer of Hollywood lust on her lightly freckled face. "Bet we can make the seismograph needle at Atlanta jump like a trampoline."

Intelligent, cute, fun-loving. She was a hell of a woman, and one of the best lobbyists on Capitol Hill. He had struggled through seven years of night school to squeeze out a B.A. in criminal justice and she had breezed through a political science program at Georgetown in three.

Ignoring his body's "leave me alone" exhaustion message, his groin responded, straining his zipper. "I wouldn't doubt it," he chuckled.

Buck naked, he crouched over her, and she greedily

gathered his genitals in both hands. Three months and she still managed to make it good for them with her low-key, lighthearted approach to their lovemaking. He simply couldn't lose himself in their love bouts. He was usually an outsider peeping at them, but that wasn't her fault. At forty-three and the long-divorced father of three children, he supposed his heart just wasn't in the mating ritual any more.

The hell of it was, as devoted as this splendid young nymph was to their mutual pleasure, he found their contortions as embarrassing as they were comforting to his demoralized ego.

His womanizing partners had been amused by his old-fashioned fidelity to his former wife Natalie, but how the hell could they be trusted with agency confidences when they couldn't even keep their own infidelities a secret?

Wendy chuckled lustily. "I like those growls you make when you're ravaging my passion-drenched, steamy orifice."

"Hey, you make them, too. Little breathless moaning sounds."

She tipped her tight little butt into the air and spread her legs, bracing herself with her hands. "Stop talking, Estevez, and show me how a real macho Latin male does it."

He complied, straining mightily to hold back until he felt her begin to come, then slipping over the edge into climax when she did.

"You're worthless," she chided him not five minutes later when he started to drift off to sleep, still half-covering her sprawled body. But she pillowed his head tenderly against her brown-tipped breasts.

The shrill ring, with the authority of a peal of thunder, interrupted his deep sleep. He rolled groggily off

Wendy and, eyes closed, cradled the phone against his jaw. "Yeah?"

"Your snitch with the Colombian drug lords. . . ." It was Reynolds.

"Yeah—L-35."

"Well, it seems he's picked up on ten million dollars worth of coke coming in from Europe. L-35's contacts in the organization say another four hundred keys of snow comes into Miami every month or so."

Tom levered himself into a sitting position and tunneled his free hand through his thinning hair. Four hundred keys was an astonishing amount. "There's a problem?"

"A wee one, Estevez. It ain't coming through regular sources. Your informant's dropping names that are European, not Latino. I want you to bust the ring—so get your lazy ass onto the next transatlantic flight to Paris."

Wendy was grazing his flaccid sacs with tantalizing fingernails. "Today?" he asked, rubbing his sleep-gritted eyes.

"What's the matter? You wanna collect your pension early?"

He hung up as Reynolds was launching into detailed directions for the proposed operation. His action wouldn't please the chief none too well, but what the hell, Reynolds oughta know by now that he was independent. Tom always gave a hundred and ten percent, but he wouldn't be pushed. Tomorrow was time enough.

He grabbed Wendy's wrist and distracted her from her teasing.

5

St. Moritz, a winding two-hour drive from Lugano, was
a cuckoo-clock alpine town, though the 1948 winter
Olympics had done much to modernize it. The center
of the Swiss village was dominated by the Palace Hotel,
which was more exclusive than the U.S. Senate, and
curled around the shoreline of a picture-perfect lake.
The main street of St. Moritz was a fur store on parade.

Doubly blessed with a breathtaking setting in the
heart of the craggy Engadine valley and good snow for
so late in the season, St. Moritz was the perch of choice
for the aristocracy, as well as for politicians, businessmen, and the film community.

Tucked away among the trees at the lower elevations
were the post-Heidi chalets and Bavarian-looking villas
of international celebrities. Murad Murarani's "cozy
chalet" looked more like a sixteenth-century palazzo.
Diana and Anne, led by the prince's flawless telephoned
directions, arrived late that morning. A valet extracted
their ski gear and overnight bags from the big T-bird
trunk.

Inside the palazzo, a housekeeper in black poplin
greeted them. "The prince and some of his guests are

already up on the slopes,'' she told the two friends, as she led them to the rooms set aside for them.

In a nearby *salotto*, two white sofas, flanked by Louis XV *fauteuils*, faced each other in front of a crackling fireplace. Diana recognized Catherine Roumey, France's top model, curled up at one end of one sofa. Diana had met the redhead on Lanvin's runways when she herself had had a fling at modeling.

Next to Catherine, stroking her neck intimately as he chatted, was a handsome Nordic man. He certainly was not her husband, who was a stoop-shouldered Milanese lawyer. A local ski instructor, no doubt.

Catherine spotted her and waved. "Do come back and have an apéritif after you settle in."

"Thanks, but I think I'll try to get in some skiing before it gets too late," Diana said.

"I'd sooner drink with the terrorists," Anne muttered darkly as they followed the housemaid up a spiral staircase. "Did you notice her leather pants? Fit her as tight as they once did the cow."

"I take it Spencer has had an affair with Catherine."

"Hasn't everyone?"

"Here is your room," the housemaid said to Diana, indicating a large Lucan empire-style bedroom, its bed draped with a blue mink coverlet.

Anne flicked Diana an amused look. "Divide and conquer. That must be the maharajah's tactics."

"The prince left word there would be a helicopter waiting at the pad to carry you up to the lodge," the housekeeper told them.

"Meet you in fifteen minutes?" Diana asked Anne, who was following the maid down the tiled corridor. Frescoes of what might have been a student of Michelangelo's graced one wall.

The chic Englishwoman turned and looked over her

shoulder. "Helicopter? *Moi?* No thanks. I've reconsidered, I'll have that drink with Lucretia Borgia."

Diana changed quickly into a U.S.-made Powderhorn vest and Hansen boots. The rest of her ski regalia was colorful—green-and-orange horizontally striped pants with an orange tank top that displayed her snow-tanned flesh. Over it she wore a matching jacket.

As promised, the helicopter—one of two kept at the palazzo—waited on a pad behind the sprawling house. The other one was probably up on the slopes, transporting Murad and his guests to the top of the glacier so they could avoid the long lines at the lifts.

The helicopter, rocking and pitching in the cold Alpine air, left her off at *Il Camineto*, the mid-mountain restaurant. She crossed to the sun deck, jammed with an avalanche of notables who had descended like locusts on the restaurant to eat or stretch out on chaise longues and soak up the double-digit sunlight.

"Diana!" a man hailed.

It was Catherine's husband, Carlo. Diana rather liked him. From an ancient lumber family of northern Italy, the lawyer was something of an intellectual who had early on bored Catherine into infidelity. With him was a balding, attractive man.

"Diana," Carlo gave her a hug and said, "come and meet Walter Vachs."

Walter turned out to be a German industrialist—and he too was bored by Carlo. She offered him her hand. His grip was firm and Teutonically hearty, and she half-expected him to click his heels as he bent over to brush her fingers with his lips.

"Diana," Carlo went on, "is the granddaughter of La Comtesse de Revillon." His introduction summed up just about the totality of her life, she thought. Carlo gestured vaguely toward the peaks. "Murad's making a run."

"Would you care for a Dom Perignon?" Walter asked her. His naked pate was already becoming pink in the snowglare.

"No, thank you. I think I'll go on up."

"I was explaining Italian eccentricities to Walter," Carlo said. "Our lira collapses, our government changes hands with mind-boggling frequency, and even the venerable institution of our Papacy is looked upon as transitory."

Walter was ignoring Carlo's prattle in order to concentrate on casting flirtatious glances at Diana. She paid him no heed whatsoever. "Carlo, you left out the worst eccentricity," she said.

Carlo's brow furrowed like a bloodhound's. "What is that?"

"The paternal care doled out by Italy's godfathers."

"Ahh, yes, our Mafia. In parts of Italy, Walter, in the antique villages, blood feuds still erupt. Newborn babies still kiss the muzzle of a pistol, and fighting ability is still the test of a man."

While Carlo elaborated, Diana snapped on her skis, adjusted her goggles over her fox hat, tucked in her hair, and picked up her poles.

"I think I will make a run myself," Walter broke in on Carlo's dissertation.

She looked Walter straight in the eye and said in German, which was not one of her more fluent languages, "I prefer the black markers." In Switzerland, a black marker identified the runs through terrain that was *very* difficult. Strictly "experts only."

Walter bowed out graciously. "Join us for raclette, when you finish. I have sampled some here, and I as-

sure you it is the most delicious you will find anywhere.''

At the lift, she waited in a double line that was much
shorter than those at the base lifts. In the crackling chill
air, she felt a pure joy at the sense of her own youth,
her strength, her perfect physical condition, which she
openly conceded was one of her major vanities.

She sensed someone staring at her, and the hairs on
her neck actually prickled. The feeling was so intense
that she swiveled her head toward the line of skiers
parallel with hers. The offender's steady gaze gave her
the sense of being momentarily paralyzed by a police
stun-gun, of being illuminated by a powerful search-
light.

She drew a deep, steadying breath, the cold, dry air
searing its way into her lungs. She forced her eyes away
from the domination of his, but an inventory of him
was still imprinted indelibly on her mind. Lean, a little
over average height, a shock of hair the color of bur-
nished gold, a handsome face with serious character
lines. Maybe forty-five. But there was something in
those cool blue eyes . . . the eyes *were* the man.

She wasn't surprised when he boarded the chair with
her, as if that had been fated. With a lurch, the chair
swung forward and upward. Everyone made small talk
during a chair's ascent, but she didn't choose to—not
this time. She was conscious of an irrational uneasi-
ness.

Irritated with the unexpectedly illogical reaction of
both her body and her mind, she appeared to become
inordinately fascinated by a narrow-gauge rail line below and off to the left. The Glacier Express, with its
quaint, oak-paneled dining car and peculiar leaning
wineglasses, was chuffing up the steep track, en route

from St. Moritz to Zermatt, with its awesome view of the Matterhorn.

Apparently her lift partner had as little desire to talk as she did. The only sound was the wind whispering through a stand of tall, snowy evergreens and singing in the lift cables. Snowflakes, almost as large as feathers, drifted around them, seeming to isolate them in a cocoon of whiteness.

At last the lift reached the top. Skis and poles ready, she pushed off from the chair and swung quickly onto the main slope. It was in the shade, and her skis clattered on the icy surface. The ski season was about over for the year, unless an Arctic front plowed through suddenly.

Her silent lift partner was right beside her, adjusting the goggles over his eyes. Just then, she realized she had seen him before—the pose was similar—in a photograph in *Le Point*, along with one of Murad and several other handsome men. The news magazine had featured a spread on the playboys of Europe.

Murad Murarani had been described as the son of the rajah of a small principality near the border between India and Nepal and the maternal grandson of a wealthy Indian who had established a clothing factory in Hong Kong in the 1930s. The company had since prospered into a multimillion-dollar business.

She wracked her memory to recall what had been written about the man on the lift. *David Mendel, scion of a prominent, centuries-old banking family and an expert polo player, fencer, and master of Jean Blanc.*

Maybe that wasn't word for word, but her photographic memory usually served her well. So, this man took his skiing as seriously as she did? Jean Blanc was considered one of Europe's toughest slopes, with a piste that sustained a expert pitch over an impressive 3,050-foot vertical drop.

She watched David Mendel schuss away into a white curtain of drifting snow. With an odd sensation of utter relief, she started off toward the less difficult runs, where she hoped to bump into Lars Thurston. The sixty-three-year-old widower was old enough to be her father but not too old to flirt with. Besides, he possessed certain information on which she hoped to capitalize.

During World War II, smugglers used to ferry across Lake Lugano from Italy to Switzerland contraband Tuscan prosciutto, cheap furs, and, surprisingly, Perugina chocolates. The smugglers then returned to bases on the Italian side of the azure water with a cargo of American cigarettes to feed the sizzling black market in nearby Milan.

Now, other items were being brought covertly into the lush, lakeside town in Switzerland's Italian-speaking Ticino canton. Money for one. A vast wealth in deutsche marks, dollars, francs, and pounds daily found their way to the banks.

The money was transferred by coded printouts, computerized telephone messages, and checks in unmarked envelopes. At the modest Lugano airport, innocuous-looking passengers with bundles of bank notes or stacks of Krugerrands in their carryons arrived every day on Saab-Fairchild Cityliners, a Swissair feeder line. To appear as if they were on a few days' vacation, some of the passengers brought their own women; others flew in with blondes supplied by Europe's high-priced escort agencies.

Shares in multinational corportions, United States Treasury bonds, shopping malls in California, real estate on the Riviera, and paintings and antiquities that reached Switzerland by devious routes—all of these often changed hands by way of the Lugano connection. At last count, more than sixty banks were located in Lugano, and new ones trying to wedge in were searching for available sites.

Lars Thurston had access to records of the documents and valuables stored in the lake city's capacious bank safes, which was why Diana sought him out. She met up with him midway down a slope, where a stand of denuded birch provided a temporary rest stop.

"You've grown up, Diana!" he told her, when she paused beside him, lifting her goggles to reveal her identity.

"Grown older," she laughed.

"Growing older is when you have to take breathers between runs," he said ruefully.

"You are not old, Lars. Why, you are as physically fit as a thirty-year-old."

"Rubbish," he chuckled but looked pleased.

She began to lay the groundwork, talking to the distinguished, silver-haired man about the antics she had participated in with his daughter and the good times she had had at his house in Copenhagen's fairyland suburbs.

On the way down the lower mountain, her and Thurston's paths crossed with Murad's. While the three were waiting at the helipad to return to his palazzo, Murad's sulking mouth made his displeasure obvious, but he was too conscious of saving face to throw one of his legendary temper tantrums. Thurston was distracted by the helicopter's approach, and Murad took the opportunity to tell Diana mournfully, "Apparently, all my prayers to Allah have not influenced your feelings toward me, chérie."

She squinted at him skeptically. "I thought you were a Hindu, Murad?"

The ends of his mustache twitched with his boyish

smile. "I am whatever I need be. If you wish, I can discuss the Christian philosophy with you—tonight about eleven?"

She laughed. "No. I don't wish." Not at all. Her Roman Catholic upbringing under her grandmother's tutelage had been a stabilizing influence in her life and it was a solid base she had come to cherish if not faithfully practice.

Over an 8 P.M. *aperitivo* to be followed by a 10 P.M. dinner, then sledding, she carefully probed Lars about his position as an officer with the Crédit Suisse branch at Lugano. They huddled in one corner of a *salotto*, populated with the usual druggies, fetishists, whores of both genders, slightly shopworn social climbers of Alpine scope, and minor European bluebloods who had come to traverse the slopes, get some sun, and slalom through a round of Murad's parties.

"Discreet banking is what we call numbered accounts," Lars said. Except for some reddish veins around his nose, he did look younger than his years. "What most people don't realize is that those fabled private numbered accounts are not in fact anonymous."

She spooned a healthy dollop of gray Iranian caviar onto a wedge of toast and passed it to the banker. "That's not very reassuring, Lars. We're led innocently to believe that banking secrecy is sanctioned by law in Switzerland."

He popped her treat into his mouth. "Sorry, my dear. But the general public has been misled. Since several key bank officers must know the customer's identity, as well as something about his personal and financial background, there's not much that goes on that the rest of us don't sooner or later find out about."

Across the room, Anne and Catherine held court with Catherine's husband and Walter and his wife, a bland, duty-bound woman named Eva. The cat-eyed Catherine caught Diana's glance and winked. "Are you married these days, darling?" she called out.

"I've been lucky enough to escape that particular brand of bliss, darling." Diana wondered if Carlo was aware of Catherine's stainless-steel syringes, the huge ones used to knock out horses, which she kept filled with Demerol.

Murad had his beringed, dusky hand perched on the sleek hip of the daughter of a Canadian cabinet minister. No doubt Murad would slake his lust with the young woman—if she didn't first take to bed the handsome athlete she had come with, a Czech tennis player who had defected in Paris two years earlier. The Czech was rumored to have spent much of the previous night drunk on the salon floor, playing with himself.

Everyone was casually dressed in jeans and pullovers. Designer jeans, of course, and pullovers with acceptable labels. Diana's jeans, which she wore tucked into shaggy goatskin boots, were an exception. She wouldn't be caught dead with someone else's name on her butt.

She refilled Lars's glass with more Dom Perignon and leaned closer. "A stolen Gobelin tapestry—didn't French authorities find it in a Swiss numbered vault last year?"

"Ahh, yes, my dear, but disclosure of bank numbers becomes mandatory in criminal cases."

"But how can officials know that what has been deposited—say a pair of diamond earrings—is the result of a criminal act?" she pushed.

"Well, that's a little more difficult. The sort of people involved in such a transaction could be a tip-off. But, usually, a wise official will maintain his counsel. After all, it is public trust that made our banks the success they are.''

"Oh, come on, Lars." She took a Gitanes from her Fabergé case and cupped her hands over his when he held his gold Dunhill to the end of her cigarette. The touch was a seductive ploy she never would have stooped to had he been even a little more sober. She exhaled a spiral of the pungent smoke. "Is that sort of thing really that common?"

"More than you realize." He lowered his voice, his breath a trumpet blast of sour Veuve Clicquot champagne. "Just last week, a South American withdrew a substantial sum from his account and deposited in return a sizable cache of gold, the sort used in Europe only by jewelers. To sell such pure gold to anyone other than a certified jeweler is illegal. An anonymous caller tipped us off to the South American's transactions."

Her heart missed a beat. "What did the bank do?"

"Nothing. South American drug overlords are valued clients and unless the bank is contacted by an Interpol agent, I seriously doubt whether the transaction will be reported."

He was dead wrong about the latter, but she said nothing. She kept on feeding him champagne, hoping he would sleep like an anesthetized patient that night and that his memory in the morning would be as fuzzy as his tongue.

6

The Hofbrauhaus brewery in Munich, significant polit-
ically as the headquarters of the original Nazi Party,
was close to the Bavarian Garten restaurant on Zwei-
bruckenstrasse, and the cloying odor of fermenting wort
pervaded the private dining room, despite its tightly
closed shutters.

Though the six men seated with their host around the
polished zebrawood table had come from all over Europe, they had two things in common—neo-Nazi lean-
ings and a commensurately complete lack of principle
or regard for human life. That afternoon they had come
to Bavarian Garten not to eat but for business. A white-
jacketed waiter distributed pewter steins of beer, then
discreetly bowed out.

The six glanced expectantly at the head of the table.
The man seated there impressed most people who encountered him as a man of the world. The pockets of
all his shirts were monogrammed and around his neck
hung a thick gold chain. On his wrist was the Rolex
President on a chunky gold bracelet. Only five feet six
inches tall, he was nevertheless a dashing figure, with
hair the color of autumn—a deep reddish brown. To

round out his bonhomie, he exuded almost Gallic charm and a truly sunny disposition.

He had, however, a darker side. Louis St. Giles was a clever operator whose dealings illuminated the dark corners of a shadow empire as large as Hitler's and as well hidden as the Pope's. Behind his guise of owner of a prestigious German publishing house, he controlled one of the most powerful criminal syndicates in the world, its operations running the gamut from international white slavery to trafficking in every sort of drug.

His name was as anomalous as the man: the hereditary product of a crusading English knight who was seduced by an Alsatian serving wench and decided to wait for the next campaign to pass through—an event that never occurred.

The blueprint for the St. Giles organization was the efficient and soulless Nazi machine of yore, with which he was as much obsessed as he was with great paintings. Oddly, his usually engaging voice could instantly develop a laser edge of disdain if he found himself in the presence of those who didn't aspire to culture—perhaps an unconscious product of his knightly ancestry.

"Gentlemen," St. Giles addressed his confederates, "we are faced with ever-growing arrogance by the Semites. Our pogrom is to be stepped up into a program of supersabotage. In the past, our intimidation and the occasional annihilation of a Jewish businessman has been small time." He smiled genially, his charming gaze riveting each of his lieutenants in turn. "Next week, we will begin by destroying a major Jewish business in every European capital, starting with Oslo."

They all had questions and they were not slow in voicing them. Louis had picked his subordinates shrewdly. André Daguerre, sentenced to death *in ab-*

sentia after gunning down a Dutch police superinten-
dent, opened the queries. "Why Norway?"

"A large explosives factory, owned by a Josef Tabosky, is located there. Tabosky does business with the
British North Sea oil companies."

"Won't it be hard to find saboteurs we can trust?"
asked a weathered, grandfatherly looking Corsican, who
by the age of twenty had been managing a chain of
brothels.

"Not at all. They already exist. There are Arab terrorists all over Europe desperate to die for their Allah."
St. Giles's teeth flashed in a reassuring smile. "No reason for any of us to make the sacrifice."

"It sounds feasible," another allowed. He was a noble looking man who could have passed as a lawyer
or doctor. In fact, he had been a hired assassin. One of
the best.

Again, Louis eyed each of his associates. "Your sub-
lieutenants will take care of the hard graft—recruiting
the saboteurs, supplying them, arranging financing. One
caveat, comrades—you must make absolutely certain no
Americans are injured or killed in the pogroms. We
don't want their CIA on our backs like monkeys."

7

The Israeli equivalent of the CIA—the Central Institute for Intelligence and Special Missions, better known by its Hebrew acronym of Mossad—was already on Louis St. Giles's back. At least, one member of the Israeli intelligence agency was.

Under the code name of Hamemuneh, the "man in charge," he was an expert in military, political, and economic intelligence, and his accomplishments were legendary. He had been involved in everything from smuggling dissident Jews out of Russia to sabotaging the plutonium nuclear reactor in Iraq to aiding the rescue of the Entebbe hostages. He was personally responsible for masterminding the stalking and capture of the infamous butcher of Lorraine, Klaus Von Heinkel.

Hamemuneh arrived at Oslo's Fornebu airport at 9:20 that morning and passed quickly through the rather perfunctory passport control. Although he was traveling on a fake West German passport with the number 430857L, it had a serious flaw: West German passports in that series had seven, not six digits.

"Hans!" an attractively dressed woman in her fifties greeted Hamemuneh and threw her arms around him.

40

Effusively, she kissed him on the cheek. "I thought you'd never get here. Daddy is asking for you. He isn't doing well."

He put his arm around her waist in an affectionate, brotherly gesture. "That's why I didn't bring any extra luggage, Ilse. I packed as quickly as I could."

His answer satisfied her.

A sidelong glance at the woman as they walked through the terminal told him she wasn't doing too well either. Ilse, usually an exceptionally fit and well-balanced person, was showing the tensions of her work. The strain of living lies had etched new lines around her eyes and mouth and deepened earlier ones.

Hamemuneh knew that danger, taken in minute doses for short periods of time, could be a potent, almost aphrodisiacal life force. Over longer periods, however, danger became like a corrosive cancer that permanently warped personalities.

Often, to allay their own growing anxieties, operatives began to survive on diets of tranquilizers, sleeping pills, and increasing quantities of alcohol. They aged shockingly and early. As he had once informed a new Mossad operative, "Each life you take diminishes your own."

The effective period of a Mossad field agent was generally five years at most. He knew Ilse had been in for three and his own Mossad service totalled fifteen. He supposed he was one of those exceptional few who had such a passion for excitement that they thrived on danger. Perhaps he possessed the singularly divine genetic characteristic that had been handed down through Jewish genealogy for thousands of years, ever since the days of oppression under the pharaohs—the Survival Factor.

Once they were seated in her gray Volvo, Ilse passed

him a folded, three-day-old edition of Oslo's daily, the *Aftenposten*, which had been lying on the seat between them. He scanned the pen-circled article, his grasp of Norwegian sufficient to understand its content.

The Norsk Explosives Factory had been destroyed by what appeared to be employee carelessness, often referred to as poor housekeeping. A drop of nitroglycerine on a dirty floor could send up an explosives factory. He read on.

"Nothing was left," said one weeping witness, *"nothing but a forty-foot hole in the ground. They all vaporized. We're finding traces of hair, but that's about it. It's anyone's guess what set off the high explosives."*

Mossad had an excellent idea what had set off the plant, and that was why Hamemuneh was in Oslo that morning. A .30-caliber rifle bullet fired into the right spot in that plant could have achieved the same results—and the slug would never be found.

"The owner, Josef Tabosky," Ilse said, her mouth stretched grimly, "wasn't in the factory when it blew and escaped unharmed—until this morning."

"What happened?"

"In the post, he received a yellow envelope with a Dutch postmark. His secretary claims Tabosky was excited about it because his hobby was gardening and he had ordered some special flower seeds from Holland."

Ilse didn't have to go on. Hamemuneh knew how such devices worked: a thick envelope, torn open, released the small spring-loaded detonator, similar in design to a mousetrap. When the striker whacked into three ounces of plastique, the violent explosion would hurl a torrent of fatal splinters from Josef Tabosky's deep desk into his unprotected body.

8

April 15th

The International Criminal Police Organization based in Paris was staffed by about three hundred persons. Perhaps seventy of Interpol's staff were liaison officers assigned and paid by the 122 member nations.

On the seventh floor of the modern glass-and-brick building at 26 rue Armengaud, perched on a hillside in Paris's western suburb of St. Cloud, Tom Estevez conferred with John Hamblin, the U.S. Drug Enforcement Agency's legal attaché, or le-at, in Paris. The bronzed windows of the austere office looked out over the Seine. From there it was possible to spot all the tourist landmarks: Sacre-Coeur's white dome on Montmarte, the Tour Eiffel, and the Arc de Triomphe at Place de l'Etoile.

Framed police institute certificates hung on Hamblin's walls, revealing that the man with the slightly graying crew cut was expert in all areas of law enforcement. A lifetime of dealing with crime and its perpetrators had blunted the deputy chief's already dry humor. Today it was missing altogether and he appeared to Estevez to be as cold and miserable as the "spring" weather outside.

43

Behind Hamblin was the American flag to the left
and, on his right, a blue-and-white banner whose em-
blem was the earth pierced by a giant sword. Interpol's
flag symbolized that, where international crime was
concerned, the world had no barriers.

"I'd like to use your computer bank, Inspector," Tom
began.

"You crossed the Atlantic to ask me that?" Hamblin
sneezed loudly into a pocket handkerchief. "You know,
Estevez, there's a little pasture outside the village of St.
Martin d'Abbat, eighty miles south of here, where a
giant antenna stands ready to transmit info to your
NLETS warehouse. Lots cheaper than transatlantic air-
fare."

Tom ignored Hamblin's gibe at the National Law Enforcement Telecommunications System, which in some
aspects rivaled Interpol's information gathering systems. "I want to go through your Special Files."

"What's up?"

"Cocaine. An elephantine load of it. We know it's
been funneling into Miami from Europe. But we don't
know who's unloading it or how."

Hamblin tilted back in his swivel leather chair and
blew his nose. His usually alert eyes were watery. "Is
there anything you narcs do know?"

Tom grinned amiably. "We know Interpol was part
of the Gestapo during World War II."

The back of Hamblin's chair snapped to its vertical
position. "They don't laugh at that joke here, Estevez."

"I didn't think they would. Well, can I use your Special Files?"

"Yeah. Go on, use them and then beat it. You narcs
give even this place a bad name."

The Special Files department was in the basement,

an immense vaultlike room where extensive dossiers were stored according to types of crimes and modus operandi. Cabinet after cabinet contained newspaper articles, lab reports, photos, crime reports—all on microfilm reels.

The metal storage cabinets were divided into five rows—Murder and Theft, International Fraud, Bank Fraud and Forgery, Drug Traffic, and Counterfeiting. A sixth cabinet housed a photographic index.

Each of the five sections held information and traced patterns of the ever-growing international traffic in crime, paying particular attention to those slippery individuals who specialized in operating between countries. Terrorist groups were usually ignored, since they could claim political motives and were thus immune from Interpol's attention.

Tom started in the Drug Traffic row of cabinets. To begin, he had two names to work with, both probably aliases: Boucheron and Donatello. After sitting in the chilly room hour after hour in front of the monitor, Tom was getting numb. Rubbing his hands together for warmth, he pored over the newspaper articles, all translated into Interpol's three languages—English, French, and Spanish. When his study of the Drug Traffic section turned up no clues, he put on his overcoat and gloves, and began working the Murder and Theft reels.

By late afternoon, Tom's eyes were blurred, his ears ached with cold, and his shoulders were crippled from hunching over the microfilm reader, but he still stayed with it. The one factor that had often enabled him to succeed where more brilliant and ambitious agents failed was his patience.

A pretty secretary, sent down to return an index file, offered to bring him a cup of coffee. When she delivered the steaming aromatic brew, he didn't even bother to glance up, only grunting a fractured *"Merci."*

Despite his fluency in his native Spanish, his French was atrocious. Natalie had told him that often enough. His mind flashed back to his last image of Natalie—in bed, her naked buttocks flagging above the Argentine polo player Luis Chamorro.

Tom wrapped his blunt, gloved fingers around the hot cup and scrolled another microfilm reel into view. Midway through scanning the third reel, something clicked. He wheeled back to the top of the article and reread it. Ali Ahmed Sciolla had been arrested and released five days before for suspicion of theft of art worth $12.5 million.

French police hunted today for a bandit who burglarized an art/auction gallery and vanished with nine paintings, including a canvas by Renoir that, the Marmottan curator said, demonstrated the bandits had the eye of "connoisseurs."

The modus operandi was nothing like Sciolla's other petty thefts, for which, Tom found, Sciolla had been convicted numerous times. His file looked like an ever-expanding family Bible, but on the Marmottan case he finally had been released without charges for lack of evidence.

So why that nagging tic at the back of his mind, Tom wondered. He glanced at his watch—past five o'clock—and shut down the reader. From Interpol's communication department, where a twenty-four-hour shift worked, came the clacking of teleprinters and the tap-tap of Morse code; since not all member countries were linked to the teleprinter circuit, radio transmitters could beam messages to twenty national central bureaus simultaneously.

The worn heels of his cordovans, their lovely deep patina betraying their age, made little noise as he crossed the vast marbled entrance lobby to sign out with the night guard. Philodendrons in the lobby's large window box seemed to huddle for warmth under two mushroom ceiling lights.

Outside, a cold, blustery drizzle welcomed him back to Paris, and he turned up the collar of his corduroy overcoat. Another degree colder and the mess would be snow. On the left bank, he went into a brasserie and ordered coffee and a ham sandwich. The decor was early Metro but the food was good.

He lingered over a second cup of thick coffee and a pungent French cigarette, watching through the window as Parisians hurried home from work through the gray, soupy mist. He had no home to hurry to, he commiserated with himself.

He supposed he should experience some Paris nightlife, but he had seen the sights eight years before with Natalie and had no great urge to repeat the experience solo. He stabbed out his cigarette and signaled to the waiter for the bill. Scanning it, he reached into his trousers for some francs—and paused. Checking the figures, he fumbled for the pen in his pocket, and began scribbling on a paper napkin.

"Monsieur, something is wrong?" asked the waiter.

Tom shook his head. *"Non."* Something was right.

He retotaled his figures and ordered another cup of the syrupy coffee, settling back to reconsider the art theft he had read about earlier.

Art thieves were enjoying a golden era. As the appeal of investing in art rather than nervously fluctuating securities brought a new group of affluent buyers to the marketplace, art prices escalated. What was more, except for conspicuously famous objects, stolen art could often be sold through legitimate auction houses to legitimate buyers, supported by false provenance documents. In the United States, it wasn't even illegal to unknowingly buy stolen art. Could a wealthy—and very private—collector have commissioned this Marmottan heist?

Realizing that nine rather well-known paintings would be difficult to turn in a short amount of time, he found the art theft at Marmottan both unique and curious. Even more curious, a little bit of figuring indicated that the value of the theft was exactly enough to purchase 400 kilos of snow at wholesale.

9

April 18th

Perspiration dampened Diana's sweatband and the hot pink leotards beneath her orange University of Texas sweatshirt, but she continued to work out in front of the wall-length mirror, flexing her arms and swiveling her upper body, as if undergoing primordial rites of dawn.

In precise time to Rimsky-Korsakov's *Scheherazade*, she moved sinuously through pliés and grandes pliés, then moved to the middle of the room for a series of arabesques and adagios. Only in ballet did she ever lose herself—or, perhaps, "become herself" was a better phrase.

Apart from her workout studio, the rest of the garden apartment mirrored her public self: oak-paneled rooms, bay windows with stained-glass panes, a dining room lined with Indian cotton, country-style kitchen with potted herbs, and an office in which to catch up on all her social activities—invitations, mail, telephone calls.

She had wanted this place on the Left Bank near St. Germain-des-Prés, rather than a quiet duplex on the ritzy Avenue Foch. She could never live in the stylishly affluent Sixteenth. That most prestigious arrondisse-

ment was one immense cemetery of apartments. No
charm at all—no bistros, no tabacs, no little brasseries.
But where she lived in the Sixth was a little like New
York—lively, with its all-night pizza establishments and
cinemas.

She went back to the barre for grands battements,
feeling at last that her leg muscles were finally warmed
up. In the mirror wall behind the barre, Peggy's reflection occupied the doorway. The starchy old housekeeper, who doubled as her secretary, supervised a
chambermaid and cook, and staunchly made certain that
no employee ever became too intimate or familiar with
her mistress. As long as she drew a breath, her sweet
lamb would not become an object of gossip and in-
trigue.

She signaled her pet now, and with a sigh Diana
crossed to the stereo and turned off the music. Peggy
never interrupted Diana's workouts unless something
important came up. After a lifetime with Diana, the
Englishwoman knew just who and what was important.

"Telephone, Miss Priss." Her parchment-smooth
cheeks were flushed. "Samuel Breckon."

That explained Peggy's flustered state. Only Samuel,
who had been at Yale with Diana's father, dared to tease
her formidable protector. "Thank you, Peggy."

Diana lifted the sweatband from her hair and shook
loose the dark honey blond mass where it was damp
with perspiration. She crossed the hall to the library
and picked up the receiver. "Sam! How are you?"

"Not dead yet," he grunted in a wry, gravelly rasp.
"Since you never bother to check on me, I thought I'd
report to you the current state of my declining condition."

"Come on, Sam, you've never been sick a day in
your life, you old crank."

She could picture him, one hand waving the constant double corona cigar as he shuffled in precise steps about his sumptuous office in a Paris-based security company, in essence a giant insurance combine. Samuel's hair was a white Einsteinian tangle, but his mustache was waxed to a foppish parenthetical curl.

"Not too sick, at least, to enjoy a holiday in Lyon last weekend. I tried to talk your father into coming, but playing teller to the World Bank is keeping Reed Dickinson awfully busy these days."

So, what else was new? Before that it was the U.N. cocktail-party circuit as America's delegate to the Economic and Social Council. She brightened her voice. "You really talked to Dad? How is he? And who is his current mistress?"

Sam's essential warmth and charm reached Diana right through his laughter. "Would you believe the wife of a well-known senator—and don't ask me to tell you which one, Diana. Ever heard of wiretapping?"

She chuckled. "What's that?"

"Actually, my dear, I just wanted to check up on the worst-behaved of my goddaughters."

"I'm your only goddaughter!"

"That's also why you're my favorite. Call me if you ever find time from your vagabond lifestyle to humor an old man." His curmudgeon manner barely masked a deep sentimentality. "We'll have a lavish high tea at the Crillon."

"That's a deal, dearest Sam," she said, lapsing into her American vernacular.

Actually, they wouldn't. She was rarely seen with him anywhere, and then only at a few of those festivities for which the brilliant *haut monde* society of *le tout* Paris turned out—opera first nights, art gallery *vernissages*, and exclusive *salons*. Their casual rendezvous were part of a meticulously crafted procedure.

"Take care, you old crank." Thoughtfully, she replaced the antique French telephone in its elaborate cradle. So, it would be Lyon this time.

In Lyon, one of France's most mysterious and secretive cities, wealth and the pleasures of the flesh had always been enjoyed behind closed doors—or high walls. Diana, however, had not arrived in Lyon for pleasure. But perhaps wealth might be proposed as the underlying reason for her presence.

Carrying only her purse, she stepped from the TGV onto the station platform. The electronic high-speed train, moving an average 260 kph, put Lyon within two hours of Paris; it was actually quicker than flying.

A black-and-yellow Peugeot taxi took her to Place Bellecour, the heart of the city, which occupied a narrow peninsula between the Rhône and the Saône. Amid a maze of tall, gaunt buildings interlaced with *traboules*, those secret, covered passages leading from one street to another, Diana entered a sullen green building, the Lyon headquarters of Credit Lyonnaise. She rode the ancient caged elevator to the second floor and went to the receptionist desk in the safe deposit section.

"*Bon soir,*" said the young man. He would have been handsome but for the close-set eyes that were perusing her long slender legs with intense Gallic appreciation.

She hadn't bothered with her contacts but wore, instead, her tortoiseshell horn-rimmed glasses, thereby disproving Dorothy Parker's bit of doggerel that men don't make passes at girls who wear glasses.

"*Bon soir.*" She presented her safe-deposit-box card, in which was embedded a tiny computer chip with an electronic record of her signature.

The clerk placed her card in a computerized tablet on his desk and offered her a pen. With the neat penmanship taught her at the Dames de St. Maur Convent in Paris and the Lycée Francais in London, she quickly signed the slip on top of the tablet.

The clerk waited while a muted whirring noise signified that the tablet was comparing her signature with that recorded on the chip inside the card. The tablet ejected the card. If it had not, her request for the safe-deposit box would have been denied. Such high-tech equipment may have been unexpected in such an old-world banking institution—but it was one of the reasons Security International had selected Credit Lyonnaise as a drop.

With a perfunctory smile, Diana accepted her card from the clerk and followed him to the vault door, which he opened with one of the keys from his master set. Another key, matching the one she had submitted, unlocked the door to her safe-deposit box. "Will you need a room, mademoiselle?"

"Yes, please."

He carried her box, as deep as a file drawer, to a high table in the first windowless cubicle. After he departed, with another fleeting but lingering glance at her legs, she opened the box lid and drew out a file folder—another assignment. Like all the previous ones, it had been left in files containing dossiers in safe-deposit boxes in the major banks of the world.

In a bank vault in Zurich, she had left a similar folder, containing a report of all the information she had managed to accumulate on the Pierluigi gold theft, with the unsuspecting help of the indiscreet Lars Thurston.

On that particular case, she had presented Security International with proof of probable cause, making mandatory the Lugano bank disclosure to authorities.

She had remained incognito—as always—providing the necessary proof for Security International to close a case without ever being in on a bust, where her cover would be blown.

Old Samuel had collected for Pierluigi the gold bars from the numbered account of a suspected South American drug dealer, and she collected ten percent of the recovery. The Pierluigi case had not yielded a recovery that equaled the value of some of the other cases she had solved—the heist of an oil tanker came to mind—but the reward was not the reason for the discontent that plagued her.

The problem with the last case was that the thief who had stolen the gold bars was still at large. The South American who had the numbered account, naturally had proclaimed his innocence in buying the illegal gold bars—from an unknown Frenchman was all he could say.

She opened the file folder and spread out the papers of her latest case: the theft of nine paintings on loan to the Marmottan Museum. She studied the details of Samuel's report. Smooth, she thought. An art auction was being held the evening of the theft and all day long workers had been coming and going—setting up chairs, installing microphones and the sound system, arranging display tables.

Scarcely an hour before the scheduled event, the curator discovered a painting was missing. His frantic verification revealed nine in all had been stolen, most of them works by Renoir and Monet, the very best in the Marmottan. Neither the French Criminal Brigade nor Interpol had come up with any clues, other than a weak suspect—a previously convicted petty jewel thief by the name of Ali Ahmed Sciolla who was one of the workers present the day of the theft. Other workers, however, testified the man had never left the building.

An attached police dossier on the thief revealed he had dropped out of school at fourteen to work on the Marseilles docks, which ruled him out as the thief. Diana doubted he had the cultural background to recognize priceless paintings. Even more knowledgeable students of the arts might not have recognized those particular nine paintings as the most valuable in the collection.

So who would?

Diana's fingers tapped a lively tarantella on the tabletop. The curator, for one. Except he had been cleared by both the Paris Criminal Brigade and Interpol.

Who else?

An art enthusiast?

The museum's director?

In a coded runic script of her own devising, she jotted down the essentials of the crime and left after locking away the box.

On the two-hour return trip to Paris, she lit a cigarette and stared unseeing at the countryside sliding rapidly by the window of her private compartment, a *couchette* of marquetry teakwood with silk moiré curtains that reminded her of the Orient Express. Lulled by the muted click of the wheels, she toyed with the few facts and assumptions she had to go on. So little. And the problem with logic was that it wasn't always enough.

She didn't have to take this case. Certainly, she had enough money deposited in banks throughout the world and set up in trusts to last her a couple of lifetimes.

Actually, her inheritance was arranged in a series of trust funds. On her twenty-second birthday she had received control of the cattle ranches and oil wells. On her twenty-sixth, a second fund interest was relegated to her, in addition to a large block of negotiable papers.

Next year, at thirty, a third fund would be opened for her and title to three enormous suburban holdings—office and mall complexes. Then, at thirty-five and every five years until she was sixty, further funds opened, including the first of five blocks of Dickinson stock. Naturally, she was also the sole beneficiary of her grandmother's prodigious fortune.

The combined sum of her inheritance was a mind-boggling prospect that would intimidate most people and left her numb. Her wealth had been an early obstacle. With enough money to visit any place, to buy any thing or any one, she had had no challenge in life. Boredom had driven her to accept the gauntlet old Samuel had flung down before her.

Who would ever suspect the rich, beautiful Diana de Revillon, playgirl on two continents, of being an undercover investigator for Security International?

"You are the only investigator I know with a one-hundred-percent success record," Samuel had once told her, during one of those rare times when they directly discussed Diana's work.

Yes, she was both thorough and persistent, qualities in which she took an almost sinful pride. She loved the cat-and-mouse duet that was her secret life as much as she loved ballet, so much a part of her public life.

Well, this time her one-hundred-percent success rate seemed threatened.

She went back to the only two possible suspects in the Marmottan case: the jewel thief and the museum director. Could they possibly have been working in tandem? All the various overlapping police agencies had interrogated the owner and probed his background—he was a successful businessman and his personal financial affairs were well in order. Besides, the insurance didn't even completely cover the current market value of the stolen paintings.

So where was the motive?

And where was the *modus operandi*—those habits, techniques, and peculiarities of criminal behavior?

Four years with Security International had taught Diana that the true criminal mind always aspired to the professional status. Generally, the criminal judged the value of his efforts solely on the basis of accomplishment. Once achieving a few minor successes, he was always loath to alter his operational procedure even minimally. His reluctance often stemmed from superstition, inertia, and sheer lack of imagination.

The Pierluigi gold thief had certainly not lacked for imagination. Because of that, he had escaped her. One day he would repeat himself and she would be there to finger him, but for now, she had another case to solve.

Arriving at the Gare de Lyon station in Paris, she collected her T-Bird from the parking lot and drove to the *Mairie de Paris*, a gothic official building with leering gargoyles on its cornices, located on rue de Grenelle.

In the commercial section, musty old rooms fortified by walls and walls of record books, she informed the clerk behind the counter, "I'd like to see the company and corporation ledger M–N, please."

The faded old factotum, who wore a Pentecostal bun atop her head, grumbled, "Second time this afternoon," and trudged into an adjoining room. Minutes later, she returned, toting the heavy ledger, her fingerprints disturbing the dust that covered it.

The ledger couldn't have been touched in months, then twice in one day. Odd. "Who else wanted the M–N ledger?" Diana asked.

"The city doesn't pay me to people-watch, madame."

Diana thumbed through the pages until she found the corporation papers for Marmottan Museum. Sometimes antique and art dealers maintained an *entente cordiale* with burglars. A roster of stockholders might reveal an unsavory character.

One glance and she was disappointed. Only five stockholders, and four bore the Tissier family name. The majority stockholder, however, was not a family member but a holding company—Kabbal Enterprises.

That name nagged at her and she drummed her fingers on the counter, deep in thought. Then she knew! Of course, the name would be familiar to her! Once, when she mentioned to her grandmother that she was occasionally dating a Jewish premed student, the aristocratic dear old lady had discoursed on the evils of Judaism and especially Kabbalism, an offshoot of Judaism that practiced mysticism.

Diana's grandmother, true to her social class and her generation, was the anti-Semite of the family. Diana was prejudiced only against criminals—and long-term relationships.

She started to close the ledger, then noticed the smudge of dust on the page. Her fingerprint? She couldn't remember. She looked at her hands. They *were* dusty. She asked the clerk for the K–L ledger. The old woman grunted at being imposed upon but brought the ledger. This one was just as dusty, and there were fresh prints on it. The clerk's only?

The Kabbal Enterprises entry provided twenty-three subsidiary companies. She let out a little despairing sigh. To track each of them down could take days. She looked over the company names again. Some of their activities were readily apparent—Tuscany Olive Oil

Company, Languedoc Road Builders, The Loire Winery. One was more mysterious. Sefirot & Company.

Slowly, a smile came to her lips. *Sefirot*, it seemed to her, had something to do with Kabbalism. *Well, thank you, after all, grandmère!*

She didn't even bother looking up the company. Whoever was the partner or owner was cunning enough to camouflage identities.

"Merci bien, madame," she called to the old clerk, closing the thick ledger and leaving it on the counter.

She left the T-Bird parked where it was and walked two blocks to the Central Bureau, which acted, among other things, as a national vehicular registry office. The Central Bureau building looked as if it had once been the target of World War II bombing and had been only hastily patched.

As in a library, few people other than employees knew all the ins and outs of the multipurpose state bureau. One division, four floors up, kept records for insurance purposes of all people permitted to operate company vehicles. The system was hopelessly antiquated, but forty-five minutes later, she found the lone person registered to operate Sefirot & Company's vehicles.

David Mendel.

Paris rush-hour traffic was suicidal, and she should have been concentrating on defensive driving—but her mind kept going back to David Mendel. Oddly, though they both made the same social circuit scenes across Europe, their paths had never crossed—until last month, when she had shared the lift chair with him.

Behind her pupils an image of his clean-cut face was reflected—and those blue eyes, so cold they burned like vapor off hot ice.

On a silver tray in the entryway, the day's mail and

telephone messages waited for her where Peggy had left them. Ignoring them, she went immediately to the studio, changed into a pair of leotards, and began her warm-ups. By dinner time, she would be pleasantly tired, hot, and sweaty. Just as the perspiration cleansed her pores, the strenuous exercise cleared her brain of the day's cobwebs—freeing her subconscious to roam when at last she went to bed. The technique was one she had heard Thomas Edison used when he was stymied by his inventions. Sometimes the method even worked for her.

In the middle of the night, she woke up thinking of David Mendel. She checked the digital alarm on her nightstand: nearly three in the morning. With a yawn, she turned over her down pillow and burrowed beneath the electric blanket and crisp Pratesi linen sheets once more—then sat bolt upright in her bed.

So that's why David Mendel had been in her thoughts! That heist of the Iranian oil tanker she had investigated—David Mendel had been one of the silent partners in the tanker company.

✣ 10 ✣

For the equine set, those maintaining an au courant social schedule, was one of the obligatory entries on the May calendar was Deauville. Within its 880 acres, one of the devout rites of the very rich took place—fast thoroughbreds, fast money, and fastidious gentlefolk—culminating the last weekend in August with the world-famous Grand Prix de Deauville.

During late spring, the lush Normandy countryside around Deauville boasted more personal wealth per square foot than any other area its size in the world. The elegant little town, constructed from the excess wealth of *La Belle Epoque*, provided tranquility without isolation, peace without solitude.

Each May, it became truly the stronghold of the rich and social racing set. Only a select crowd of international luminaries was invited to join the high-stakes social circuit. The first big draw of the season was the yearling sales. Prices at this horse auction, the largest in France, rose to astronomical heights.

Except for the Rothschild family, who had a stud farm in Calvados; Sheik Mohammed al Maktoum, who had one in Kentucky; and Stavros Niarchos; Diana and her grandmother were probably the best judges of horse-flesh present that Sunday for the auction. To the un-trained eye, the task was formidable: how to distinguish a $300,000 horse from a $3 million one.

The fashionable spectators seated in the small audi-torium of the Hall des Ventes were garbed in everything from tennis attire to dinner jackets. Diana's grand-mother, La Comtesse de Revillon, was as scrupulously majestic as Britain's Queen Mother in her rose pink suit with matching wide-brim hat. The patrician older woman invariably wore a hat or carried a parasol to protect her pampered camellia skin—and just as invari-ably lectured testily to her suntanned granddaughter about the necessity.

That afternoon, Diana, in a white linen three-piece suit, was sporting a wide-brim straw picture hat that dipped flatteringly in front. She had selected it not be-cause it protected the flawless skin she had inherited from her doting grandmother but because it partially concealed her features.

On a dais toward the rear of the roped-off stage, the three-man auction crew, dressed in white tie and tails, took their seats behind a table. Behind and above them, the electronic auction board flashed to life, and the au-dience quieted in tense expectation. From the left side of the stage, a man in a red coat and black bow tie led out the first horse: a sleek, shiny filly with a numbered patch on her flank.

"Ladies and Gentlemen, we have hip number 218," said the announcer. He spoke in a fairly rapid but clear cadence. "Number 218 is an outstanding daughter by Green Dancer out of the exceptional brood mare My Caroline by Carroll. You will please note that this year-ling filly is a half sister to a champion two-year-old in Great Britain. Bidding will now begin."

At that point, the auctioneer—the man in the middle—took over, while the man on his left prepared to record bids. "The opening bid is one hundred thousand dollars. Do I hear one ten?" Though he spoke even more rapidly than the announcer, his voice was quiet, well modulated. The auction did not resemble the tobacco scenarios perpetrated by television but was more discreet, like those at Sotheby's or Christie's.

At the base of the stage, six ringmen, also wearing black ties and dinner jackets, had already taken their stations in various parts of the auditorium. These bid spotters now moved up and down the aisles in their assigned sections, eyes alerted for the merest movement of a hat or perhaps two fingers that would signify a bid. That bidder then became their responsibility. They worked the audience with discretion, one ringman subtly pitting his bidder against an opponent in another ringman's section.

Diana's casual glance slid over the racing people in the audience, most of whom, like herself and her grandmother, had flown into Deauville-Saint-Gatiens International Airport in chartered planes or private ones sporting the colors of their racing silks on their tails.

An assembly of titled aristocrats and moneyed gentlemen who disported with women who were not necessarily ladies were also following the bidding, if not actively participating. A few of the seatholders were out in the paddock, watching the horses walk, feeling their legs, writing down everything—or else were on the lawn, drinking, talking, and gaining respite from the high-priced tension inside.

A bearded sheikh, dressed casually in a lavender polo shirt, had his own agent, who handled the bidding, seated next to him. To the center right of the stage, she spotted Robert Sangster, the English betting-pool mag-

nate. A representative of the BBA, the British Blood-
stock Agency, was bidding for Sangster. It was all an
elaborate charade, with no one wishing to get caught
bidding. Most of the prospective buyers already knew
which horse they wanted to buy well before the auction
began; they had examined the young thoroughbreds for
those telltale signs of a potential champion.

At last, her gaze fixed on one person in particular
who was just taking a seat toward the left rear of the
auditorium. David Mendel wore body-hugging white
jeans, a bold patterned Claude Bonucci black silk shirt,
and, she noted, deck shoes without socks. A tremendous thrill shuddered through her, perhaps what a
jockey must feel, she thought, the split second before
the bell rings.

Accompanying David Mendel was a petite, exotic
beauty in an eye-dazzling poppy-colored pantsuit.

"Who is that woman, *grandmère*? The one with the
raven hair?"

Through her tinted Bronzini bifocal glasses, the
countess directed a probing squint in the direction Diana had indicated. "Maja bint Fadine, a great-
granddaughter of the last sultan of Turkey. She's a new
name on the scene."

Diana settled back, prepared to watch and wait. The
display board indicated that hip #218 was sold for
$865,000. Most of those present were aware that the
corpulent Stavros Niarchos had won out on the bidding.

"Now, *mesdames et messieurs*, I have for you hip
number 219, a foal by the renowned Top Hat, out of the
incomparable brood mare Sultana. You will note that
Top Hat's sire, Our Folly, was a multiple stakes winner."

Though the colt didn't have quite as illustrious antecedents as the previous filly, he was nonetheless magnificent. Diana would have wanted him for her grandmother's farm in Provence for that, if no other reason.

There was, however, another reason for her interest to be piqued: David Mendel was perking up. He leaned slightly forward in his seat, his vivid blue eyes intensifying. At his side, Maja said something, and he inclined his head to listen, without taking his eyes off the yearling shuffling restlessly in the ring.

The display board cleared. "Bidding will now begin," the auctioneer said, his words already quickening. "Pierre, what do you have?"

The bid-spotter in the center aisle signaled a dollar figure, and the auctioneer said, "Bidding has opened at seventy-five thousand dollars. Do I have eighty-five?"

The bidding continued rapidly in increments of ten thousand. Then, just as it appeared that Francoise Sagan, who owned estates and stables in the emerald Calvados countryside, would win, David Mendel made a slight gesture—his forefinger and thumb extended against his chest. At once, the bid-spotter of that section picked up his bid and relayed it to the auctioneer.

"I have two hundred fifty thousand dollars," the auctioneer responded at once. "Do I hear two sixty?"

The auction slowed down, while Sangster's crew huddled. It looked as if the bidders were prepared to let David Mendel have the colt.

Diana touched her fingers to the brim of her hat. Her bid-spotter immediately relayed her bid.

"I have two eighty," called the auctioneer. "Do I hear more?"

Immediately, the tension in the room rose like the mercury on a sorching Riviera afternoon. A duel was on. From across the room, she could feel David Mendel's dissecting scrutiny. He responded with another subtle finger gesture.

"Three fifty for Sultana's Folly," said the auctioneer. "Jean-Paul, do you have higher?"

She barely nodded to her bid-spotter, Jean-Paul. The young man in the tux couldn't conceal his pleasure at the way the bidding was going. He relayed her signaled bid on to the auctioneer, and the electronic board flashed the most recent bid, hers for $400,000.

A ripple of astonished whispers rolled across the auditorium, then ebbed in expectancy of her competitor's response. Desperately, she wanted to light a cigarette, but she remained motionless, dispassionate and regal, waiting. After all, patience and perseverance, that was her game.

David Mendel responded to her coolness with an astonishing jump in the bidding—to $750,000.

Jesus Freudian Christ.

Maja bint Fadine cast him a dubious look. Obviously, Diana thought, the late sultan's great-granddaughter was as astounded as was she and everyone else present.

Coolly, Diana signaled a $150,000 increase when she bid, and her grandmother sucked a hissing breath that quickly expanded her already ample bosom. "Have you lost your mind, Diana?"

Abruptly, David Mendel raised the bid. He could certainly afford to keep pace with her bidding, but the businessman in him surely recognized the senselessness of raising the bid on a thoroughbred yearling beyond its worth—unless, perhaps, the competitor in him goaded him into taking unnecessary risks purely for the pleasure of it.

Satisfied now with what she had been wanting to know, she let the bidding pass her by.

As she and her grandmother walked up the aisle toward the exit, the display board winked SOLD and the amount: $1,000,000.

With a soft sigh, Diana slid deeper into the tiled tub, its water drawn, not by the maid, but by the gardener, and then covered with gardenias, hibiscus, and orchids.

Everything about Deauville's Hôtel Royal reeked of elegance—from her room terrace overlooking the heated seawater swimming pool and the English channel beyond, to the doormen and bellhops, who still wore fitted monkey suits with brass buttons and pillbox hats. The traditional French breakfast of warm brioches and croissants with aromatic coffee was served on leather-lined trays, no less, so rattling china and crystal would not awaken the guests who were still sleeping.

Leaving her grandmother contentedly playing poker at Deauville's summer casino, the Casino d'Été, Diana had the entire evening to herself. She closed her eyes, letting the image of David Mendel fill the screen on the back of her lids, dominated by the unforgettable blue eyes that were so shrewd, with a strong male's predatory intensity.

She usually relied on her hunches, what foolish and shallow men often called "a woman's intuition." But then, she started searching for objective reasons, for motives.

She could find no reason for a man like David Mendel to risk his fortune, reputation, and family name on a common crime like theft. A crime of passion, yes. But not the robbery of items that often yielded less than Mendel would make in a month. Items like gold bars from a Valenza jeweler that turned up in Lugano. David Mendel had been in the vicinity that week, skiing. But then so had thousands of others, including herself.

The *modus operandi* of the thief she was seeking was

extraordinary—and David Mendel was brilliant. Was it the challenge after all? The afternoon's yearling sale seemed to confirm that suspicion.

Still, she needed more. This week at Deauville might just prove she was on the right track—and the racetrack was where she would begin tomorrow.

May 2nd

The daily races at the Hippodrome de la Touques, with its Norman architecture of overhanging eaves and half-timbered walls, lasted from two to five in the afternoon. At least that was the time the fashionable and trendy, the *bon chic bon genre*, put in their appearances. Business and pleasure mixed seamlessly.

Diana observed the horse-racing enthusiasts through her binoculars.

"Another one of your love interests?" the Comtesse de Revillon asked her granddaughter.

The two women were seated in the silver-haired *chatelaine*'s private box. The grounds below were packed with spectators: men in gray top hats, ascots, and tails and the women parading their glamorous *chapeaux*. The venerable countess carried a dotted swiss parasol to ward off insolent shafts of sun. Diana wore a turned-up-brim straw hat banded with the same black-and-white houndstooth silk charmeuse of her Bill Blass creation.

She lowered her binoculars. "What are you talking about, *grandmère*?"

The regal old lady nodded toward a box one aisle down from hers and several sections over, on the far right. "That is not the winner's circle you have your binoculars trained on, Diana."

Diana smiled wickedly. "Kindly grant me my hedonistic pleasures."

The countess rolled her eyes. At seventy-one, her carriage was as erect as a Benedictine nun's. "I thought the year in the convent would dilute that vulgar strain of American carnality that pervades your veins. Such morals!"

Bitter recollections of the convent's rigor and sparseness assailed Diana, but she merely said, "You might recall that a French courtesan's blood also runs through my veins."

"Bah. Your ancestor was a Montmorte; not even Louis Quatorze's blood was that royal. Now, who is this man who captures your fancy?"

"David Mendel."

"The man you bid against yesterday?" Her grandmother's lips, artfully rouged, pursed in a network of fine wrinkles. "He's the scion of that Jewish banking family."

"I know." She rested her hand over the doyenne's warm, veined one. "It's all right, *grandmère*. I'm not planning on marrying the man."

Confusion furrowed the countess's brow. "But why did you drive the bidding up on him?"

"Well, I certainly wasn't being a female Shylock and taking my own pound of flesh, though I know that would have pleased you. I was just doing a little harmless flirting. Now stop worrying and enjoy the race."

She raised her binoculars and refocused them. With a roselike smile, Maja was pointing to a name on David Mendel's program. The girl had a frail, childish, and sweet beauty.

"What do you know about him, *grandmère*?"

"Who?"

"You know who, *grandmère*," Diana singsonged.

La Comtesse de Revillon clicked her tongue at Diana

disparagingly. "He was married for several years to Esther Reinholt."

"Any kin to the Israeli scientist?"

"His daughter. She has the kind of looks that remind
you of an Egyptian queen, a Nefertiti beauty, but she
has never remarried. Devoted herself to the arts—
something both she and her former husband seemed to
have had in common. Diana, dear, why don't you find
some eligible and—"

Without lowering her binoculars, Diana said,
"*Grandmère*, when will you accept the fact that I don't
ever plan to marry? I'm perfectly happy with my life as
it is. Why complicate it with compromises?"

David Mendel was signaling to the waiter. Was it
possible this influential and powerful force in the European economic community could have pulled off the
Pierluigi caper? And the Antwerp diamond theft she
had read about? And absconded with the Marmottan
paintings, as well as masterminded the heist of the Iranian oil tanker?

"It is all your parents' fault," the countess said.
"They battled and bickered until it well nigh drove me
crazy, not to mention having a devastating impact on
you. Then that awful Ladshaw and the way he ruined
my Nicole didn't help your impression of marriage."

"At least I won't have to worry about leaving the
same impression on my children," she said, cutting
short her grandmother's unhealthy reverie. As Diana
was her only grandchild, she knew her grandmother
despaired of the Revillon line's dying out.

"It would be just like you to have a child on your
own, outside of marriage," the countess said indig-
nantly.

"The next race begins in five minutes. Do you want
to place a bet?"

Her grandmother fluttered a beringed hand in dismissal. "I'll save my wagering for the casino tonight."

"Bottom Dollar is running in this one." The horse was a half sister to Full-Length Mink, out of the countess's own stables.

"That horse doesn't stand a chance," the old woman pronounced.

Her grandmother was usually right about horses. Before the racing began, they had gone to the back track to get a feel for the day's events. Having grown up in that earthy milieu, Diana still knew about half of the jockeys and trainers.

She lifted her binoculars again—and found David Mendel's glasses focused on her! For a full ten seconds, she trained her sights on him, then shifted away smoothly to the horses prancing nervously toward the starting line.

Perhaps, without realizing it, she had been wrong when she told her grandmother she wasn't being a female Shylock, taking her pound of flesh.

11

May 3rd

In the predawn darkness, the great dolorous bell tolled as pairs of vacant-faced Benedictine monks filed from the cloister in through the side door of the Abbaye Notre-Dame du Bec. Occasionally there came a cough or the sound of a nose being blown. Wakening birds in the surrounding Normandy forests chirped a hymn to a new day, even though the sky was still smeared faintly with stars.

His face partially hidden by his black cassock hood, Frère Jean-Paul, père hôtelier, or guest master, led the visitors toward the guest refectory. From the rope belting his white wool robe, keys on a large ring clinked musically in counterpoint to the drone of the Gregorian chanting of the monks at early mass. Blank-eyed statues kept vigilant along the thirteenth-century corridor of squat Roman arches, staring dispassionately at the newest visitors.

The sense of serenity and age-old ritual comforted Hamemuneh. The monastery was a world apart, with a discipline that purified and strengthened the spirit. He wished he could undergo that revitalization before leaping back into the frenzy of life in fifth gear.

Since their foundation in the tenth century, the abbeys and monasteries of Europe had stood like beacons; they had acted as hospices and way stations and offered shelter to pilgrims and succor to the troubled. There, names were never asked, never used. Nor did the monks ask what a person did, where he came from, whether he believed, why he was there.

In the late nineteen eighties, Europe's monasteries were no longer refuges for Catholics alone. They had become places where men, women, couples, families, those of the faith and those in doubt, could set aside temporarily their daily concerns and become part of the monastic life.

Hamemuneh and his two companions sought out the Abbaye Notre-Dame du Bec for none of the traditional reasons, but rather for privacy and anonymity. The very idea that three of Mossad's top officers were meeting in a Benedictine abbey an hour's drive from Deauville would have been preposterous, even unthinkable, to the opposition.

The trio bypassed the abbey shop where a peach-fuzzed young lay brother perched amid jars of honey, packages of herbs, fruit-paste candies, and demijohns of the tart Normandy apple cider.

The guest refectories were a cluster of pink, half-timbered houses, roofed with bluish slates and latticed by gardens and arbors. The refectory assigned to Hamemuneh and his companions was secured by stone walls, awash in early dawn rosiness. A tiny lizard, disturbed from its sleep, streaked off the worn stone sill and disappeared into the mesh of nearby pine needles. Inside the stone-floored building, the men climbed a winding, narrow, wooden staircase smelling of beeswax. The upper room was small, white-washed, and ascetic, and its dormered windows were close to the floor at one side of the space.

After Frère Jean-Paul departed, the senior Mossad officer, a man of seventy or more, who wore a traditional black beret at a jaunty angle, opened the dormers. Outside, an owl hooted eerily, and scents of wild thyme and cypress drifted into the room.

Each man washed his hands and face in the icy water of a basin on a dark-wooded chest of drawers, then, as he finished, took a seat around a long wooden table rubbed to satin by the hands of centuries of pilgrims.

The mood in the room was restrained. The old man in the beret, Yashiv Yadan, was the first to speak. He was an early recruit to Mossad, when it was organized before World War II to mastermind the illegal immigration of persecuted European Jews into British-mandated Palestine.

At that time, Mossad consisted of exactly ten people, spread over half a dozen European countries and entrusted with the agonizing decision of singling out which names, from among hundreds of thousands of candidates, would be placed on the coveted passenger lists of the secret refugee ships.

Yashiv Yadan's twinkling faded blue-gray eyes never reflected the tragedies he had witnessed. "Your gold bar operation set up the South American superbly, Hamemuneh. That is one drug dealer who won't be offering asylum to any more Nazi renegades."

Hamemuneh didn't say anything, and Yadan didn't expect a response.

Rabin, the third man, became impatient. His head was skull-like and shaven, the dark eyes deep in their sockets, his skin almost cadaverously taut on his bones. Against all odds, he had survived the Treblinka concentration camp. "It seems we have another problem," he put in. "We're faced with a step-up in anti-Jewish terrorists attacks. What about Oslo?"

"You have the report?" Yadin asked.

Across the table, Hamemuneh rubbed the bridge of his bladed nose, one of the very few times he ever permitted himself a gesture that expressed his great weariness.

He had been trained in cover, concealment, and camouflage, in night detection and operations, in the handling of grenades, mines, small arms, and booby traps, along with nuclear, biological, and chemical defenses; still, he couldn't shake off his feeling of futility and ineptitude that crept over him whenever he was with old warriors like Yadan and Rabin and the other war horses. For Jews like them, revenge would never be sufficient.

"A stringer in Oslo's police department showed me the bomb fragments—burlap, paper wrappings, a piece of twine. Some particles clinging to the twine provided information under a microscope." Hamemuneh almost droned his report. "The twine came from a farm, the lab report said, where would be found a fast-running stream, pine trees, black and white rabbits, a bay horse, red chickens, and a light cream-colored cow."

Rabin shook his head and flicked a skeptical glance at his senior officer, who merely said, "Let him continue, Rabin."

"The paper was traced to a Marseilles pharmacy suspected of drug dealings. A week of watching netted three buyers, one of whom was presently working on a farm just outside Marseilles that matched the description suggested by the twine. The man is a second-generation French-Algerian *pieds-noir* who goes by the name of Sciolla."

He broke off as a burly monk with thick glasses came in, bearing a breakfast tray. The fare was simple—fried eggs, baked brown bread, a kettle of coffee and warm milk, and, surprisingly, pungent herbal liqueur from the abbey's precious cache. Hamemuneh found his morning-pure palate appreciative of the light meal.

After they finished, he continued his summation. "I think Sciolla is the man responsible for the factory explosion and Josef Tabosky's death, but I think he was recruited by someone else. At a dockside cabaret on the Quai des Belges, I bought him several rounds of cheap wine. The name of Andre Daguerre slipped over his lips with the wine."

Yashiv Yadan glanced at Rabin and asked, "Ever heard of this man?"

The gaunt man shook his shaven head. "No."

Hamemuneh rose and went to the open window. In the courtyard below, a fan-tailed white pouter pigeon strutted among large terra-cotta pots, ablaze with red geraniums. Beyond, bees hummed in hillside hives and cows grazed in pastures dotted with moss-thatched cottages.

Without turning, he spoke to the two behind him. "I tracked down Daguerre in Amsterdam. He's a production manager at the Heineken Brewery. His daily routine is fairly consistent—except for a trip he made to Schiphol Airport. He greeted one of the arriving passengers—from Munich—then left."

"That's all?" Rabin asked. "He simply returned home or whatever?"

"That's all, as far as Daguerre is concerned. I boarded the departing plane, telling the stewardess I had forgotten my jacket. I didn't find my jacket, of course, but I observed the seat number of the passenger Daguerre had greeted earlier. The passenger list showed seat 16C belonged to a man by the name of Louis St. Giles."

"Still doesn't mean anything to me," Yadan said.

"All I've been able to find out is that St. Giles is the

head of a reputable publishing house in Frankfurt—and that he is a collector of objects of vertu. But from certain things I've picked up on, I believe this St. Giles may be the head of a neo-Nazi fringe organization.''

"Then we set a trap for him," Rabin said, "and see if he nibbles.''

"I've already done that," Hamemuneh said, "using Sciolla as bait.'' He rarely worked with anyone on an operation and then only undercover. With Sciolla, though, he had put himself into the open. "Hiring Sciolla as an accomplice, I now possess some art masterpieces St. Giles would dearly love. Naturally, St. Giles will learn from his employee that I happen to possess the stolen masterpieces.''

"You don't waste time, do you?'' Yadan said warmly.

Hamemuneh was slightly disgusted with himself at his involuntary flush of pleasure. With these two old men, he was still a boy, seeking approval from the father long gone, roasted alive in a Nazi crematorium.

"In the meantime," Yadan continued, "we'll see what else we can find on our friend, St. Giles.''

Hamemuneh braced his hands on the windowsill. The bucolic scene below made it difficult for him to believe death and destruction were a part of his life, that racial and religious bigotry still flourished more than forty years after the Holocaust, after the horrors of Auschwitz and Dachau and Bergen-Belsen, horrors that staggered even the unfettered imagination.

The contrast was an infinite perplexity to him.

✤ 12 ✤

May 4th

So many affluent Parisians escaped to Deauville during its short spring season that the town was known as Paris's Twenty-first arrondissement. Despite its international racing regattas, car rallies, film festivals, and tennis tournaments, Deauville remained an old-fashioned residential watering place of tree-lined, winding streets and half-timbered Norman houses with flowers spilling from every window box.

The town collected scandals as a woman did jewelry, and the place to flaunt both was the fabled Boardwalk. Early each morning, through the light summer mist, came the sound of hooves clopping on the hard sand as racehorses galloped past the Boardwalk in training. Few jet-setters observed this ritual, since they rarely arose before eleven o'clock.

By midday, the sun was warmer, and rows of bright green, yellow, red, and blue parasols stretched for three hundred meters along the sand in front of the Boardwalk. Here on the sun-bleached *planches*, everyone took their constitutionals in the invigorating sea breezes. Further out, billowing yacht sails patched the horizon.

For changing, there were the tall, slim, and colorful

78

tents with their baroque canopies that reminded Diana of a Matisse painting in motion. Her grandmother thought differently. "They all look like a tumult that belongs in a Cecil B. De Mille Biblical epic," she sniffed.

From their vantage point on the chic Le Ciro's terrace they could watch the vast spectrum of the elite sunbathing in old-fashioned wooden deck chairs or strolling the boardwalk behind balletic high-stepping, white borzois and chunky Siberian huskies.

Diana had her eye on one person in particular. Laughing, Maja bint Fadine and David Mendel splashed ashore in the wake of the roiling tide. With the build of a competition swimmer or avid snow skier—wide shoulders, narrow hips, and muscled thighs and calves—David Mendel had clearly escaped the inevitable paunch that was the by-product of money and age. He was so tanned and fit, it was difficult for her to judge exactly how old he was, but there was enough gray in his blond hair, coupled with the fan lines at his eyes and mouth, to place him well into middle age.

Observing him and Maja gathering their thick hotel towels, preparing to leave, Diana asked herself—was he athletic enough to scale a twelve-foot-high, spiked iron fence?

Where had he been yesterday? Secluded away in his hotel room with the lovely Maja? The entire day?

Perhaps all these years I've underestimated the power of fascination.

"You haven't touched your Dover sole," her grandmother chided. The naturally stylish old lady looked as if she had just that moment stepped off the Champs-Elysée. "Try the caviar with blinis and *crème fraîche.* It is the best I've tasted in months."

Diana set her napkin to the left of her plate. "Let's go browsing, *grandmère.*"

"Browsing? I thought you wanted to go to the polo

match this afternoon. Competition for the Championnat Mondial Cup begins.''

"There's plenty of time."

With as much a frown as the old lady permitted her well-preserved features, she put down her half-empty glass of Perrier and said, "This is highly unlike you, Diana. You have always been contemptuous of what you called the idle pasttimes."

Diana lifted her shoulders in a Gallic shrug. "Perhaps I'm degenerating."

"More rapidly than I thought. Honestly, Diana, you must find more to devote your life to than occasional modeling, ballet practice, and charity balls."

Diana signed the bill and collected her purse. "Like mother, like daughter?"

Instantly, she regretted her remark, but the countess waved the remark away. "No. Devote yourself to a family. When you get to be my age and there is no more family left—then you can take up a hobby like horse breeding. But, until then, life is passing—"

"Please," Diana said with a broad smile, "don't mar this lovely day with your serious lectures about my frivolous life. Please, *grandmère*."

The countess acquiesced with a slight shrug of her designer-padded shoulders and insisted to the waiter that he carry the table parasol as sun shield for her and her granddaughter all the way to the waiting chauffeured limousine.

The waiter and Diana cheerfully humored her eccentricity. In a world that had turned upside down for Diana as a child—being shuffled from continent to continent, from father to mother, to father, to mother and stepfather—her grandmother had been the one solid foundation in a transient life of illusions.

The big black Mercedes bypassed the busy stalls in

Place du Marche, where a melange of antique clothes and linens was intermingled with fresh fruits, vegetables, and the incomparable Norman farm cheeses.

On Boulevard Eugène Cornuché, behind huge family villas and the majestic white summer casino, squatted pseudo-Norman houses with thatched roofs. Most were occupied by the best of fashionable Paris jewelers and couturiers, and it was there that spontaneous elegance and worldly cachet came into sharp focus.

Diana ordered the chauffeur to pull up in front of the celebrated jewelers, Vacheron-Constantin.

"Jewelry?" the countess asked, descending from their leased Mercedes. "I really prefer Van Cleef and Arpels or Bulgari baubles, Diana. I found a little gold trifle there that—"

"I'm not interested in gold, *grandmère*. What I have in mind is diamonds."

"Diamonds? You have never liked them. I distinctly remember your saying on your seventeenth birthday that you didn't like cold things touching your skin. That diamonds reminded you of ice."

Ushering her grandmother through the timbered door the chauffeur opened for them, Diana barely glanced at the brightly lit vitrines. "I thought you said you wanted to browse," the countess protested.

"I've changed my mind," Diana muttered. What she had in mind had only just occurred to her, as she was watching David Mendel leave the beach.

A soft chime announced their entrance. The interior was decorated in modern accents—all glass and chrome, splashes of yellow and orange on the silk-upholstered walls and a plush white carpet.

As she and her grandmother seated themselves on chrome stools before one display case, a little man with a pencil-thin mustache entered from a back room. "La

Comtesse de Revillon, *n'est ce pas?*'' The man asked with
a glance that managed to appear aloof without offending.

"It is," her grandmother responded in the haughty
manner that only the French can affect instinctively.

"Vacheron-Constantin welcomes your patronage,
mesdames," he said, his manner warming degree by
degree. It was a harmless charade demanded by the
beau monde. "May I show you something?"

"I'm interested in diamonds," Diana said. "Possibly
a ring and bracelet set."

"Vacheron-Constantin has a baguette ruby and sapphire bangle bracelet with diamonds set in eighteen-karat
yellow gold—and it has a matching ring. Because it features the three American colors, we call them our star-
spangled bangles. The Americans have all but emptied
our stock. Of course, *chère* madame, those are also *our*
colors." He brushed a manicured finger past the end of
his mustache and very nearly simpered at the countess.

"Show us what you have then," La Comtesse de Revillon said.

He withdrew a velvet-covered tray from one of the
display cases. "If you'll kindly accompany me to one
of our viewing rooms, I shall be most pleased—"

"I am interested solely in diamonds," Diana emphasized, smiling charmingly at the man. "You see, I would
like to match a ring and bracelet parure with an absolutely
exquisite little necklace that I bought in an Antwerp shop."

"Ahh, yes, I understand. However, we are able rarely
to match pieces."

"Oh, really. How interesting."

The clerk was more than ready to display his wealth
of knowledge, and within minutes she had her answer.
Only another Orthodox Jew could have possibly pulled
off the Antwerp diamond theft.

13

To Tom, the charming bistro cafés lining Deauville's sidewalks never seemed to close and they were frequented by customers who never seemed to sleep. *He* hadn't slept more than five hours straight for weeks now. Sciolla was doing his damnedest keeping him busy, wandering from city to city like an American tourist taking advantage of a favorable exchange rate.

Except Sciolla was French—and spending money that a temporary worker didn't usually possess. Nor did the bourgeoisie of France ordinarily choose Deauville for its *vacances*.

So, why was Sciolla here? To take advantage of the short-term influx of disposable income? The overgrown cretin was totally out of place in a town of clubby bars and exclusive dining rooms, and he certainly didn't fit in with the high-powered habitués of the horsey set.

For that matter, Tom thought, he himself didn't exactly fit in with these people who seemed to drift through their days—wandering in and out of pricey boutiques, wining and dining in intimate private restaurants or sunning themselves at the open-air cafés, always seeking some brand of impulsive, instant graftification.

From the green turfs of the race course to the green baize of the gaming tables, these people occupied themselves in a devoutly plotted campaign to exchange their money for pleasure.

Tom had come to know them well; they were like Natalie's people, and they practiced the theory that if money couldn't buy happiness, it certainly bought an acceptable, however fleeting, facsimile. On his salary, he had been unable even to *rent* that kind of happiness for the French ambassador's daughter.

He had known all along that her infatuation with him—the tough, Hispanic narc—would eventually turn to disgust. There was the ultimate damned irony of their marriage. She had married him hoping to change him, to smooth over his bumpy edges, and he had married her hoping she would never change. Ultimately, they had both been disappointed.

Wondering where he might get a cup of coffee that didn't taste like sulphur molasses and a cigarette that wouldn't sear his lungs, he signaled to the waiter. Just then, in the bistro across the street, Sciolla got up, dug a wad of francs from his trousers pocket, flung them on the table, and scurried away.

Without waiting for his bill, Tom went after him, dropping a more than adequate collection of francs. Tailing Sciolla was a cinch. His features were far from ordinary: a flat nose and jutting chin and dark, oily ringlets that dribbled over a high forehead. And today, he was wearing a purple and green plaid shirt.

To be most effective, shadowing by foot required at least three operatives to minimize the risk of detection by appearing in the subject's line of view too often or being forced to make abrupt changes of direction. Two followed the suspect from equal distances, and the third stayed approximately opposite him on the other side of

the street. Well, Tom didn't have the luxury of two partners, and keeping up with Sciolla had been wearing on
him for days. His surveillance, however, now looked as
if it might pay off. Sciolla was following an exotic-
looking young woman, who hung on the arm of a man
dressed impeccably in a three-piece, hand-stitched, gray
silk suit and black oxfords. He might have just stepped
off London's Bond Street or from the pages of *GQ*.

The man dipped his head, apparently excusing himself to the woman, and stepped aside to talk to Sciolla.
The conversation was brief, then the two parted.

Without hesitating, Tom let Sciolla go. Instead, he
followed the couple. Sciolla had rarely spoken to anyone since he'd been shadowing him, and then the other
person was usually a bellhop, a waiter, a street vendor.
Once he tried to pick up a college girl outside the Sorbonne. Another time, he drank himself into near obliv-
ion with a dockworker at a Marseilles quayside bar.

Why would Sciolla converse with a man who was so
obviously from a vastly different social level? What
could they possibly have in common?

Paintings?

A love of art masterpieces?

Casually, Tom ambled into the elegant jewelry shop
in time to hear the clerk greet the couple with, "Monsieur Mendel, so good to see you in Vacheron-Constantin once again!"

"There it is!" said the raven-haired woman on the
arm of the man called Mendel. Her dark eyes were fixed
avidly on a particular piece, her voice lilting with
delight. "There is the black pearl necklace I was talking about."

But her escort, Tom noticed, was not looking at the
necklace. Tom caught a brief exchange of glances between Mendel and a stunning blonde with tawny golden

legs. Although momentary, the glance enabled each of them to take the measure of the other . . . even more . . . there was an almost blistering, sensual appraisal.

14

Motive.

Without one, Diana had no basis for establishing as her prime suspect in a series of spectacularly staged thefts a man who lived like a Renaissance prince. Nevertheless, she had a gut feeling, as Sam called it.

So, a little gossiping was in order.

She slipped her glasses on and thumbed through the invitations mounded on a corner of her desk. Yes, there it was—a grande soirée hosted by La Baronne de Rothschild in aid of the Musée des Arts Decoratifs, which was opening the doors to one hundred new rooms at the Louvre.

If Esther Mendel was a patron of the arts, she would most likely be there. Not a conducive atmosphere for gossiping, but Diana knew that David's former wife, like most of Paris's high-profile women, would spend that day in one of the cosmetics houses that reminded Diana of grooming kennels, with all the cubicles and stalls. Perfect for eliciting information.

But which cosmetics house?

She lit a cigarette, all the while doing some mental inventory. Then she picked up the telephone and dialed

Maria Vitani, the Duquesa de Montoya y Villaferia, who was on kiss-kiss terms with society's *crème de la crème*.

"Maria, *chèrie*, this is Diana. So good to hear your voice. Where have you been cavorting lately? Yes, I plan to attend the Rothschild soirée, but I think I want to change my style of makeup. After five years with Dior, I am ready for something different—perhaps a bit more exotic. I've noticed Esther Mendel's look this season and rather like it. Can you recommend a salon? *Dernier?* Yes, I am familiar with it. An independent, isn't it?"

The call paid off and Diana placed another one, sweetly asking the secretary at *Dernier* to book her at the last minute.

An appointment with a cosmetics salon meant an all-day affair, or pampering, as Diana thought of it: face masque, massage, hair styling, manicure.

Despite the eight o'clock rush-hour traffic, she arrived early the next morning at the salon, a converted Belle Epoque palace fifteen kilometers outside Paris. Undressing in the cubicle assigned her, she slid into the thick white terry cloth robe with the monogrammed "D" emblazoned in gold across its back. A covert glance of the secretary's open appointment book informed Diana that Esther Mendel had already been checked in.

Dernier was more like a spa, where marble halls, crystal chandeliers, an immaculate staff in crisply starched uniforms, and an indoor/outdoor pool were all vital parts of the overall grooming services. Serenity was the hallmark of the place, whose treatments were enhanced by the charming music of a chamber orchestra in the main pavilion.

Diana's morning began with a visit to the medical

staff. Here an herbal wrap and mud body pack from the Borghese collection were prescribed. She recognized an old friend of her grandmother's undergoing hydrotherapy. CeCe Blount, the estranged wife of a Texas oil tycoon, was getting an inhalation treatment. The woman could spend three million on jewelry in a single day in Switzerland or loot a Fifth Avenue bookstore of nearly every decorative volume in an hour. She made Imelda Marcos look like a bag lady.

In a private *cabinet* decorated with a plush ultramarine carpet and flowered-fabric walls, Diana stretched naked on a sheet-covered bed. One of the spa's experienced therapists took handsful of the heavy steamy paste and glopped it on specific points: face, arms, shoulders, waist, and legs. Towel around her head and wrapped in a sheet, Diana rested in the gunk for twenty minutes. In the next cubicle, Esther Mendel was undergoing the same gooey treatment. Eyes closed, Diana listened to the chatter between Esther and her attendant.

"After the marine-algae wrap, a body peeling, followed by ozone steaming, and, of course, an Evian water hydrotherapy."

"What do you think I should do with my hair?" Esther Mendel's voice was low and cultivated.

"A highlight will really bring out the brilliancy in your black hair, Madame Mendel. Some russet, perhaps. We'll run you through the color charts just before lunch."

When Diana went to soak in a hot mineral bath to dissolve her mudpack, Esther was already reclining in the circular pool, eyes closed, head tilted back against a folded towel on the tiled rim. Even through the hazy steam, the woman's noble profile really did resemble

Nefertiti—a long neck, almond-shaped eyes, high-bridged nose.

When she felt Diana enter the pool, Esther opened those dark eyes and turned her head toward her. "This water's marvelous," she said with a soft sigh in flawless French.

"Mmmm," Diana acknowledged in a lazy voice. She wetted the body sponge she had been given. "Makes you want to forego the rest of the day's treatments."

"Not at this price."

Diana chuckled. "I couldn't help but overhear part of your discussion about highlighting. My hair has been lackluster lately. I haven't been able to do anything with it. Did your stylist recommend any particular brand?" ·

"Well . . ."

Instant rapport. As they moved languorously through the various stages of the day's indulgences, Diana kept her end of the conversation light and easy. "I did hear," she said, smiling through the smoke of an after-lunch cigarette, "Lady Banes-Leigh had asked for a waxed bikini cut and ended up totally pillated!"

Esther laughed, thoroughly entertained. She leaned her head closer to Diana and confided shyly, "I've always had a fear of just such a thing happening."

"I'm certain a husband would raise some questions. Fortunately, as I am single, I don't worry about that."

Thus encouraged, Esther asked later, when they both were alone and waiting for their makeup to be spritzed with mineral water, "Why have you never married?"

"There has never been just the right man for me. Childishly, I believed in that crazy notion that sparks fly and violins play and your chemistry cells go berserk." She let a hollow little laugh escape. "Now, when I know better, it's too late for me to change my independent ways, I'm afraid. What about yourself?"

Esther looked away, her mouth tightening. "It is possible. At least, it did happen to me, although I doubt the same thing happened to David—my former husband. There's an old saying—when the gods want to punish you, they answer your prayers."

Diana repressed a sympathetic response. Instead, she asked, "How did you two meet?"

Restlessly, Esther rose from her padded chair and strolled about the makeup room, her graceful long fingers toying with bottles and jars and boxes. She had a lithe gazellelike beauty.

Diana felt slightly ashamed of her prying. "I didn't mean to bring up such a grim subject."

Esther lifted her gaze from a jar of emerald-green glass in which she had seemed absorbed. "That's all right. My family isn't affluent—not on David's level, at least—but we can trace our lineage back to Queen Isabella of Spain. My father is a nuclear physicist, who until recently lived here in France," she said with obvious pride. "Now, he works in the Negev for the Israel Mining Company, searching for and extracting uranium."

"I've heard of him."

"David and my father became acquainted in Tel Aviv, when David was there transacting business with his firm's Tel Aviv branch. David was almost thirty and, I suppose, aware that he should take a wife.

"The first time I saw him was at his chateau outside Paris—in Rueil-Malmaison, where my father and I had been invited to spend the weekend with some of his other guests. I was reminded of that other David—Michelangelo's. David left his poolside table and came to greet us. The violins, the bells . . . I heard all of them."

Quietly, compassionately, Diana said, "But your marriage didn't last. . . ."

"No. I could never get through to David, to become that nebulous 'one' with him. He has the temperament of a restless warrior-scholar. That's the only way I can explain him. He always holds himself apart, despite his gentle ways and caring attitude."

"It sounds like you love him very much."

Esther's voice became bitter and brittle. "I do. Unfortunately, his endearing and charming ways cover a terror of emotional commitment. The only times I ever got close were those moments after he awoke from one of his dreams. Half-asleep, he'd let me comfort him— perhaps I should say suffer my comfort—until he had coalesced within himself once more."

"What kind of dreams?"

"Oh, you know—nightmares. About the concentration camps. The war years left a lasting impression, though he never would talk about it later, after the nightmares, after he had regained control of himself."

15

June 1st

The throng of international press and fashion buyers who make the twice-yearly pilgrimage to Paris were at the Tuileries for the fall/winter fashion collections, featuring a panoply of designer furs.

Separate sections were reserved for star journalists, star buyers, and just plain stars. John Fairchild of *Women's Wear Daily* and Polly Mellen of American *Vogue* were among the journalists and Marvin Traub of Bloomingdale's was among the buyers.

From the celebrity grouping, the show was stolen by Boy George in a butch look and leggy and lean Princess Stephanie of Monaco in a punkish hairdo featuring a purple-dyed swath of hair, good for fifteen minutes of pros and cons. Sitting together in the front row, the pair gave new meaning to the term androgyny.

Female international clothes horses jockeyed for position in the frenetic burst of paparazzi's strobes with the men who designed their frocks. Other celebrities and socialites—Anouk Aimée, Marie-Hélène de Rothschild, Claudia Cardinale, Catherine Deneuve, and Diana de Revillon preferred anonymity while they watched the Balenciaga show, at the end of which the designer took his traditional walk down the runway.

The collection, Diana felt, deserved plaudits. She knew *haute couture* inside and out. Not only had she modeled in her late teens for Lanvin for a paltry sum, compared to that of photographers' models, but she had also worked later on for Ungaro during her lost, purposeless years. That was how she defined her early twenties, when, as a *mannequin du monde*, she wore exclusively the clothes of a single designer and was seen often in his company.

She had learned that *haute couture* was a costly distinction, which only a score or so successful designers could claim legitimately. The Ministry of Industry imposed strict controls on the label. Each *haute couture* house had to have at least twenty employees working in production and had to present two major runway shows a year for buyers and the press, featuring at least seventy-five outfits—as well as no fewer than forty-five additional shows a year for customers only.

The melodious strains of Brazilian bossa nova introduced the collection of Thierry Mugler, *enfant terrible* of Paris fashion. Rumor had it that tickets to his fashion show were being scalped by hotel concierges for $500 and more.

The spectators began taking notes. Diana's pad had the words: "Psychedelic prints, Lucite accessories, bold color, body-conscious shaping, tarty style."

Then the name "David Mendel."

Sitting beside her, Sam, obviously out of place in a rumpled white linen suit, read her note, fingered his equally white mustache, nodded slightly, and said, "Your father has updated your trust at Tours, my dear. You might want to go over it."

Next to him, the twice-titled Margo Adolfo flared her

aristocratic nostrils and snapped at Sam, "Monsieur, would you kindly extinguish your cigar?"

Forty-eight hours later, Diana drove away from her penthouse in the T-Bird. She had one stop before she left town: Paris's ancient public library, in the heart of the city, a gothic structure with buttresses, turrets, and a crenelated roofline. The place reeked with the chill, musty smell of a crypt. In the archives department, she asked the down-at-the-mouth male librarian for the microfilms of European newspapers for the month of February.

Every crime had a personality, a mind, and that was what she was banking on. She was very lucky. In less than an hour of eyestraining concentration, she found what she was looking for: a report of a diamond fraud totaling 125,000 Belgian francs on the second page of Antwerp's largest-circulation French newspaper, *Gazet van Antwerpen.*

In an edition dated a week later, she was rewarded for her thoroughness. Buried among the small, miscellaneous items, she found where a New York rabbi had reported an anonymous donation of 125,000 Belgian francs, earmarked to aid the resettlement of families arriving in Israel.

She reached Tours, in the lush Loire Valley, in just under two hours. Despite the wartime bombing, le Vieux Tours had managed to retain the charm of a peaceful provincial center. She parked on rue Colbert, a narrow and attractive street with some picturesque old houses, including one on the site of a slightly earlier shop where Joan of Arc had bought her suit of armor in 1429 before setting out for Orléans, where she routed the English.

Although the bank on rue Colbert was modern, the

product of the postwar reconstruction, there was a certain coziness in its underground vault. In the safe-deposit section, she aligned her hand with the impression on the metal board, an electronic palm reader. Her palm and fingerprints had been recorded a year before, and the computer screen above the metal board flashed its recognition of her as an authorized entrant.

Behind the four-and-a-half-ton door and the thick steel-reinforced concrete walls, bank employees went quietly about their tasks. Some tended the shelves laden with clients' gold: little boxes holding bars of many sizes, like so many foil-covered chocolates or small brown cloth bags, sealed and coded. Others wheeled in dollies bearing old and new bond issues, all wrapped in plastic.

Diana overheard connoisseurlike murmurs: "Ahh, a fine blue paper . . . An intriguing one, ten percent, I'd estimate. . . . Lovely! Imperial Japanese government, 1910—the last coupon!"

Alone in a cubicle, she opened the safe-deposit box and withdrew the file folder that had been placed there only the day before. The dossier contained data on David Mendel: his position as CEO of Mendel Banking House; president of Infodex, which provided information through a computerized advertising medium; and director of the philanthropic Europrogramme Fund; as well as an European equivalent of a D&B report on the financial standing of his companies.

Aside from business, Mendel was described as a patron of the arts, expert skier and fencer, polo player, and horse-breeding enthusiast.

A list of his holdings indicated a Paris townhouse, the country house in Rueil-Malmaison, his famous yacht—*The Star of David*—a private Mitsubishi jet, a 1935 Aston-Martin, a Rolls-Royce Silver Cloud, and thirteen other grand cars as well as a Harley Davidson. Also included was a health record detailing his height at six feet even and weight at 180 pounds, along with an indication of an appendectomy.

On a separate page, she found what she wanted under the heading of DACHAU. Apparently, David Mendel's life hadn't always been filled with aimless pleasure.

In 1943, twenty-eight freight trains transported 13,000 Jews to Dachau. David Mendel, five at the time, and his family were passengers. His family was subsequently exterminated. David Mendel survived and, after Dachau, was liberated, eventually returned to Vienna and the family business, run by family friend and employee, Otto Dagenfeld.

The next page detailed his schooling.

David Mendel was educated at a small English preparatory school, Summerfields, in St. Leonard's-on-the-Sea, near Hastings, Sussex. He went on to become an Oxford scholar-athlete, majoring in economics, and finished his education at L'École des Sciences Politiques in Paris.

She replaced the file. She had a suspect and now she had a motive—a probable cause: After one beat the gas chambers, what could ever equal such a feat in intensity? Beating the legal system. Where boredom had driven her to work for the legal system, it must have driven him to work against it.

16

June 5th

"Noooo!"

David bolted upright in the bed. Sweat coursed damply through the valleys created by his sinew and muscle. Slowly regaining control of himself, he ran his fingers through his rumpled hair. In the dark, he fumbled on the nightstand for a cigarette.

Had Angeletta, or whatever her name was, heard his scream? Obviously not, or she would have come to the door connecting his bedroom to the guest one—his Sleepover's room, as he wryly thought of it. Esther had never liked the separate bedrooms, but she had loved him and endured this idiosyncrasy of his.

He regretted the breakup of his family, and a different woman every month didn't begin to assuage his loneliness. But then Esther, wise Esther, like her namesake in Jewish history, had known from the beginning that his loneliness was of his own devising.

With the first inhalation of the soothing cigarette smoke, he relaxed and lay back against the mounded pillows, soggy from his perspiration. Gradually, his phantom pain receded. The digital clock gleamed 4:17. He wasn't sleepy now, and he thought about showering.

Then, surprisingly, he thought about Diana de Revillon. Or, maybe, not so surprisingly.

She was a woman of unusually good taste and she had a well-developed sense of deportment, a marvelous *élan* and thrust. But it was more than that. She also possessed a relaxed erotic power and a tremendous presence that, combined with the spangled flash of her arrogant eyes, proclaimed, "I couldn't care less what you think."

He had never seen a woman who appeared more independent, more capable of going after whatever she wanted—but who, at the same time, was so straitlaced and almost virginal.

He had met and bedded more sexy women than he could remember, but they depended on low-cut dresses and wriggling hips to distract one from what they really didn't have. Diana de Revillon was beautiful, clean-looking, clean-smelling. Furthermore, her quiet intensity had gripped him at first glance.

Why, he didn't know, but he felt as if he had known her all his life. Oddly, he felt when he looked at her as if he was seeing a feminine reflection of himself.

🐝 17 🐝

June 5th

Otto Dagenfeld's mansion was just off Via Vittorio Veneto, a wide tree-lined thoroughfare that had been the gathering place of Rome's aristocracy since the beginning of the century. Its ornate palaces shared the district with luxurious hotels and elegant shops.

The home of the Mendel banks' retired senior vice president resembled a small-scale Villa Borghese. Dagenfeld greeted Diana at the door himself. He was a tiny man, whose wizened yet innocent dim blue eyes were set in a face as wrinkled as a day-old baby's.

"I was on my way out to the garden, Mademoiselle Signoret," he said in careful French and held up hands covered by cotton work gloves. "We can talk there."

"Thank you for seeing me on such short notice."

"It must be important for you to fly from Paris the same day." He led her along an arched corridor where classical statuary and ancestral portraits stood sentinel. In front of a *succo d'erba* fresco, she recognized a bronze of Pope Clement VIII.

"I had an appointment in Napoli, and it was easy enough to arrange a layover in Rome between flights."

"Ah, Napoli, the city of lovers," he said with twinkling eyes, "regardless of what the Parisians may claim."

Outside, the brilliant Italian sunlight was blinding. Shielding her eyes with her hand, she glanced about. Graceful loggias, Ionic columns, and stone escutcheons bearing coats-of-arms adorned the mansion's rear terrace.

The grounds were a glorious disarray: herb gardens fragrant with the scent of valerian, red-leafed sage, lemon balm, and rosemary; meandering blue pebble paths; a cherub fountain surrounded by creeping thyme and lavender; a low, mossy marble bench.

"I rather like your garden," she told him. "No straight lines, no cramped formality."

His smile was cherubic. "I think a garden properly reflects the lifetime philosophy of its owner." In slow, measured steps, he started down a path leading to what looked like a gardener's house—a charming, gray stone cottage roofed with red tiles and almost obscured by overhanging oaks. "How can I help you, Mademoiselle Signoret?"

"As I told you, I'm a stringer for *Paris Match* and I would like to do a piece on David Mendel."

The old man pushed open a wrought-iron gate. "Not very original, mademoiselle. He's been done before. Several times."

"I know that, but always from the angle of the European playboy. I suspect there's much more depth to the man than that."

"And you want to do an in-depth piece."

She smiled innocently. "Yes. If anyone could give me glimpses and insights into the man behind the playboy image, you could."

"No, if someone could, David could." He opened

the door to the gardener's house and held it for her.
"Have you asked him, Mademoiselle Signoret?"

"Call me Gabrielle, please, Monsieur Dagenfeld."
There *did* exist such a stringer for *Paris Match*. Diana
had checked out that fact just in case Dagenfeld decided
in the interim between her telephone call and arrival to
verify her credit claims with *Paris Match*.

Inside, it was damp and cool, and the air was sweet
with floral scents, chlorophyll, and other earthy aro-
mas. Along one wall was a potting table littered with
an assortment of gardening tools, empty plastic pails,
and terra-cotta pots. Difficult to believe that outside the
sleepy walls of the villa compound, a frenetic city bus-
tled about its daily affairs.

"You know yourself, Monsieur Dagenfeld, your
mysterious banker refuses to be photographed or interviewed. Besides, whatever answers he would give me
would be one-sided. I want your viewpoint. You know
him, I think, better than he even knows himself, perhaps."

"You are a most astute young woman." He crossed
to the table and picked up two small pots of purple and
white lavender. "Can you imagine a century ago laun-
dresses would dry their freshly washed linen over rosemary and lavender bushes to absorb the scents?"

"You're not talking to me about David Mendel," she
chided lightly, wagging a beautifully manicured finger
at him.

"So I am not." He picked up a pair of pruning shears
and slit the side of a plastic bucket. "What can I tell
you? That his spacious office is rumored to be the power
source to end all power sources?"

"Is that truly so?"

Dagenfeld shrugged. "Who can be certain? But I do
know that when Gianni Agnelli wished to sell ten per-

cent of Fiat to Khadafi, he first had to ask David's permission.''

''Tell me more.''

''Such as?''

''Such as what kind of person he is?''

''For one thing, he shuns the limelight. He is a bit shy, a private person, a master of quality and ease.''

She had suspected all that. ''How was he as a boy?'' she persisted gently.

''He was an exceptionally bright child and he demonstrated incredible feats of memory and reasoning that astounded even the Talmudic scholars.''

''How could he have done that?''

''Let me begin at the beginning. The Mendel name in banking is as venerable as the Rothschilds. David's family was highly intellectual and brilliantly multilingual. The Mendels have had an extraordinary influence on European affairs. Sometimes they supported wars, sometimes they prevented them by denying armament loans.

''I was present in March 1938, when Hitler's troops goose-stepped into Vienna. At that moment, the Austrian capital ceased to be a center of European culture and erudition.''

''What happened to the Mendels?''

''The family prepared to go into hiding. Since I wasn't Jewish, David's father, Judah, felt I would most likely escape mistreatment by the Nazis. He asked me to keep intact what I could of the family bank. I was there when the Nazi looters invaded the Mendel palace, carting off priceless *objets d'art*, crystal, silver, chandeliers, furniture, even the English sporting-print wallpaper right off the walls. Anything and everything.

''During those years of the *Anschluss*, when Austria was annexed to Germany, there were . . . terrible . . .

terrible atrocities. I was not a Jew, so I did not react. I merely closed my ears to the horrifying stories I heard and turned my eyes away from the depravities in the streets—revolting orgies of rape and vicious cruelty.''

His back to her, the old man thumped the root ball of lavender against the potting table, and its pot-formed earth crumbled away. For a moment, he was silent, then he sighed. ''I apologize, Mademoiselle Signoret . . . Gabrielle . . . I have been reliving my old guilt, not telling you about David.''

His gnarled old hands sprinkled gravel, then charcoal, into the bottom of a Delft-blue ceramic pot. ''During those years, I stayed busy, extremely busy, trying to hold the Mendel bank together—its branches ranged from Napoli to Paris to London. Then, in April 1945, when the British and Americans liberated the camps, I waited for the Mendels to come home to Vienna.''

Dagenfeld's voice dropped to almost a whisper. ''When no one appeared, I began my ancient mariner's journey—searching for them. Eventually, I learned from the International Red Cross that they had been separated. David's two sisters were the fortunate ones—they died the day they were arrested. They had been taken to a local slaughterhouse and stripped. Their heads had been chopped off and their bodies, stamped with the word *Kosher*, had been hung on meathooks.''

Diana choked back the nausea that rushed toward her mouth.

As the old man went to work on the lavender roots, gently repotting the plant in the jar, his voice was dry, crackly, relentless. ''David's father was put to work in a death camp—that charnel house of horror at Bergen-Belsen—shaving the heads of the dead. One day he shaved his own wife's head. I learned that he had died—

in a crematory—two months before the British liberated the camp.

"After that I searched the relocation camps scattered throughout central Europe and, almost a year later, through the Jewish Board of Deputies, I found David in a camp in Lorraine, working in the coal mines. When he was taken away from Vienna, he was a strapping five-year-old. By the time I found him . . ." the old man's voice became hoarse with deep-felt emotion, "he was eight and I could encircle his thigh bone with my forefinger and thumb."

When Dagenfeld turned to face her, his face seemed centuries old. "About those three years of his life, I can tell you nothing. And about the years since then—well, all that is a matter of public record."

"You've been immensely helpful, Monsieur Dagenfeld," she murmured. His lovely little garden house reeked now of rot and decay, and she could hardly stop herself from fleeing headlong from the gardens.

18

June 12th

For the dinner honoring the visiting president of Turkey, Diana wore an Oscar de la Renta ruby silk crêpe gown and jewel-encrusted bolero. Amid the elegance of an era past, the hundred-odd guests—international intelligentsia of all political persuasions—mingled at the seventeenth-century Hôtel de Lauzun on the Île St. Louis, since 1928 the official reception hall for the city of Paris.

Some of the dignitaries arrived by boat, mounting quayside steps to the sumptuously elegant townhouse, restored to its original grandeur with lovingly refurbished furnishings from the Louis XVI, Directoire, and Empire periods.

Diana's escort was one of her few friends left over from the Sorbonne days, Baron Alexis de le Sueur, a world-class roué. Next to every place setting on the tables was a deluxe party favor—leather-bound Vuitton notebooks for the men and Gondola perfume for the women. Diagonally across from Diana was the wife of the prime minister of France—and next to la Madame sat David Mendel and his dinner companion, the Mar-

106

quise du Gruyn, a lovely, refined widow with her ash-
brown hair done in classic half length.

Diana was acquainted with most of those present—
friends and other acquaintances she recognized from
similar past events whose guest lists were drawn from
that most exclusive of social and genealogical hand-
books, the *Almanach de Gotha*. Ironically, considering
her past, by nature she was shy—walking into a room
full of strangers was always a nerve-wracking experience. Often criticized behind her back for being too
regal, her icy poise usually concealed her private terror.

Alexis had taught her the vital lesson of how to relax
in the presence of pesky paparazzi. After all those years,
his profession was still a mystery to her—he had something to do with investment counseling, but she wasn't
certain just what it was. Handsome, generous, and
amusing, he had a single major defect: the sole objective of his existence was a hedonistic desire to have a
good time. The night before, or early this morning,
rather, he had pulled down his pants at a trendy disco
in Monte Carlo and poured Scotch all over himself.

He leaned close and whispered in her ear, "Diana,
my sweet, come home with me tonight."

How long had it been since she had last felt the intimate touch of a man? Her breasts ached for a man's
caress, but her mind simply refused to submit to the
compromises needed to admit a man into her life.

She smiled charmingly at Alexis. The affair was be-
ing videotaped for later broadcast on French television.
"I'm afraid, *cher* Alexis, that I hold to the traditional
European view that the man should wear the pants."

He had the dignity to redden, though his cheeks were
already ruddy from alcoholic excess. "You heard what
happened at Jimmy's?"

A white-gloved waiter interrupted their tête-à-tête to

place on the table with a flourish a silver bowl of truffle-flavored *sauce Périguex* to complement the beef Wellington. At that instant, Diana looked up to discover David Mendel's eyes locked on her. Like the moment in Vacheron-Constantin's, she experienced a similar sudden deprivation of air in her lungs and a flush of heat that seemed to singe upward all the way to her scalp.

All at once, she felt foolish—that this most accomplished of criminal minds could generate such a feminine reaction from her. You arrogant stallion, she threatened silently, you aren't going to elude me as you have others.

Boldly, she held his stare. He had a most invincible presence, an essence she had encountered only a few times. Mother Theresa had it. So did the philanthropist Ross Perot and the sinister con man Charles Sobhraj, and Diana wasn't certain what the common thread was. Charm and the power to attract were so elusive.

David inclined his head, almost as if making her a promise, and in that fleeting second she had the sinking sensation she might succeed in acquiring everything in life she had ever desired.

Four times recently their paths had crossed and he had yet to say a word to her, or she to him, beyond the superficial acknowledgment during the table introductions that very evening. Over ice cream in cookie cups from Maxim's, she only half listened to Alexis's gossip, straining instead to catch fragments of David's conversations with those seated closest to him.

On her other side, the Greek Archbishop Marsekopoulos, dressed as befitted an ecclesiastical prince in red and gold satin and white lace, led a discussion on the subtle and dangerous power of the World Bank. He punctuated his sentences by thumping the floor with the massive gold-headed staff leaning next to his chair.

The World Bank was one subject she could discuss in depth but wouldn't deign to touch. Besides, she would learn more by listening to David Mendel, although she was really too far away to understand fully what he was saying; mainly she heard only the fluid overtones of his baritone voice.

Surreptitiously, she studied him, noting that he wore no personal jewelry. She sensed a restraint in him, an unexpected dimension, as if he were held in check by an unknown force. She suspected he was more erudite, more complex, than even he allowed himself to express, which made him difficult to gauge—and, therefore, the most dangerous of opponents.

She had to admire, too, that he was playing the game as coolly as she, but playing it he was. She was highly accomplished at using her beauty, whose sensual eloquence had caused plenty of men to lose their heads over her, although she had a well-established reputation for complete indifference to flattery.

Just as she knew how to employ her beauty as ammunition, David Mendel knew how to take advantage of his magnetic presence. After all, he possessed a chimerically tantalizing personality. Behind those eyes, the overcast grayish blue of the gelid North Sea, smoldered fires that could incinerate her if she wasn't exquisitely cautious.

Playboy meets playgirl.

Who would finally relent and make the first approach?

19

June 15th

"Money means never having to kiss ass," Gregorios Aristos pronounced Delphically, his smile disarming, his eyes flashing recklessly behind the mask. The Levantine millionaire was a glittering rhinestone in the rough. Olive-skinned and gangly, he had not come into the money of his industrialist father until he was almost thirty-five and now, at forty, was thoroughly indulging its enormous power.

"That's why Joan Rodger's lips are so tan," he continued. "Not even films guarantee the kind of money she spends."

"You ought to know," Diana said. "You helped finance her film. A risky business, isn't it?"

"Do tell," Greg said. "You know, Diana, there's a rumor flitting around that she was caught one night last week in a phone booth at the Longchamps racetrack with a jockey. They say she left the booth with mincing steps—her panties hobbled about her ankles!"

Diana vaguely knew Joan Rodgers, or rather knew of her films—epic lust adventures. Still, despite the crush of masked revelers, it wasn't difficult to pick out the summer-white blonde. The darling of *cinéma vérité*

110

posed amid a covey of fawning admirers, while her low-cut dress struggled to contain her breasts. Her black net mask flattered her button nose, prominent cheekbones, and pouting lips. Nearing fifty, she had held her looks gracefully. Her career was in its second revival, and she had become the center of something of a cult.

Shit, Diana murmured to herself. She and Joan Rodgers were both wearing identical Ralph Lauren lilac silk satin gowns with emerald beaded tops, a wasted outlay of $3,000.

There was a lot of nearsighted squinting from behind the outrageously ornmented masks of the seventeen-hundred-odd revelers who converged that night on the grand ballroom of the Paris Opera House for the masked dinner and ball to benefit the French National League Against Cancer.

Diana's grandmother had more than once told her, "In the twentieth century, you should know how to type, change a tire, and raise money." The guests had paid 40,000 francs each for their invitations.

For the *bal masque*, the guests turned out in an assortment of garish masks, creations that ranged from peacock feathers to bugle beads, sheep horns, porcupine quills, metal, and zippers. Diana wore an original ruffled gold mask of Austrian crystals made by McLaughlin of New Orleans, costing a cool $750.

Even a marble bust of Mozart became frivolous in its black demi-mask. "The Phantom of the Opera," Diana said, and Greg tittered.

She suspected he went both ways. Regardless, he made a marvelous escort for the functions she had to attend, mostly because he never high-pressured her into going to bed with him. She did know some women who had gone to bed with him; they claimed he was more than adequate in the arena of lovemaking.

However, she hadn't selected the tall, lanky Greek as her escort on the basis of his sexual preference. Greg had financed the veteran American actress's latest film along with David Mendel.

From a passing waiter's tray, she plucked a gold-rimmed flute of champagne. Holding it in her gloveless left hand, she watched idly as couples danced to one of the three orchestras playing in various parts of the Opera House that night. From her right hand dangled her elbow-length white kid glove and her beaded bag, containing a mandatory pack of Gitanes to get her through the tedium of the evening.

Three days had passed and David Mendel had made no move to contact her. Had she overestimated her power to allure? More importantly, had only she felt that visual impact at the sight of David Mendel, an impact she had labeled as High Voltage? Was it possible he had felt nothing?

She knew that he was listed on the invitation as one of the sponsors of the French National League Against Cancer and therefore he had to be at the masked ball. But where was he?

Then, ten meters beyond Joan Rodgers and her sycophantic throng, beneath a flower-festooned arch, she saw a man, deep in conversation with two other masked gentlemen wearing top hats and tuxedos. The object of her scrutiny looked gorgeous in white tie and tails. She was positive the man, who was now staring intently at her, was David Mendel, if only by her treacherous body's unconscious response: a tremor of anticipation that raised gooseflesh on her bare arms. She was certain, too, that he recognized her behind her mask.

David Mendel represented a challenge, but there was something else, too. The echoing music, the burbling chatter, the crystalline clinking of glasses against silver

trays and each other—all were muted by what seemed
like to her a time warp.

"Diana, did you hear what I just said?" Greg
grumped. "You're really not flattering my ego."

"I'm sorry, Greg." She forced herself to interrupt
that tenuous but persistent force that was binding her to
David Mendel. "What was it you were saying?"

Greg snagged one of the buttery, de rigueur canapés,
spread fanwise like playing cards on a silver tray, and
she chose a crystallized violet. "What I said, Diana,"
Greg emphasized archly, "was that Joan Rodgers's
current financial problem is the result of her well-
documented taste for pink champagne and eighteen-
karat-gold-plated Daimlers with zebra-skin seats."

"So finance another film for her," she tossed off
carelessly.

During dinner, a benefit auction was held, and Diana
watched Joan Rodgers contribute her two-minute ego
trip at the mike. Her glossy voice thanked everyone for
their generosity. Then, oh so reluctantly, she handed
the microphone to the auctioneer.

Lynn Wyatt applauded when her donated auto-
graphed copy of Somerset Maugham's *The Moon and
Sixpence* went for $6,750. Louis Jourdan's offer to sing
Thank Heaven for Little Girls over breakfast in bed
brought $2,500.

As the last item was auctioned, a week at Monte
Carlo's Les Terrasses Baden-Baden, Diana daintily fin-
ished off the meagre desert, a scrumptious petits four.
Tomorrow she would double her workout regimen.

A hand gently removed the empty champagne flute
dangling from her fingers. She looked up into David
Mendel's challenging gaze. "I would like to dance with
you," he announced. He set her glass on the table.

She laid aside her paper napkin, imprinted with the

monogram of the hosting charity, and rose from the table. Without directing a glance at the startled Greg, she let David draw her onto the dance floor. The black-tie orchestra had just begun a romantic tune, one she didn't recognize, but then at the moment she doubted whether she would have recognized the Pope if he'd suddenly appeared in full ceremonial robes.

"You've been following me," David said. He danced well, his right hand placed firmly at the small of her back.

He was slightly taller than she; in three-inch heels she reached just over five eleven. She tilted her head a bit. "Suppose I make the same charge? *You* have been following me."

"Why did you bid against me at Deauville?"

"Pourquoi d'autre?" She shrugged ever so slightly. "I merely wanted the horse for my grandmother's farm."

At that, he smiled, a dazzlingly open smile. And yet, she sensed he was a man who kept his own counsel, who cherished his privacy. With his dark blond hair, his high forehead, and his nose so straight and so un-characteristically un-Semitic, he could have passed for Aryan. "Why is it that I doubt your wonderfully dis-ingenuous statement?"

She matched his smile, her perfect teeth the result of teenage years spent in orthodontial agony. "Because you have obviously never learned to trust others."

"Do you?"

"Do I what?"

"Do you trust total strangers?"

"I operate on instinct."

"Are you ever wrong?"

"Never."

Their verbal sparring was stimulating, the more so because she suspected she had met her match. He was as masculine as her father, but younger, richer, and far more powerful. Had she married David Mendel a decade earlier, she would easily have trumped her father and his domination.

When the dance ended, he turned over the gloved hand he held, his lips going unerringly to the tiny oval patch of exposed skin at her wrist, near the first pearl button. "Thank you for the dance, Mademoiselle de Revillon. It was most enlightening." Behind the black domino, his eyes were laughing.

She flashed him a sassy smile. "D'accord." Then she did the unexpected. She curtseyed. And winked at him flirtatiously as she rose.

His sudden full-bodied laughter at her mock obeisance drew startled glances that shifted quickly away when, his hand at the small of her back, he returned her to Greg's side, bowed himself, and disappeared back into the crowd.

Now what? she wondered. Pursue him more avidly, and she would blow any chance to nail him.

"My, my, aren't we the belle of the ball," Greg bitched, nodding toward another man who was approaching, his hands bulking the pockets of an ill-fitting dinner jacket.

Of average height, but solidly built, the swarthy man looked vaguely familiar. Beneath the demi-mask, his square-set jaw had a bluish five o'clock shadow, but then the "Miami Vice" scruffy look was fashionable now. Somehow, maybe because of the way he walked— an I-don't-give-a-damn amble—she didn't think he was the sort who pursued ephemeral fashions.

"I haven't seen you since the birthday party," he rumbled in execrable American-accented French. His yellow-brown eyes, studying her through the slits of his mask, were world-weary and almost sad.

"I didn't have a birthday party this year."

"I was referring to mine."

"I don't remember you."

He waggled his thick brows up and down. "You were that smashed? I would never have known it."

Now Greg was really bewildered, glancing back and forth at them as if he were watching a tennis rally at the net.

There was something magically uninhibiting about masks, Diana thought. People worked out their fantasies behind them or did reckless things they might not ordinarily do. "Aren't you going to ask me to dance?" she said.

"Last time you trampled all over my shoeshine." He grasped her elbow and fairly propelled her out onto the floor.

She was his height, but he gave the impression, even though she was standing close to him, of being taller because of his Ramboesque proportions. Instead of tapering, his waist was a blocky continuation of his barrel chest, a build she found unusually appealing. "Most men try to use more finesse when they make passes at me."

"That's why I'm dancing with you and those 'most men' aren't. *Grandes dames* quickly become bored with mere finesse."

So he was educated. His unshaven cheek rasped hers, yet the masculine feel of him was strangely reassuring. "Now why is it I feel you mean 'dames'—as in the American vernacular?" she said, switching to English when she spoke the word.

Lips beside her ear, he chuckled and, reverting to English, also, said, "Do I really come off so crass?"

In the line of his shoulders and the solid strength of his arms, she deduced the kind of power achieved by someone who played racquetball for at least an hour every day of his life. "How did you get in? The invitations were very exclusive."

"How long have you known David Mendel?"

He nodded off to her left, where she spied the financier, or whatever he was, dancing with Joan Rodgers. "Longer than I've known you."

"Let me correct that right now. My name is Tom Estevez, I was forty-three my last birthday—the one you got smashed at—and I'm a boat broker from Miami."

"Boat broker" triggered a file photo image of the yacht *The Star of David*. "And you want an introduction to David Mendel." She sighed dramatically. "I should have known it wasn't my fair beauty that attracted you."

"It wasn't your graceful dancing, either. I've danced with . . ." he groaned as she purposely trod on his instep with a stiletto heel.

"I'm so sorry, Don."

"It's Tom. Tom Estevez."

"Tell you what, Don, you have my full permission to introduce yourself to David Mendel, using my name—as a *new* friend."

"New as opposed to old?"

"No, new as opposed to used."

"I'll call you and let you know how well your name serves me as an entrée," he said, stepping gently but steadily on her foot.

Mercifully, the dance soon ended. After Tom returned her to her escort, who had been on his fifth glass of champagne at her last count, Greg said, "An old friend?"

"No, a used friend."

At least, she hoped that might be so. The overbearing "Don" Estevez could very well prove to be the link she needed to David Mendel.

20

June 16th

The Star of David.

As the taxi rattled erratically along Boulevard Haussmann in typical Paris fashion, Tom settled back in the rear seat and lit up a cigarette. He had thought New York traffic was bad, but in Paris it fairly took your breath away. So did the pungent French cigarettes.

So did Diana de Revillon.

A savvy lady. Behind that playgirl image was a Gallic toughness he suspected most people never perceived—a steely yet casual aura that implied she could handle whatever came her way. French women were like padded steel, he thought. Natalie included. They ran the country but their men never realized it.

Despite her European manners, Diana was American, too—and he had the feeling this was one savvy lady who didn't play games. Real ball breaker. In some ways, she represented everything he usually found repellent in the upper crust—not only were they often shallow and frivolous, but completely lacking in ethics or commitments.

But in other ways . . . he summoned a vivid image

118

of her . . . tall, delightful ass, and blessed with a wide and inviting mouth.

He grunted out a helix of smelly blue smoke, thinking about how Diana managed to intimate a steamy, sexual passion existing beneath her cool and cultivated exterior . . . she was a paradox, all right, enormously strong and wildly vulnerable at the same time . . . he remembered how she never looked down when she walked, as if she took for granted that her path would be safe, without traps or stumbling blocks.

Damn it. How had she become hooked up with David Mendal? And why would someone with Mendel's immense net worth bother with theft, even on the scale Tom had uncovered? Most art thefts were committed with the purpose of converting the booty to more negotiable currency such as cocaine and diamonds, snow and ice.

He wondered if he was on the right track at all—the art museum corporation papers left a suspicious trail that could take forever to track down unless the tracker knew exactly what to hunt for, and at that moment Tom was like a green kid in Paris. There had to be another way.

The Star of David.

The same niggling thought kept intruding, bringing him back to Mendel's incredible yacht. The front as a ship broker had only occurred to Tom as he was putting on his rented tuxedo the night before. When he worked the Miami district, he had picked up enough jargon in the marinas and along the cargo wharves to pass himself off as a boat broker to David Mendel.

Tom flipped his cigarette butt out the taxi window. He wished he had a cigar like the Havanas the Miami office used to confiscate. He was almost ready to concede that his morning-long perusal of ship registrations had been a waste of time. At least he had learned something about *The Star of David*, which carried Italian registration.

The 170-foot yacht was equipped with a landing deck for an August 109 helicopter, satellite communications capability, and navigation systems rivaling those of a naval destroyer—autopilot, three radars, satellite guidance, an Atlas echosounder and aeronautical VHF and SSE radios.

Strictly for recreation, Mendel had installed 260 phones, an olympic-sized pool, two thirty-foot Riva ski boats, a discotheque complete with light show, and a cinema with an 800-film library.

The Star of David.

An ego thing, this play on Mendel's given name? Or something else?

Abruptly, he shouted at the taxi driver, "26 rue Armengaud," changing his destination from his hotel to Interpol headquarters at St. Cloud.

When Tom arrived at his desk, John Hamblin looked up from the papers scattered across its surface, sneezed, and, whipping out a pocket handkerchief, grunted at him, not exactly hospitably, "You're back."

"I know that thrills you." Tom drew up a chrome chair and, turning it backwards, straddled it. "Wasn't one of the notorious Nazi Gestapo chiefs the wartime president of Interpol?"

Hamblin blew his nose, emulating a foghorn. "That's not something Interpol likes to brag about. Memoranda will tell you that Interpol headquarters, then in Vienna, rapidly became nonexistent in 1938 when German forces occupied Austria."

"But . . . ?"

"But the files and staff were removed from Vienna to a large house in the Berlin suburb of Wansee under the KPK—the German abbreviation for Interpol. The president you're talking about—'' Hamblin paused to sneeze again— ''. . . was Reinhard Heydrich himself, the infamous Hangman of Czechoslovakia. Picked by Himmler, who was often called Hitler's terrible high priest. Heydrich was a born intelligence officer—a living card index. Like Hitler and Himmler, the fellow had a mania for the aristocracy of Aryan blood. He was the one who perfected the Final Solution—the total annihilation of the Jews.''

''What happened to the files during those years?''

''Technically they were purged, but the Allied occupation recovered certain folders in July of 1945.''

''Any Jewish names in them?''

Hamblin squirmed uncomfortably. ''Quite a few, actually—but a former General Secretariat explained them not as Nazi holdovers but merely as religious identities.''

Tom hunched forward over the chair back. ''I don't understand.''

''In the post-Nazi years, Interpol kept those Jewish criminal files supposedly to contrast with, let's say, those of the Catholic or Greek Orthodox faith. Interpol interpreted the Jews as rarely committing those offenses that require a man to drift away from society and to adopt a purely passive stance.''

Once again, Hamblin wiped his reddened nose with his handkerchief, then went on. ''According to Interpol, what appeared from their statistical comparisons was the preference of Jewish offenders for offenses calling for craftiness. On the other hand, the comparisons also revealed a common abhorrence of violence.''

''Where are these Jewish files?''

''As I said, technically they don't exist. As recently as 1972, a former Nazi SS officer, who had served with the dreaded SD—the intelligence and espionage arm of the elite corps, the SS—was president of Interpol.''

''That explains the *technical* disappearance,'' Tom said. ''It's also a little unnerving to think of Interpol's power. Like an Orwellian dream, isn't it?''

''You're asking me?'' Hamblin sneezed loudly. ''We Americans might spare a thought or two about the IRS connection.''

''Suppose I wanted to see one of those missing files?''

''You might try Interpol's archives—after five o'clock, naturally. Damn this cold!''

Color tabs in the archives designated each subject's country of birth. Tom found Mendel's file under the yellow tab representing Austria.

For more than half an hour he read, beginning in 1943 in the Munich suburb of Dachau with David Mendel's assignment at five years of age to a nearby underground munitions plant. Feeling utterly sick to his stomach and nauseated by humanity, Tom finished his research by reading Himmler's statement: ''Anti-Semitism is exactly the same as delousing. Getting rid of lice is not a question of ideology. It's a matter of cleanliness.''

21

June 17th

"You have an appointment at three with your couturier, Miss Priss," Peggy reminded her, as she followed Diana to the studio doorway. "Last minute alterations to the Christmas gown." The housekeeper's pen checked off the message. "Also, monsieur said to tell you that the red brocade you selected is being ordered from the factories in Lille."

Diana tucked stray blonde wisps under her sweatband. "Call Jean-Claude back and tell him I can't make the fitting. He'll just have to use the dummy."

"Lastly, Madame Spalding-Hyer is on the telephone. Shall I tell her you'll call her back?"

"No, I'll take it in here."

Picking up the receiver, Diana answered more tersely than she intended, and Anne was quick to react. "Bad night, huh?"

"And a worse morning." Long-distance static crackled in her ear, and she asked, "Where are you?"

"Heathrow. Any chance you could put me up for a few weeks, Diana? I've left dear old Spencer and being alone in London has been a frightful drag."

"Oh, darling, I'm so terribly sorry things didn't work

123

out for you! And, of course, you can stay as long as you like. You know that. You must be feeling awful. If you're up to it, let's talk about it when you get here. You know, one of our infamous all-night gab sessions.''

After Diana hung up, however, she stood there biting her lip, worrying about going on with her investigation of David Mendel with Anne living right under her nose.

Putting the question aside with a microscopic shrug, she switched on the stereo and began her warm-up exercises before the unforgiving mirror. A night spent stewing about David Mendel, rolling from one side to the other of her bed, turning like an old dog until she was temporarily comfortable, had left smudgy gray half-moons beneath each eye.

If he had held onto the Marmottan paintings, he was certainly too smart to keep them at any of his various premises. So, where were they and what did he intend doing with them?

She flexed her arms. He'd get rid of them, no doubt. How?

She stretched her legs, feeling the tension in her calf muscles. Would he destroy them?

No, he was too much an art connoisseur.

She put herself through a series of pliés. Would he sell them?

No. Too well known, too hot to handle.

Then some grandes pliés. But not if the buyer dealt in hot merchandise.

David Mendel might already have washed himself of the loot, but she doubted that. Something like that took concentrated time.

As if he had been conjured up by her concentrated thoughts of him, she looked in the mirror and saw him, standing in the doorway, his hands thrust in the front pockets of his jeans. He was so casual, in a denim shirt rolled above his elbows, she almost didn't recognize him. Regardless of his costume, that supercharged energy he radiated would have given him away anywhere.

Behind him, Peggy stood agitatedly, her parchment cheeks crimsoned. "I told him you were busy!" she bit off.

"I'd like you to come out for coffee with me," he informed Diana, ignoring the housekeeper's petulance.

Diana nodded at her housekeeper, and Peggy retreated from the hallway, but not without directing at David an indignant and frosty glance that only the British could do so well. "What in heaven's name took you so long?" Diana said, smiling. "I almost gave up on you."

"You knew very well I'd take the bait," he said with a smile that matched hers—a smile born out of anticipation of both excitement and danger.

"Let me change first," she said. In minutes, she had slid into all black T-shirt, pants, and blazer. A single gold hoop earring was all that eased the severity of her ebony ensemble.

At midday, the Paris boulevards were congested. The exhaust of David's motorcycle popped merrily. Riding any motorcycle through the kinetic city was a form of Russian roulette. Ahead of them, the Arc de Triomphe shimmered miragelike in the heat waves. A taxi darted out of a side street on the Champs-Elysées, followed by a cyclist balancing piled-high laundry in a willow basket, and Diana's arms tightened about David's waist. When he shot deftly between the cab and the bike, exultant laughter bubbled past her lips.

"You take the long way round for coffee," she said, after he parked his top-of-the-line Harley outside the Twickenham, a cozy English-style pub in the heart of the publishing district, the Seventh Arrondissement.

"Well, I do enjoy the ambience here," David told her with a smile that generated a megawatt sincerity.

Inside the dimly lit barroom, everything was either polished mahogany, brass-studded leather, or beveled mirror. At the rear of the pub, several patrons were engaged in a darts contest, but they, like everyone else in the pub, paused to stare at the arrivals, and Diana knew it was because she and David made an unusually attractive couple.

At one table where two men were holding court, one of them, whose chin sprouted a shaggy beard, hailed David, and he led her over. She took a seat in the deep leather armchair he drew out for her. "Diana, may I introduce Henri Lévine and Bernard Gaillard. *Mes amis*, Diana de Revillon."

"Bon jour," she said to the long-haired Henri and the bearded Bernard, both of them looking like middle-aged hippies.

"Do join us!" Henri said cordially. "We were just discussing the properties of beauty."

"Beauty as in what?" David asked, signaling to the waiter for two cups of coffee and baguettes.

"Beauty as in 'Beautiful People,' " Bernard said. "With Diana's presence in our midst, we have the perfect subject."

"Certainly, gentlemen, I can tell you something about beauty," she began easily. Her college days had prepared her well for the biting cynicism of café philosophers like these, and she would not be intimidated. "First of all, beauty carries an obligation. It is far more a burden than a benefit."

Bernard's mustache dipped sullenly into his beard. She couldn't pinpoint it, but there was something about him that put her on edge.

Henri said, "You're not very modest, are you?"

She drew her silver cigarette case from her shoulder bag and plucked out a Gitanes. "Why should I be a hypocrite about the obvious?" Her cool fabricated smile chastised them both. "If you think looks don't matter in men as well as women, then you've been out of touch with the real world, *messieurs.*"

When David leaned over to light her cigarette, she saw a faint tic of barely restrained amusement at the corners of his mouth. What did *he* think about her? Did *he* find her beautiful?

Henri hunched forward over his tankard of stout, absorbed by her statement. "Then will you also admit candidly that beauty bestows power to women—*n'est-ce pas?*"

Slowly, she exhaled. "Most certainly, but most women haven't the foggiest notion of what to do with it."

"But you do?" David asked, more as a statement than a question.

"Certainly, because I manipulate the manipulators."

"Apparently we have a true feminist in our midst!" Henri declared, raising one eloquent eyebrow.

"There might be some nonenlightened men who have that trite image of me," she nodded, laughing lightly.

The waiter set two large china cups before her and David, and when the waiter left, David said, "You realize that statement about manipulating manipulators comes across as a challenge to some men?"

"To you, for instance?" she asked.

He smiled, but his eyes were thoughtful. "Especially to me, Diana. I rather enjoy confronting challenges."

"As well as the risks that usually accompany them?"

Bernard cleared his throat. "I feel as if the conversation has just soared over my head like an old Montgolfier balloon. David and you know very well that this is our bullshitting domain you are trespassing on.''

"My apologies for upstaging the two of you, *mon vieux* Bernard,'' David said with that easy charm Diana was so determined to resist.

Half an hour later, after the two café philosophers had departed, he said, "Do you know this American, this Tom Estevez?''

She stared into her half-filled cup of black coffee, her hands cupped around it. "So, he called you after all. A boat broker, isn't he?''

"You don't know him either?''

She looked up at him, eyes twinkling. "Not at all. I set him on you in retribution for your rudeness at the masked ball.''

"When did you think I was rude?''

"You were staring at me.''

"Surely, Diana, you are used to being stared at—a former model for Lanvin?''

"No,'' she answered honestly, "not the way you were.''

"How was I staring?''

She was surprised to feel her cheeks reddening. "How did you know I worked for Lanvin?''

"An article in *Paris Match*.'' He reached in his rear jeans pocket and pulled out a crumpled clipping. "I knew I had seen you somewhere.''

She glanced at the wrinkled article.

. . . one of the legendary beauties of Paris and New York . . . a socialite who changes boyfriends the way some women change outfits . . . haunts Paris's modish nightspots with most of her nocturnal forays ending at L'Aventure disco.

"I knew you would be at the cancer society *bal masque*," he said. "Just as you have been at most of the other functions I've attended this last month."

She swallowed the last of the coffee in her cup before asking again, "That article's more than a month old."

"I know. When I saw it, I tore it out with the intention of cornering you with it. I recognized you from St. Moritz, last February."

"Yes, in the lift line, wasn't it?"

"So, you admit to remembering. Do you also admit you purposely drove up the bidding at the Deauville auction?"

"Of course. You paid far more than that horse was worth, you know."

"It was worth it to me to see how far you would be willing to go to attract my attention."

"Well then, your male ego must be quite flattered," she said, smiling through a haze of blue Gitanes smoke.

"Come on, Diana, I'm old enough and experienced enough not to fall into that trap. Let's just say I'm intrigued."

"I had hoped you would be." She looked at her watch and stubbed out her cigarette. "Sorry to put an end to such a fascinating conversation, but I've got to get back. I'm expecting a friend to arrive from England."

"We'll have to meet again some other time," he told her when they pulled up in front of her apartment and she climbed off the motorcycle.

Was he suggesting he wanted to see her again—or was the comment merely a polite good-bye? She'd never before worried, or even cared, whether a man was interested in her or not. Her attitude toward David was a whole new experience for her. Trying to discern in those fathomless eyes of his some indication of what he was thinking was an impossibility for her, who prided herself on an almost mystical perception of others.

She combed her fingers through her wind-tangled locks. "I'd like that, David," she said finally, smiling as her eyes bored into his.

Then, before she could react at all, he placed his hands on both her cheeks and kissed her gently. She could sense the hesitation in his touch, in his lips even, then she went week-kneed, as if her bones were cooked spaghetti, a physical phenomenon she had heretofore dismissed smugly as mere cliché. As if under orders, their lips interviewed each other through the medium of their kiss . . . who *is* this stranger? . . . I know you as I know my own reflection . . . what do you want of me? . . .

He broke the kiss, removed his hands, and stepped back. She saw that his lips were curved into a devil-may-care half smile. "*Au revoir, chère* Diana."

With her feelings in a four-alarm uproar, she watched him wheel into the afternoon traffic. It was really foolish and unprofessional of her . . . letting herself become enthralled with a criminal.

Peggy opened the door. "Miss Anne is here," she announced by way of greeting.

And so was Tom Estevez. He had one hip propped on a padded window seat and nearby, Anne lounged on an Art Deco sofa. Its tangerine color coordinated with the rest of the living room, which Diana had done in various shades of orange, from persimmon to pumpkin. Both her guests had wineglasses in their hands and were laughing cheerfully about something.

When she caught sight of Diana, Anne rose and strode quickly across the room, arms wide open, her empty Baccarat balloon dangling from one hand by its stem. "Di darling, thanks so very much for taking me in like this on such short notice."

They hugged, and Anne stepped back, her sweeping hand taking in the brawny American. "As you can see," she said wryly, "I've already found a gentleman to comfort me in my *mélancolie*." She batted her eyelashes at Tom Estevez along with a provocative leer that only the ebullient Anne could possibly get away with. "Oh, I say, and do please pardon me for enquiring, but are you by any chance a fortune hunter, Tom?"

He grinned at her gibe, his uneven teeth glowing against his swarthy face. "Sure am, honey, a genuine fourteen-carat rhinestone fortune hunter."

Diana noted there was a dose of disingenuousness in his manner—a humility affirmed by a vehement dose of arrogance yet balanced by his laid-back, informal, oh-so-American personality.

"Jolly good!" Anne shot back. "I certainly had no desire to get mixed up with anyone who could possibly become serious."

Smiling affably, Tom set his half-empty crystal wineglass on the window sill. "I told you the other night I'd let you know how my talk with Mendel went, Miss de Revillon."

He was so casual, so offhandedly Yankee, it was difficult for her not to be annoyed by his presumptuousness. She flipped her shoulder bag onto a tufted chair and went to the sideboard to pour herself a glass of wine. For some reason, she decided not to mention she had just been with David. "So, is he interested in buying a boat from you?"

Tom's pale brown eyes seemed to narrow on her speculatively. Had he observed her and David from the window? He lifted his bull-like shoulders in an indolent shrug. "I've persuaded him to talk to me about buying one that I'm handling."

"Tom and I are going out to one of those steamy African discos tonight," Anne said. "Want to come along?"

"I don't think so," she answered. "I'm going to catch up on some reading."

"You may borrow my well-thumbed copy of *Tropic of Cancer*, if you think you'll need it," Anne teased.

"Don't tell me you even brought that with you."

"I never realized when I packed in London that I would be lucky enough to have this charming American for company."

Charming, eh? Diana smiled at Anne's chirpy enthusiasm, but over the rim of her glass she observed Tom Estevez. He was a swift mover, all right. What could his heritage be—Puerto Rican? Mexican? Possibly Cuban, if he was actually from Miami, as he claimed. Whatever, there was definitely something about him; she couldn't put her finger on it . . . yet. Maybe he was a fortune hunter, after all.

She should run a quick check on him for Anne's sake. Then again, she was probably overreacting. Matching wits with the elusive and charismatic David Mendel could short-circuit a person's analytic mechanism.

"Diana, do you remember when we first worked up the courage to buy the forbidden green-covered book?"

"We? Who was the shaky-kneed customer who ended up stuttering in Shakespeare & Company all by herself?"

"Reminds me," Tom said, "of the first time I went into a drugstore to buy a rubber. I was thirteen years old and sweating like an altar boy waiting outside the confessional with a mortal sin on his mind."

Anne giggled, and Diana, smiling, said, "You must have been a raunchy thirteen-year-old kid, Tom."

Tom leveled his hard male gaze on her but said pleasantly, "I *was* an altar boy, you know. But at one of the High Masses I decided to load the thurible with extra charcoal and incense. Within minutes, the chapel looked like a smokehouse. Father Luke almost excommunicated me."

Anne laughed again and said, "I can see this is going to be an entertaining evening."

Diana was barely listening. In the back of her mind flashed unbidden a scene: she and David confronting each other in Vacheron-Constantin—and Tom Estevez looking on.

22

Tucked away on a dimly lit side street of rue Pigalle, the safari-decorated Afruidisiaque was the premier discotheque of the espresso society, where a sophisticated underground aristocracy coalesced with a guild of exiled monarchs and their courtiers.

Outside the club, the usual tabloid paparazzi poised like carrion birds, and when Tom and Anne squirmed out of the Renault taxi, camera strobes began stuttering until they reached near-epileptic frenzy.

Once past the towering Senegalese security man at the door, those selected as patrons mingled as best as they could. The dance floor was rump to rump with throbbing blank-faced couples, as were the aisles between the tables, couples exercising their rhythmic urges even there. Some were perched on the backs of their chairs, faces tilted hopefully toward the air vents.

Guests were screaming *bon mots* from table to table, and requisite magnums of Comtes de Champagne and Dom Perignon were sucked dry at the end of each frenetic set. Afruidisiaque was hardly the place for any serious conversation. Tom would have preferred a secluded bistro, but he intended to make a go of it, so he asked the captain for a table well away from the dance floor.

Scanning the diamond-dripping crowd, he felt out of place in his one good business suit. The other patrons were mostly French and German, of the "de" and "von" variety.

"You could easily lose count taking a total carat survey of the ears and necks and fingers in here," he half yelled into Anne's ear when they were finally seated at a lilliputian table. The music wasn't quite as decibel-shattering where they were.

"People come here the way others go to take the waters," she screeched back.

Lady Anne Spalding-Hyer was a very attractive brunette. In another fifteen years and two more divorces, he figured she would wind up on the arms of a parade of oily gigolos.

His thoughts must have sneaked into his eyes, because she said caustically, "You Americans have a not-very-discreet contempt for European idleness, passivity, lack of order, and immorality, don't you?"

"Do we?" he asked, grinning.

"I think I like you, Tom Estevez."

"Your friend Diana de Revillon is an American," he pointed out.

"Half American."

"Does the European half of her fit into the category of idleness, passivity, and so on?"

She took a joint out of her opal-inlaid cigarette case. "Diana passive or idle? Hardly. I remember when we first met—in college—she seemed determined to swallow all of life's offerings in breathless gulps. She was so caught up in protest marches and love affairs and whatever else caught her interest at the moment that eventually she failed her final year."

He shook his head when she asked him if he wanted a hit or a joint of his own. "And what does Diana do with her life now?"

Anne grinned impishly. "Oh, she stays busy with charities and some occasional modeling when the whim strikes her. The remainder of her time is spent disporting in the usual bacchanalias, just as the rest of us do—parties, traveling, skiing, and more parties."

Glitter and rhinestones, he thought, and just as insubstantial.

"I get the distinct impression you don't care for my friend."

"I don't know your friend."

"She's really much more than she seems, Tom. She devotes an astonishing amount of time and goes to great lengths to cement her serious friendships. She has quite an extraordinary ability to concentrate on her friends, even when she's basking in the limelight of some festivity or other."

For a while they studied the dancers, comparing their styles. Sometimes they were comfortably silent and sometimes they talked about things they had done, good and bad. A slow piece was playing at last. "This sounds as close to my style of music as we may get tonight," Tom offered. "Shall we dance?"

She moved fluidly with him, and he responded to the feel of her in his arms. She melted against him. "You make me feel very much a woman, Tom," she said. Her eyes were unnaturally bright—no doubt a combination of the marijuana and the drinks they'd had.

"You are very much a woman."

"Come back to the apartment with me," she whispered, her lips nuzzling his ear.

Trembling slightly, he pulled back to gaze at her

upturned face. "How do you know I'm *not* one of those fortune hunters?"

"You're not the sort, Tom. I'm afraid you have an idealistic image of yourself—a real man-of-integrity hang-up. That's why inevitably you will always be small time."

He laughed at her gentle dig. "Won't Diana mind if I stay with you?"

"She's lived on this side of the Atlantic far more than the other and is quite liberal minded, let me assure you."

It was almost two and the scene in the disco was building to its usual hot, crowded and supercharged climax somewhere between four and five A.M. "What you're inviting me to do, Anne—nothing good comes from rebounds in bed."

"Does that mean you're turning me down, Tom?" She asked so softly that he read her lips more than actually heard her words.

He shook his head. "I'm no fool. Let's go."

When Anne let them into Diana's apartment, the household was dark. She took his hand and drew him down the hallway to her room, where she turned the light on dim and turned to face him. Vulnerability glazed her eyes. "Tom, please . . . I'm not asking for a grandstand performance . . . just hold me, if you care to."

He dropped the jacket he had slung over his shoulder onto a black velvet padded stool in front of the dressing table and went to her. "I'm too old to care about making grandstand performances," he said and reached behind her to unzip her silver lamé dress. It slithered to the floor to reveal what he already suspected: she wore only pantyhose.

She cupped her curiously firm breasts, smiling apologetically. "Implants."

He grinned. "That'll be fine."

She reached up and wrapped her arms around his neck and kissed him lightly, tentatively on the lips. Her breath smelled warm, almost narcotic. "I think, Tom, I've had a bit too much drink."

"Does that mean you'll be sorry tomorrow?" He smiled gently.

Her tremulous lip-twitching response was almost childlike, with a sort of lost look to it. "I don't think I will," she said seriously.

Bending, he scooped her into his arms. She was slight, like a child. He carried her to the four-poster bed, which had already been turned down. She had obviously aroused him, but with all his clothes on, he merely lay on the bed with her cradled against him, letting her set the pace.

"I'm lonely, Tom," she whispered against his collar, "so lonely."

"We all are, Anne."

"And only frenzied fucking can keep that loneliness at bay?"

He knew she was trying to shock him. "Right."

Gingerly, he placed a finger under her chin, and lifted her face to his. Her lips parted readily, and her tongue tenuously fenced with his. He took over then, disrobing them both and forcing her to lie passively as he began a veritable siege of her body. Because she was so anxious and tense, he took a long, gradual time with her. When at last he entered her, she erupted into a burst of grinding, panting determination.

"Hey, slow down," he said quietly, raising up to look straight down at her, "this isn't some kind of competition, Anne—where you have to have a climax or you're not sexually normal.''

She let out a small, whimpering sigh. He lay there half atop her and talked about insignificant things like his first car, as he felt himself go slack.

"Yeah, it was a 1955 pea-green Plymouth convertible. What a bomb. I pulled out the back seat and put in some lawn chairs. We used to take it to drive-in movies."

She chuckled sensuously at his ploy, and he was aware that she was warm and wet and swollen and that he was starting again to grow steadily harder inside her. Only then did he begin that ageless ritual of intimacy . . . hearing her passionate sighs and groans in his ear, feeling her muscles becoming soft as butter and, afterwards, smelling the bittersweet fragrance of their secretions.

After a while, as they lay with limbs interlocked, she said, "Thank you, Tom."

"Nothing to thank me for."

"Yes. For not putting on a performance."

"I'm beginning to suspect that the attitude of the yuppies' generation—the how-you-perform-at-the-moment-is-what-it's-all-about—explains their deep frustration with sex."

"Is there a wife—or a steady woman—back in the States, waiting for you?"

When he was about to reply, she placed her fingertips over his lips. "No, don't say anything, darling. Let's not spoil the moment."

He kissed her fingers. "You're a wise woman, Anne."

She yawned. "Not wise enough to make my marriage work."

"Want to talk about it?"

She shook her head, sleepily. "Not tonight. Under the delightfully numbing influence of spirits, I might reveal something foolish I'd regret later."

As her already deep breathing eased into the steady but shallow tempo of slumber, he lay there thinking that for a few illusive moments their coupled bodies had staved off that essential need to reject the stark fact that every person was alone. Absolutely alone. But now it was over, and they were once again merely two relative strangers in a damp and rumpled bed.

After a bit, he got up, drew on his pants, and made his way down the darkened hall. He bypassed what he suspected were more bedrooms. A wrong turn led him into what must be a workout studio. Another door opened on an office/library. Closing the door quietly, he turned on the desk lamp. Papers were strewn messily across Diana de Revillon's desk—invitations, bills, a few personal letters that seemed innocuous enough.

Perhaps he was wrong in his suspicions.

He tried the desk drawers. Locked. The high-carbon steel three-inch jimmie on his penknife easily tripped the lock mechanism. File folders filled the larger drawer, but a quick scan of them revealed nothing incriminating.

In another drawer was a metal box with a combination lock, the sort of box sold in any office supply store, and he soon chivied it open. Inside was an assortment of keys—numbered and engraved with the names of banks in a surprisingly varied list of European cities.

Why did Diana de Revillon need so many safe-deposit boxes?

23

Keeping a string of horses at the French Riding Club, Le Société Vivant du Cheval, signified one's ultimate arrival into the uppermost echelons of the gold-silver-platinum-edged Gallic society. As a result of its petulantly particular membership committee, the Club had a two-year waiting list.

David Mendel had been a member in good standing for almost ten. He rode his mount, a red and white pinto Creole, with the same deviously imperceptible skill that carried him fleetly down the ski slopes of Mount Blanc. Diana was riding the million-dollar thoroughbred he had battled her for at Deauville.

She suspected he took a certain taunting enjoyment in mounting her astride Sultana's Folly.

"Awfully expensive animal to ride just for pleasure," she said.

They were walking the horses along one of the trails in the Bois de Boulogne, a wooded park of nearly twenty-five hundred acres that had been a Royal Hunt preserve in the seventeenth century and during the Revolution a refuge for the pursued and the destitute. The afternoon was overcast, threatening rain, and the humid

141

air was redolent with the warm, heady smell of horses and late spring.

"I do nothing except for pleasure."

"I'm beginning to believe you," she said, nodding ruefully.

The few riders they passed wore lavishly expensive riding habits, but David was dressed casually in worn jeans and scuffed western boots. That meant, of course, discounting his shirt, a cream-colored custom-tailored pure silk from Charvet, the luxurious gentleman's emporium. Diana knew the shirt had to cost at least $350, the jeans a lot less.

Funny thing about David Mendel, she thought—he handed out cash all over the place, as if it were Monopoly money, but seemed to take no voluptuary pleasure in his grand cars, boats, or villas.

Could it be that he was never fingered in any of his grand thefts because he never kept any of the proceeds? If so, he couldn't be traced—especially if he donated the spoils anonymously to charitable organizations around the world—in effect laundering it.

"You handle Sultana's Folly rather well," he told her.

"I spent much of my childhood at my grandmother's restored *mas* in Provence," she said, leaning forward to pat the well-muscled neck of her coffee-colored steed. "You saw my grandmother with me in Deauville. She breeds horses as a pastime."

In the leafy shadows, his blue eyes were as sultry as the steamy air. "What do you do as a pastime?"

She looked away from him into the trees. "Are you asking how I deal with life's empty spots? If so, I deal with them by not dealing with them."

"Would you care to explain?" His smile was encouraging.

"I simply stay on the fast track."

"Mmmm, I see. So, the empty spots at the side of your road are merely a blur."

"Something like that."

The bridle path narrowed, forcing him to drop behind her, and in passing, their legs brushed. This time, she anticipated the electrical charge that surged through her, turning her veins into a writhing snake's nest.

"Why have you never married?" he asked from behind her, raising his dark voice. She could almost feel the heat of his stare on her shoulders, waist, and hips.

"I watched my mother struggle through two unhappy marriages. They were warning enough."

"You speak of her as if she were dead."

He was able to draw even with her again, and she looked hard at him for a beat. In a dry, flat tone, she said, "She might as well be. She's in a sanitarium not too far from here, near Chantilly. She sought the great, peaceful nirvana once too often and the last time she almost OD'd. She doesn't even recognize me any more."

Few knew that sordid story, and Diana was surprised and somewhat chagrined that she had revealed it so readily to an almost total stranger. Some quality of David Mendel's encouraged confidences.

"Does she recognize anyone else—your grandmother, her husband?"

Her momentary indiscretion, a major lapse in privacy, she realized, caused her to fire back. "My mother's husband, my stepfather, couldn't be more delighted with her indisposition. He turned Mother against me, against my grandmother, you know. He controls the trust my grandmother arranged for my mother as well as the money my father settled on her at their divorce."

David's level gaze was penetrating but he said nothing.

Instantly, she felt a childish contrition, then the phantom pain as unhappy memories invaded her thoughts. There was nothing childish about her voice, though; it came forth as crisp and definite as a nutcracker shattering a walnut.

"While she languishes in her hospital room, he spends her money on a porno star, far past her prime."

"It must be very difficult for you."

"I try to make my mother's hospital room as homey as possible for her: her favorite sheets, fresh flowers, family pictures. The last time he visited her room, four years ago . . ." Disgusted, she didn't bother to finish her sentence.

"Was he hard on you when you were a child?"

"I was twelve when they married. He had been part of the French Resistance and later reached the rank of colonel in the army. He constantly lectured my mother about my irreverence and rebelliousness. I think that's partly what attracted Mother to Ladshaw—he offered her the stability and strict discipline that her life had lacked. Jesus Christ, that discipline of his! Because he forbade it, I was forced to read Socrates, Spinoza, Aristotle, even *Oliver Twist*—under the covers at night! As if those works were pornography! I was forbidden all frivolous pursuits—no swimming with my girlfriends, no movies, no makeup."

"But you did all those things anyway."

"Not at first. After two or three years . . . I don't remember how long . . . I rarely think about it anymore . . . my mother became disillusioned with her loveless marriage or her rigid personal life, however you want to put it. Ladshaw made no move whatever to prevent her from turning to drugs. Sometimes I even think he encouraged them. Thank God, my father and grand-

mother stepped in before he took complete control of
me, too."

"But not without leaving you prejudiced against permanent male-female relationships?"

"Even Freud would have a time with that one. What
about you? Have you no prejudices?"

He reined in his horse and said, "That's the only
luxury I do not allow myself."

"You evade my questions with a skill Lewis Carroll
would have admired."

"Do I?" His eyes seemed to smile, but her work as
an undercover investigator had taught her never to trust
men's eyes. They were an unreliable indicator of character. She judged men by their mouths, and David's lips
possessed a steely strength in the sharply angular delin-
eation of the upper lip. The bottom was full, sensuous,
and she found herself staring, recalling his kiss.

Ultimately, she knew she'd have to seduce him. In
the world of espionage, she was the swallow, the se-
ductress who lured the quarry into her honey trap. "I
was afraid I wouldn't see you again," she said softly.
"I was glad you called this morning."

"I'm twenty years older than you, Diana."

"You're more than twenty years older than your *petite amie*—Maja bint Fadine."

"What makes you think Maja is my mistress?"

Diana glanced away from his bemused stare. She jiggled the reins and the two mounts moved forward in
unison into a trot. "I don't know why I said that. It's
really none of my business."

It began to dawn on her that it was *she* who was being
subtly seduced—by the swallow's male counterpart, the
raven. It was a treacherous position in which to find
herself in her profession.

Few undercover investigators lasted long in the business. The stress and tension that were the by-products of living with an assumed identity months at a time invariably undermined an operative's family life. Then, too, sometimes a propensity to enjoy too assiduously the role of fast living caused an investigator to sell out to the opposition.

Because Diana had no intimate family life and what was a "role" to others was for her a "reality," she had been extremely successful undercover. She meant to continue her achievement, because without her work, she was sure she would wind up like so many of the poor-little-rich girls—like her mother and Anne, who would one day OD on heroin or drift through lives of ennui in alcoholic dazes.

"You never talk about your father, Diana. Who is he?"

"He's American."

He lifted a questioning brow. "That's all? Just an American."

"That's all."

"You must love him very much."

She jerked her head around and stared blankly at him. "Why do you say that?"

"The cigarette case you carry. It's engraved, 'To My Daughter, Diana.' "

"You're very observant. How do you know it's not from my stepfather?"

He shrugged. "Either way, you would hardly have kept it, if you didn't care for the man who gave it to you."

"Perhaps I keep it to remind myself not to equate expensive gifts with genuine affection."

"Is that, also, why you don't use your father's surname?"

"I legally opted to use my grandmother's house

name, because here in Europe the use of de Revillon merely makes things less complicated.

David made no reply, and they rode for a while in comfortable but tense silence. In the distance, thunder rumbled. At the sound, she said, "I suppose we'd better turn back."

"Or else," he said, grinning, "risk getting pneumonia." He paused, then said, "Diana . . . Tuesday I'm taking my yacht on a two-week cruise that will end up in Sardinia, where I'm having a grand opening at a hotel I've financed. Come with me."

"Just up and leave everything?"

"Leave what?" he countered.

She was reminded instantly that this was a man who reveled in challenges. She had to choose every word carefully around him. "David, I will not be your kept woman."

"I don't need a *femme entretenue*, Diana. There are no conditions, no strings on your presence. I wish to enjoy your company on the voyage. Whatever might occur beyond that is up to you entirely."

Their silence after his comment was punctuated only by the crunch of dead oak and chestnut leaves beneath hooves until she said, "Let me think about it."

And thinking she was—very rapidly. A long yacht cruise would create a perfect opportunity to fence the paintings in another country . . . Sardinia itself, for instance. It would be a cinch to conceal the canvases somewhere on the yacht. It was enormous enough—and there was virtually no need to worry about customs inspections.

"You may invite anyone you like," David said. "Your grandmother, the friend who is staying with you. There will be other guests on *The Star of David*." He grinned and added, "I thought I'd even invite our mutual acquaintance, Tom Estevez. He's trying to convince me I need a second yacht, a three-masted schooner, so I thought I'd let him have a firsthand look at *The Star of David*."

"Anne would like that. Tom is helping to ease her way into divorcée status."

"We weigh anchor at Aber-Wrac'h at ten A.M. Tuesday. I hope you'll be there."

The last seemed almost like a dare. She stared at his handsome, haunted face, knowing that she could decline his invitation and evade a possible threat to her emotional security—the danger of falling in love with him.

If she did decline, David Mendel, were he the art thief, would go scot free. An integral part of her would not permit that to happen. There was a relentless determination in her that made her one of the best criminal investigators in the world of law enforcement.

24

June 21st

David Mendel's pied-à-terre on smart, ultra-expensive Avenue Foch consisted of a drawing room, library, dining room, bedroom and bath, bar-clubroom, and a tiny but complete kitchen. Although his public lifestyle exhibited the brisk meticulousness expected of any influential businessman, his private lifestyle appeared to be one of indescribably charming clutter.

His library was a shambles. The desk, big as a door, was buried under a heap of papers, magazines yet to be read, all sorts of parcels, and poking out from under the stack, an open box of Godiva chocolates. A pair of dusty English riding boots lay on their sides in front of a coffee table, where two kings, a queen, a bishop, and two knights waited to resume battle on a marble chess board. A cerise cashmere pullover was flung over a high-backed chair, currently occupied by a dozing black and tan Yorkshire terrier.

Anyone searching the flat for any indication pointing to a master spy would throw up his hands at the first sight of the room, which was exactly the effect David wanted to create. Who would expect to find a code book cleverly concealing its true function within a dusty tome on breeding horses?

Master spy! He grunted his disgust. This master spy wasn't even master of himself. He was meant to be nimble-witted and resourceful, versatile enough to conjure credible reasons or excuses for being in any place at any time, mentally quicker in order to take instant advantage of any opening or any barely perceived weakness in an opponent.

Now he had a potentially fatal weakness—for a cultivated and intelligent much-too-young woman with sun-streaked hair as shiny as a page from *Elle* and a sabra's soldierly self-reliance and toughness packaged in an otherwise ladylike exterior. Could she really be like the sabra, the Israeli cactus: hard and prickly outside and sweet and tender inside?

Or was she other than she appeared, something very much more? That way she looked at him sometimes— with an aristocrat's inbred disdain and so steadily, without a trace of self-consciousness, created chaos in his imagination. Beside all that, she had that ineffably magic and intense beauty.

Little details about her popped into his mind at the unlikeliest times. At the masked ball, the sound her gold satin dress made when she walked past reminded him of a grazing racehorse swishing its tail.

The doorbell proclaimed a visitor, and a gravelly voice over the apartment's intercom announced that Tom Estevez was on time. A few moments later, David's stonefaced manservant ushered Estevez into the library. David stood up and shook hands across his desk. He genuinely liked this man and his easy Latin style. That morning, he was wearing a tweed jacket and was tieless. "Just scoot Monsieur off the chair, Mr. Estevez.

That Yorkie is so old, he's almost toothless. He might gum you fiercely, though," David smiled.

Somewhat gingerly, Estevez picked up the torpid ball of fur and ensconced it on his lap after he was seated. "Little fella reminds me of a shaggy mutt I had as a boy. Had so much hair covering his eyes, I felt sorry for him. Stupidly, I took the scissors to him and whacked it off. The bright sunlight drove old Pedro crazy. Literally. He began to run around in circles. Never did stop."

David leaned back in his chair. "What happened to him?"

Estevez's expression turned grim and formidable. "My family was too poor to afford a vet. I had to shoot him."

"Whoever said childhood was the best times of our lives was either monumentally insensitive or had amnesia as a child. Would you care for a cognac?"

"Too early. Thanks."

"You wanted to discuss the details of a boat you are brokering—a schooner?"

"I have in mind a yacht built for one of the richest men in England by Amels."

"Amels? I'm not familiar with the firm."

"It's a family-owned ship and yacht yard at the edge of what was once the Zuider Zee. Their naval architect, Hendrik van der Vries, has solved the problem of maintaining high standards in boat finishing by keeping a crack workshop on the payroll and subcontracting the rough work. They usually specialize in passenger liners, and they have a two-year backlog of orders."

"How did you get involved with them?"

"One of the brothers is retired and spends a good part of the year in Palm Beach. For buyers of the finest yachts, Holland is where it is happening."

"It's always been my understanding that luxury boats, bargains, too, only with pizzazz, are usually built in either Italian or German yards, with their hi-tech assembly techniques. The Milanese marine engineering firm of Giorgetti e Magrini built *The Star of David*."

"Amels's are floating diamonds, David. Dazzlingly finished, rock-solid, and beautifully structured from stem to stern. They build according to the 100 A-1 classification of Lloyd's of London—the most severe standard of quality construction in the world. Yacht, after all, is a Dutch word."

"You seem to know your business, Estevez. What about brokering for me?"

"You want to sell *The Star of David*?"

"Perhaps. I'm taking her on a two-week cruise day after tomorrow. There's some business I have to attend to—the grand opening of a hotel I financed in Sardinia. Would you like to come along and get the feel of her?"

Estevez's oversized hands scratched behind the Yorkie's ears. "Why not?" he said, after a thoughtful moment. "I could use the rest."

After Estevez left, David had two free hours before his next meeting, and he went to work on decoding the latest communiqué from Mossad, which carried the awesome mission name "Wrath of God"—describing the present operation, a Nazi hunt by certain members of its revenge squad.

David met Sciolla in Luxembourg gardens at the boat basin, where children, old people, secretaries on their lunch hour, even vagrants watched as scale-model yachts and sailboats navigated the basin's calm waters, as they had for almost sixty years. For six francs, the miniature boats could be rented from a concession.

David was content to sit on a wrought-iron bench and

watch the little armada traverse the Luxembourg seas. As a lover of boats, his presence there would not be questioned nor would the apparently idle conversation he was having with the other bench occupant—a flat-nosed man with ruthless eyes and a penchant for sadistic pleasures, if Mossad's follow-up report was accurate.

When one of Sciolla's prostitutes broke the so-called iron law of silence by denouncing his pimping gang, he had them take her to a lumberyard at closing time, where she was tied to a crossbeam and rented to sixty men in three hours. Next Sciolla personally booted her till a vertebra in her spine cracked, then jammed a rough, wooden club into her vagina.

The man's slow feral eyes slid from a listing sailboat toward David. His voice lowered to a sibilant hiss. "Suppose I turned you in to the police?"

David lowered his voice, too, but he smiled warmly. "I have an alibi, Sciolla. And who do you think the police will believe—an upstanding citizen like myself or a scum like you who was present the day the paintings were stolen?"

"You're not so smart as you believe you are. I wrote down the license number on the van you rented that day to transport the paintings."

"That number plate, *mon vieux ami,* was off a wrecked vehicle, and the van is now a block of scrap metal a few centimeters high and wide. Now, of course, if you wish to renew our discussion on a certain transaction . . ."

The ends of Sciolla's scarred mouth turned up in a gruesome death mask. At last, David thought. Common ground with this bastard. The pleasures and profits of trafficking in coke Sciolla could well understand and relate to.

"That friend I told you about in Deauville," Sciolla said sotto voce, "he's okayed the deal—400 keys for the paintings. He just wants to know when and where the exchange takes place."

"There is a condition," David said. "I will do business only with the buyer."

"Why? You don't even know who he is."

"No, but when we meet, he should know a *Sunrise* forgery from the real thing—then I'll know if he's a genuine art connoisseur."

Sciolla's square face was puzzled, as if he could hardly imagine why two men like St. Giles and Mendel would go to such lengths for some paint-daubed canvases. "When and where do you want to make the turn?"

"July the seventh. Porto Rotondo, Sardinia."

25

June 23rd

"What can this friend of yours, this David Mendel," he sneered the name, "offer in the way of entertainment, *chèrie*, that I cannot?"

"Not a trace of pressure, Murad," Diana said, taking the glass of Scotch and water Tom was passing to her. She and Murad sat opposite Tom and Anne in the passenger compartment of the Indian's customized Mercedes limousine. A telephone rested on the console between them.

Murad's sleek white German car, with its blue velour interior, sped through the idyllic forested countryside of mysterious Britanny, the Celtic province, passing scores of medieval stone-walled farms, handsome abbeys, and turreted castles that echoed a magical past of Tristan and Iseult, Guinevere and King Arthur. Ahead, the crown of Finisterre's windswept peninsula, was the fashionable yachting center of Aber-Wrac'h.

Ice cubes clinked in another glass Tom was filling for Murad from the electronic bar between him and Anne. Beneath the sweep of his ebony mustache, the corners of Murad Murarani's mouth dipped sulkily, his gargantuan Eastern male ego completely overcome by Diana's studied lack of infatuation with him.

She had invited Murad along on the pleasure cruise, Tom supposed, to play off the Indian prince against Mendel. Murad, with royalty's typical disregard for conventions, had in turn invited two other couples Tom didn't know.

"Walter Vachs and his wife, Eva, along with Carlo and Catherine Roumey," Diana had informed him, while they waited for Murad to pick them up. "Not that David Mendel will care. With a yacht as large as his, we might never encounter each other."

Anne had rolled her eyes. "With that nympho aboard, she'll have all the men playing musical beds."

"Who is this?" Tom asked with lifted brows.

"Catherine Roumey," Diana said. "She and I modeled together for a while for Lanvin. She's a vitriolic keg of nitro."

Tom settled back in the plush seat and swallowed his drink. Ten in the morning was a little early for booze, but this was one of the few times he'd ever got to ride the high road in his line of work.

Taste alone told him the amber elixir was the best of Scotches, just as Diana was the best of her kind, and he couldn't help being intrigued by her. It was like watching a female scorpion in that final mating dance before she stings her willing mate.

That morning she had on some kind of khaki jumpsuit that he estimated had to cost a fat grand. Damn, a thousand bucks for car mechanic's coveralls!

He noticed that she was watching him, so he said, "A penny for your thoughts, Miss de Revillon."

"A penny only? Surely, my thoughts are worth more."

"I suppose that's why you're wealthy."

"You don't like me, do you?"

"A male dog and female cat," Anne drawled. "And I've got to spend a two-week-long cruise with you two.

You're both going to ruin the trip.'' She passed her empty glass to him. ''Another, please?''

''Friends?'' Diana offered, a hint of mockery on her lips and in her tone.

''Friends,'' he confirmed and turned his attention to replenishing Anne's glass.

Behind them, a TV set, the sound turned low, was running a French-dubbed version of ''The F.B.I.,'' and he was reminded of his conversation with Hamblin that morning. Between snatches of sneezing, the Interpol le-at informed him that the various safe-deposit boxes registered in Diana de Revillon's name also carried the signature of Samuel Breckon, a top official for Security International.

Tom was pretty certain Diana was operating as an undercover agent for the giant insurance combine. One of those fiscal sleuths. If so, she was playing at being one just as she played at life. Well, he didn't have time for any games and he certainly didn't need her screwing up his investigation.

Aber-Wrac'h's split-timbered houses and slate-faced shops were intermingled with a few luxury hotels that proclaimed the village one of the newest English Channel resorts. The medieval town was poised on a granite spur overlooking a lovely inlet, or *aber* in Breton, where multimillionaires' yachts were berthed in serried ranks like ungainly shoals of fish.

David Mendel's 3,500-ton polished-steel yacht with its bronze reflective windows was easy to pick out of the crowded maritime throng. From a mast on the heliport deck waved the French Tricolore, as well as that of David Mendel's mobile empire's port-of-call, Aber-Wrac'h. Below the others flew the owner's private signal— the gold star of David on a cerulean field. In yard-high gold letters on the bow was the ship's name.

As Murad's chauffeur, a brown-skinned Hindu in a

Nehru jacket and blue turban, backed the Mercedes into a parking place, two stewards trotted down the yacht's ramp to collect the guests' luggage. Murad led Diana aboard as Tom, with Anne's elbow socketed safely in his palm, brought up the rear.

Toward the bow, as they were stepping onto the deck, he made out Mendel in cut-offs and sweat shirt, descending from the bridge, most likely giving a tour to the long-stemmed beauty with him. Tom recognized her: the American film star, Joan Rodgers; he remembered her, too, from the masked fête at the Opera House.

Behind David and Joan trailed Greek entrepreneur Gregorios Aristos, Diana's escort that fateful night, and Maja bint Fadine, the young woman who'd been with Mendel at Deauville.

So, it seemed David Mendel could play Diana's game, and very well too. Tom almost chuckled aloud. This cruise was going to be quite a jaunt; with any luck at all the two antagonists would outduel one another, keeping themselves busy while he went about his own nefarious business.

The two groups merged on the main deck, where Diana and David—the Golden Couple, Tom couldn't help but think of them—handled themselves admirably, each cordially introducing the pawns they'd brought along for the midgame festivities.

"I'll show you to your rooms, first," Mendel said with an impartial smile for each of the new arrivals, "then, after you've had a chance to rest and clean up, we can meet for lunch on the upper deck by the pool. Tom, maybe you and I will have time before lunch to tour the ship. I'm sure you'll be interested in her finer points."

Damn right, I will! "It would appear to be a technological masterpiece at the very least," Tom said, rubbing his fingers absently along the teakwood railing. Somewhere aboard the yacht were likely hidden nine priceless works of art. Where they might be stashed interested him less than where they were headed—to whom—and for how much.

As the crew prepared to weigh anchor, Mendel escorted his guests to their various suites, each named for precious and semiprecious gems. "I had all the living quarters constructed with a circular pattern to enhance intimacy and comfort," he explained.

Tom's suite was the Ruby, so of course everything was coordinated in vivid reds, including the candy-striped, padded sleigh bed of Goliath proportions. A tour of the bathroom widened Tom's eyes. Bath suite was a better term. The bathroom certainly had come out of the water closet: redwood dry sauna, stereo, TV, VCR, exercise bike, and, to fill the empty space next to the toilet, one of those bidets to provide the Continental touch. The faucet's solar-powered digital readout ensured that he wouldn't have to put his piggies in the gold leaf tub and get scalded.

After a white-jacketed steward had deposited Tom's single piece of luggage in a mirror-paneled closet and departed, Tom opened it, moved aside a .357 magnum, and took out a small device he had packed with one purpose in mind.

After several wrong turns, he found the engine room, painted a blinding white and color-coded in green. The place was as immaculately clean as the steward had been. The two 3,000-horsepower diesels were noisy enough to conceal his presence as he wandered through the immense room.

In a sideroom, he found what he was looking for— the bridge telephone. To install the direct tape, it took only minutes for him to attach a set of wires to a specified pair in the communications box and run them into the pocket-size tape recorder he concealed behind a nearby electrical cable junction box.

After climbing the engine room steel-mesh exit ladder

to the deck, he ran into Mendel at the entry, who said, "My chief engineer told me he thought he saw you go down there." The financier's eyes were suspicious.

"God, David, I was so impressed by what I had already seen," Tom said with an enthusiastic grin, "I couldn't wait to begin looking around. I noticed all the wiring is shielded. Two-inch-thick teak decks. Diesels powerful enough to run the U.S.S. *Enterprise*. Quite a boat you have here."

"Yes, isn't it," he said, and Tom couldn't be sure his answer had allayed the man's obvious suspicions. "She draws over fifteen feet and can make eighteen to twenty-one knots."

His hands jammed in the back pockets of his jeans, Tom let Mendel lead him away from the engine room. "The others are already on the upper deck, waiting for lunch," Mendel announced.

Had Mendel seemed slightly anxious about his guest wandering alone in the engine room? Tom wasn't sure.

On the upper deck, sheltered from the sun by a beige and white striped awning, was a dining area that, by Tom's reckoning, looked as if it could seat sixty.

"There are two main kitchens, backed up by three deck pantries," Mendel said so easily that Tom wondered if he could have been mistaken about the reason for the man's earlier concern, which could have been merely concern for a guest's safety. Somehow, though, he doubted it. He was virtually certain Mendel was his man.

Diana, Anne, and Murad were already seated at one of the large round tables, with Joan Rodgers and the Aristos guy, tall as a redwood and thin as a sapling. Tom couldn't remember the Greek's first name right off, but he had come dressed for the part—navy blue blazer and white duck slacks.

There were two other guests Tom didn't know—a bald,

athletic-looking man, whom Mendel introduced as Walter Vachs, ". . . who was responsible for coordinating the financial planning for the winter Olympics that West Germany hosted some years ago," Mendel said.

Walter's wife, Eva, sat with downcast eyes, shoulders slightly hunched. Her figure was lush and abundant, and if she had not been so large-framed, she would have been overweight. Eva Vachs was blunt-featured, with a smooth, hanging crown of graying light brown hair. When they were introduced, she offered Tom a tight, rather nervous little smile.

In the nearby Olympic-size pool, a studious-looking man named Carlo called out a greeting. As he did, his wife Catherine's head broke the surface. A stunning redhead, she put her palms flat on the cool deck, vaulted up gracefully, and pirouetted onto the edge of the pool, sleek as a seal. She was topless. Interesting, Tom thought.

Mendel made the introductions, and Catherine called, "Join us."

Not on his life. This was no time to go swimming with a man-eating shark. "Later."

Several more guests, the women also topless, cavorted in the pool. A black French photographer by the name of Noël and his sandy-haired, teenage girlfriend were installed on a king-size mattress, sipping a fruity cocktail of some kind. Noël wore flamboyant rhinestone sunglasses and a dripping wet, bright pink silk scarf.

"Welcome aboard, Yank," the short, sandy-haired girl said. Her name, she told him in broad Aussie accent, was Tanya Gordon.

Tom figured these were the usual beautiful people who rode happily along on the coattails of the rich. But why did the jet-setters tolerate them? Were they that lonely? That insecure?

He stepped over a stack of high-pile Hermès beach

towels and headed toward the nearest table. Once seated, his eyes were drawn unerringly to Diana. Like Catherine, she had a lithe, lissome build, tall and rangy. But Diana's expression was charged with energy and she overwhelmed the others like a sun among planets. The sea breeze ruffled her sun-streaked golden hair.

Murad sat on her left, his arm draped territorially on the back of her chair, while she smoked one of those stinky French cigarettes, her *salade Niçoise* untouched. Tom was glad he had picked up a box of cigars beforehand, stick-length stogies.

He settled back into the deck chair and, while he ate, studied the others. Anne was unusually quiet, while Joan went on in a silky voice about the new television series she was doing.

"I play the villainess, a really vile bitch, and the hate mail has already started to pour in."

Watching her, Tom couldn't help thinking she was sultry, sophisticated, and completely plastic. When she glanced at others it was as if she were gazing into a mirror, evaluating her performance by their reactions.

"Every day the mail is brought into my dressing room in these enormous canvas bags, and the studio has even hired a fucking security guard to go through it to check for those bomb things!"

A sad-eyed, slender man, who Tom learned was the yacht's doctor, somebody Corneille, said, "That's not the kind of mail I'd expect you to get." He bit into a B.L.T. and, mouth crammed, mumbled, "Obscene letters, things like that."

"Oh, I get those, too."

While they ate, the Brittany coastline slipped lazily by— awesome rocky headlands, where the waves burst into spray, alternating with secretive, sandy coves. Occasionally a town, enclosed by gray granite medieval ramparts, could be spotted teetering on a windswept promontory.

For a moment, Tom was reminded of his kids. Marc and Luann and Deedee would have loved a trip like this. He missed the hell out of them. And he missed Wendy's uncomplicated passion, too.

A waiter set before him a dish of lobster with cream sauce—*"homard à l'armoricaine,"* Anne cued him discreetly—but his attention was focused on the waiter rather than the regional dish.

Sciolla!

When the conversation reached a lull, Tom decided to draw Mendel out. "Doesn't your investment banking firm oversee the appraisal and sale of special assets— for instance, works of art?"

Diana purred cigarette smoke through her nostrils, and leaned back in her chair, quite feline, but Tom sensed she was also just as alert as a cat.

"Occasionally," Mendel replied easily to the camouflaged question, laying his napkin beside his plate. "Recently, one of our trust officers arranged the sale of a ten million dollar collection of paintings, but we specialize in managing personal assets. For clients with portfolios of two million dollars or more."

"You're talking to the wrong man," he told Mendel. "I wouldn't know an equity from a debenture."

"Speaking of art collections," Diana said, "did any of you hear about the theft of some Renoirs—the Marmottan Museum, wasn't it?"

Mendel met her contemplative gaze. "Not all of them were Renoirs. I believe there were several Monets, too, his *Rising Sun*, for one."

David glanced around the table. "Anyone for swimming?"

26

June 24th

The pool water was like unchilled Perrier. Diana did a few slow lengths then gradually pushed herself, just as she did before the barre . . . changing the kick beat, stretching and punishing the long muscles of arms, shoulders, back, thighs, and belly, drawing in precious air and bubbling into the water layers of staleness from the depths of her lungs. Her brain was mushy as an oyster's, and she forced herself to swim that one extra lap, repeating the mantra, *Just one more, oh just one more.*

What the hell was David Mendel up to?

And one more.

In the vastness of the yacht, with all its nooks and crannies, the paintings would be about as easy to find as the Holy Grail.

And one more.

At last, muscles aquiver, heartbeat accelerated, she levered herself onto the poolside, flipping her wet hair back from her face. The deck's pebbly surface was pleasantly warm against her stomach and thighs, and she closed her eyes lazily, willing herself to drift . . .

164

with the tide . . . with the day . . . as the yacht slid
into Spanish waters along the recherché Algarve Coast.

By the standards of avant-garde travelers, the day had
scarcely begun; it was about eleven, and she was the
only one at the pool. The pool bar, a half-round,
thatched-hut structure, wasn't open yet. Joan Rodgers
wouldn't swim, of course, because, like Diana's grandmother, she never let the sun touch her skin . . .
couldn't afford to take the risk of a wrinkle.

Anne, Diana suspected, was still abed, luxuriating in
a night spent in the arms of Tom Estevez. The man was
homely handsome and, despite his rough half-polished
appearance, was reportedly capable of gentle lovemaking.

"It's nothing acrobatic, Di—God knows I've had
enough of those lovers," Anne had said yesterday
morning, while they were packing for the cruise. "No,
it has nothing to do with rocketing stars and explosive
climaxes, but, damn, the man's attentive, tender, con-
siderate . . . you know, what the romance novels corrupt into twenty-four-hour foreplay. He's also divorced
and brutally honest, which is something I appreciate
after the mealy-mouth toads I've crossed paths with."

Honesty was one of the few traits Diana would have
attributed to Mr. Estevez.

"Sleep well?"

She squinted up, one hand shading her eyes against
the fierce sunlight, and made out the unmistakable sil-
houette of David standing over her. "Very, thank you.
But then those of us without guilty consciences always
do."

"So if I didn't sleep well, I should attribute it to
guilt?"

"You could," she emphasized with an ameliorating
grin. As her eyes adjusted to the sunlight, she mar-

veledat his well-built body, clad simply in shorts and polo shirt. He wore thick rope-soled sandals. A sweat-dampened towel dangled around his neck. His legs were suntanned, solid, muscular, and fuzzed with sun-bleached body hair. Had he slept with Maja last night? "Don't tell me your yacht also has a workout gym?"

"It's a regular floating minicity." He reached down and took the hand she held over her eyes, tugging her to her feet. "I was wondering if you carried concealed oxygen tanks in that skimpy swimsuit."

"No," she said, laughing. "I just take to the water like a kid on a summer vacation."

"Come along, I want to show you something."

She knew he had noticed the way she flinched at his touch, but his expression gave away no reaction on his part. He led her to the railing and her eyes followed the direction of his outstretched arm.

"Dolphins!" she said, her awe instilling a trace of breathlessness in her voice. The gray-black streamlined bodies arced gracefully in and out of the yacht's frothy bow wake. "They're absolutely beautiful."

David turned to face her, his hands braced on the railing. Salt spray formed a momentary halo around his head, which was canted, as if he were weighing her beauty from a solely objective point of view. His pupils, even in the sun, appeared to dilate in order to take her in. "So are you, Diana, but I don't think you were always beautiful. Were you?"

"How did you guess?" She rolled her eyes. "As a schoolgirl, I was gawky—too tall—and my nose developed well before the rest of my face."

"Did your mother ever reassure you that it would all come together one day?"

"She . . . she never said much one way or the other. I remember we did clash frequently over makeup, be-

cause I wore a lot of black eyeliner during my early
teen years. As I told you, my stepfather wasn't particularly well disposed to black eyeliner. Neither were my
father or grandmother for that matter.''

"The ugly-duckling-turned-swan complex?''

"Worse. I still haven't reconciled myself to my face.
It's difficult for me to look at pictures of myself.'' She
surprised even herself with the admission, so she re-
versed roles and became inquisitor. "What about you?
Did you have a difficult childhood?'' She waited for the
words that were slow to form.

"My parents and sisters were killed by the Nazis.''

"I'm sorry.''

He shrugged philosophically. "Few European families were untouched by the ravages of the war. Anyway,
a conscientious friend and employee kept my family's
banking business intact while I was being trained in the
proscribed life of an international financier. I was always alone among my other classmates, who, at least,
went home for the holidays. After I finished my education, practical training followed at a London advertising agency and branches of the Mendel Banks in
Madrid, Frankfurt, and Tel Aviv.''

She tucked a swath of hair behind her ear, blown dry
by the steady ocean breeze. "You know, David, I don't
hear any enthusiasm in your voice.''

"That's true. I had no desire to emulate my father
and his father's father, but banking was one of those
legacies that was inescapable.''

"You could have jumped ship, so to speak. Just aban-
doned it all and bummed around the world.''

"No. I couldn't do that. Something in me responds
to a challenge—and to succeed at an occupation to
which I was indifferent was a great challenge.''

"Is that why you've asked me to join this cruise—

because I'm not one of your easy amorous conquests and, therefore, a challenge?''

"Maybe I'm intrigued by a quality not even you can see. Look at us, Diana—we're a matched pair.'' He was smiling, but his eyes flashed with that flagrant intensity that had first captured her interest. "In more than just looks, too, I suspect," he added, his fingers entwining a lock of her hair the wind had spooled toward him.

"Oh, David,'' Joan called from behind them. She had on a pair of Givenchy sunshades and a bright orange and green Polynesian wrapper that covered her from her slightly crêpey neck to her ankles.

As he turned toward her, she said, "You're proving to be a very poor host.'' She spared an obligatory smile for Diana but concentrated all her attention on David. "I've been searching all over for you. Your guests are dribbling one by one into the dining saloon, and we're famished.''

"My apologies. A brunch is being served—to be followed by a screening of *Out of Desperation*.''

"How marvelous, darling!'' She linked her arm in his. "Is there anything you can't manage?''

As Diana collected her ankle-length lace cover-up, she said, "Maybe he can even manage to procure an Oscar nomination for you.''

"Not a bad idea,'' David said, removing his arm from Joan's talonlike clamp. "We could start promoting *Out of Desperation* now for the Cannes Film Festival.''

"Marvelous,'' Joan said again, but less enthusiastically, as two thin lines formed shallow parentheses on either side of her artfully drawn mouth while she observed her prey taking Diana's cover-up from her hand and helping her into it.

Odd, Diana thought, how his touch alone could set her off, decalcifying her bones instantly. Her grandmother would be quite distressed if she knew that the man who ultimately had reached through the wall of distrust Diana had built was a Jew. Yet, much as Diana loved her grandmother, she felt she should follow her own good instincts instead of her grandmother's prejudices.

Three chefs—French, Chinese, and American— prepared a variety of dishes that were being served buffet style. As the living quarters were, the dining salon was circular, its walls draped in heavy gold damask. Vermeil flatware and Spode crystal graced each table, at which, incredibly, fresh flowers—daisies, asters, and carnations—served as centerpieces.

David presided over the festivities with a congeniality and animation that made it difficult to believe he had planned anything for the cruise but the enjoyment of his guests. Catherine and the doll-like Maja came in late and took empty seats at the table where Carlo sat, with Walter, Eva, Joan, and Murad.

The Indian was still sulking over Diana's rejection of his request to occupy his bed and arms the night before. "Why did you invite me on this boat then?" he had asked, rather grumpily.

"Because I like you," she had answered, honestly, if not completely so.

Occasionally a guest would stop by from another table and David would introduce him or her, reminding everyone of the screening after lunch.

While baked Alaska was served, David and Tom discussed the yacht and the possibilities of its sale. The imperturbable American had on Levis and a faded blue shirt with its long sleeves rolled to his hairy forearms. "*The Star of David* should fetch you around seventy million dollars," he was telling David.

"Want a hit, Di?" Anne asked.

Diana glanced at the toke her friend was offering and shook her head. "Thanks, Anne, but no. Too soon after eating."

"This is Turkish stuff," Greg said, exhaling a slow, pungent haze. "I have a mule, an old Pakistani woman, would you believe, who brings out only the best keys. Come on, give it a try."

Having passed up one too many joints to maintain her playgirl image, Diana accepted one but smoked it slowly. Her mother's Lotusland dependence on Percodan and Dilaudid—and all those other little two-tone capsules Ladshaw allowed to pervade the house—had left Diana with a deep aversion to drugs of any kind.

David, she knew, did not smoke; she wondered if he used any of the harder drugs? At the pool, she had scanned his body swiftly for needle marks and there were none. If he was snorting cocaine, then he wasn't into it heavily enough to have acquired the so-called "rat's nose," which left the nose red, with enlarged mucuous membranes, and constantly dripping so that the user was constantly sniffing like a rat.

What he had acquired, however, was a barely discernible scar on the inside of his forearm.

Through the veil of whitish haze that she exhaled, Diana caught Tom eyeing her speculatively. "Could that be a look of disapproval?" she asked him quietly, coldly. His manner definitely put her on edge.

At her barbed query, the conversation around the table ebbed into expectant silence. Anne rolled her eyes, as if to say "they're at it again."

Tom leaned back and lit up one of his obnoxious cigars. "Well now, I guess you could take that look however you want," he said in a mock Western drawl.

"I will take that as signal to adjourn our little gathering to the movie room," David said, pleasantly but firmly.

An elevator outside the dining room was waiting to take the six of them down two decks. "I've brought along some refreshments," Greg said, holding up two bottles of champagne as he stepped into the elevator. "Hope you don't mind my robbing your larder, David."

"My pleasure." At his side, Joan was carrying a glass that had been refilled before she left the table.

Eva said quietly, "Does anyone mind if I get on last?" She stood before them with an intuitive ducking of her head, her eyes peeking up from her lowered countenance rather charmingly.

"You see, she has this fear of closed places," Walter explained patently.

"Have you always had claustrophobia?" Diana asked.

Eva fairly beamed, delighted at the attention for once. "I was trapped in a basement bomb shelter when I was just a little girl. You know, it was when the American planes were bombing Berlin, and . . ."

Whatever Eva was saying, Diana missed because Murad drew her to the back of the elevator to whisper in her ear, "Joan Rodgers couldn't act her way through rice pudding, *chérie*. Let's leave once the movie begins."

"Sssh," she warned him with a glare. Ducking out, however, was exactly what she had in mind.

A sprinkling of couples was already present in the small auditorium, which looked as if it might seat seventy-five. Diana maneuvered Murad so that she was seated on the aisle. Beside Murad, Catherine lit up a turquoise cocktail cigarette. Her face was a porcelain mask that hid her boredom and her eyes were quite composed, almost exactly as they were when they stared out of glossy fashion magazine layouts.

David signaled to the projectionist and the lights were dimmed.

In the dark, Joan laughed and said, "I deserve an Oscar for this one if for no other reason than managing to look in love with my leading man. The prick is into little girls. And I mean little."

A fanfare preceded a three-foot-high close-up of the actress's sensual face, rendered flawless by a gauze filter and extremely careful lighting. The credits followed, as the lens widened to a shot of her and the male star, whom Diana didn't recognize, grappling lustily beneath a not-very-concealing sheet.

Diana settled back, prepared to endure fifteen minutes. She made ten, before quietly excusing herself to Murad and slipping out of the room. Instead of going into the nearest ladies' room, she made her way by a back stairwell to the deck, where the main sleeping quarters were located.

She knew to search a yacht the size of *The Star of David* effectively would be a formidable task, with its hundreds of recesses, which would at least demand special mirrors to examine.

Nevertheless, to hide paintings as large as the nine stolen ones would be rather difficult, unless they had been removed from their frames and rolled. That prospect put her right back to square one—and the most likely place to begin: the private office David had shown his guests the day before, when he had given them a tour of the boat.

He had locked the door afterward, and she could only hope that he hadn't entered the office since then. She tried the knob, and the door opened readily. Before going in, she plucked out the segment of toothpick she had surreptitiously lodged in the lock to jam it.

Enough sunlight spilled through the rectangular porthole for her to find her way easily about the room. David's desk was built into the wall and extended its entire length. Mentally, she assessed its multitude of drawers—too narrow and shallow to hold even rolled paintings.

She glanced around the office, conscious that time was slipping rapidly by and that she would soon be missed. Across the room was a door that looked as if it might open into a supply closet. "Shit," she muttered when the knob wouldn't give.

"Didn't anyone ever tell you what happens to little girls who play where they shouldn't?"

Her hand still grasping the knob, she spun around. Tom Estevez blocked the doorway, one arm braced indolently against the door frame. "I'm sure you know the answer. Now, let me ask you a question, Mr. Estevez. I have a right to be here. Do you?"

"I don't think Mendel would recognize your right—not if he knew you were an undercover investigator for an international insurance agency. Security International, I believe."

Spasms of utter shock leeched her legs of their normal strength, and only her hands on the doorknob at the small of her back supported her weight. "You Americans watch too many movies," she managed to get out along with a chiding smile.

Hands in his jean pockets, Estevez ambled across the thick carpet to stand before her. "You know, Miss de Revillon, you're damned clever. I admire your chameleonlike ability to act the playgirl while all the time you're a supersleuth. It's only because I'm a socially ignorant American that you didn't succeed in convincing me of your cover.''

She tried for sarcasm. "Why, thank you.''

"Problem is," he continued amiably, "I don't think you've got what it takes to burn Mendel. I've seen the way you look at him. You're falling into that psychological trap all undercover agents must deal with—losing touch with reality.''

Anger fueled her and she straightened to her model's full height. "Who the hell are you to lecture me about—''

"A detective, also, ma'am. Course, not in the same classy league as yourself, just a street dick—a narc to be precise, with twenty years' experience though.''

She should have expected as much, after remembering the imposter was too-coincidentally present in Deauville's Vacheron-Constantin. "I may not have twenty years' experience, Mr. Estevez, but I have a one-hundred-percent success record.''

"Oh, I'm sure you do," he drawled, a trace of contempt tinging his tone. "I'm sure that you take whatever risks are required to accomplish your assignments, don't you?''

"I'm a professional, Mr. Estevez.''

"I suppose if that includes sleeping with Mendel, you'll do that also?''

She flashed her warmest $500-an-hour smile at him. "You're a chauvinistic bastard, aren't you? Perhaps you'll allow me to point out that quite probably you are sleeping with Anne for less than honorable reasons yourself.''

"Filthy work we have to do, isn't it?" he grunted with a mock grin of lechery.

"Are we quite finished with this scenario? Because

if we are, you should know that I'm going to take down David Mendel, and then I'm going to light into you."

Estevez had turned away while she talked, which made her more furious. At the door, he faced her and said ominously, "Mendel is mine, lady." At that moment his face was far more ugly than handsome. "I'm gonna punch his ticket—and his supplier's—when he tries to fence those stolen paintings for drugs, so leave—"

"For drugs?"

"You heard me. So, leave the artwork wherever it is. One more thing: if you get in my way or screw up this operation, I'll blow your cover in every major daily across the face of the earth. After that, not even all your money will buy you an undercover job."

She crossed her arms negligently. The corners of her mouth lifted in an arch smile. "I might point out that I can and will blow your cover just as easily."

She might as well have waved a flag in front of Attila the Hun. "Lady, if you want a war on your hands, you've got it. As far as I'm concerned, the race is on to see who gets Mendel first."

"May the best woman win!" she called out on the door that was yanked closed.

27

David had to feel the electricity that coursed between them, Diana was certain; she could see desire smoldering in his eyes. Regardless, he had made no attempt to seduce her. It was that steely restraint that beguiled her above even the inexplicable magnetic attraction she felt as a throbbing beat that pounded through her veins and agitated her blood.

They were standing on the bridge, David pointing out its state-of-the-art navigational equipment, all encased in gleaming brass, steel, and chrome. Gauges, levers, wheels, telephones, many buttons and digital readouts. Behind them, the uniformed, mustached Italian gleamed, too, his own pride as captain of *The Star of David* obvious.

"Italians have been the best navigators throughout history, haven't they?" she remarked to him in Italian, smiling.

Capitano Antonio Fernetti's chest swelled visibly, until it appeared as if it might turn his double row of shining gold buttons into flying shrapnel. "*Si, signorina*, and I come from the best, a direct descendant of Cristoforo Colombo himself!"

The vessel was beginning to make its way through

the thirty-two-mile-long Strait of Gibraltar, bound for the warmer, calmer, bluer waters of the Mediterranean. Along the Spanish shoreline, no more than twelve miles from Africa on the narrowest point of the strait, sixteenth-century ramparts and modernistic military installations stair-stepped up into the gloriously curved and hilly coastline. Just ahead on the port side rose that commanding limestone headland towering almost fifteen hundred feet above the water: the Rock of Gibraltar.

"It's awesome," she said.

"Those steel towers, *signorina*," Captain Fernetti said, "are the electronic eyes and ears of NATO and keep watch over the strait."

"Want to go ashore?" David asked. "It's like no place you have ever been."

And he was like no man she had ever known. She was still horrified by Tom Estevez's statement that David intended to make a drug buy, apparently a hefty one if he meant to fence the paintings for the drugs—if the narc agent was to be believed. Tom Estevez might be as abrasive as a pumice stone, but her usually infallible instincts told her he was honest, which in her occupation impressed her mightily. "You've piqued my interest."

Soon the landing was arranged, so she changed into a yellow tiered sundress and low-heeled walking sandals. The yacht's two black Rivas transported not only her and David, but Walter, Eva, Murad, Carlo, Greg, and Anne into the battleship-guarded harbor. The amorous attention Greg was lavishing upon Anne was something new. Was Anne perhaps showing off for her Latin lover, Tom Estevez, who seemed to be dropping her?·

Diana suspected Joan was languishing in her beauty sleep. And Maja and Catherine said they preferred a lazy afternoon sipping mai-tais by the pool. Maja's reserve had relaxed enough around the uninhibited Catherine for the Turkish girl to bare her breasts to the sun. They were small but perfectly shaped, pleasingly proportionate for her size. Catherine's breasts were flat and egg-shaped against her long, lean rib cage.

Surely not even Estevez believed David would try to fence the paintings in a British colony, or he would have come along, too. No doubt he planned to search the ship in their absence. Looking up from the Riva as it sped away from the mother ship, she saw Tom watching from the railing, arms folded indolently. He was wearing that same billed black cap, with *Chicago Bears* stenciled on it in red script, that he had worn that morning. He waved casually, and she wriggled a finger back at him.

The bastard.

The Riva, piloted by a cretinous-looking character called Ahmed, quickly covered the distance between the yacht and Gibraltar's wharf. "The fortress of Gibraltar was built in, above, and around the Rock," Carlo said, quoting from a travel folder, while Walter crossed the wharf to hire two taxis. Walter, Diana noticed, made himself seem indispensible, always working, doing deals. She knew his kind, always thinking, "Who's important, who might help me with this or that?"

"The town of Gibraltar lies on the western and southern slopes of the peninsula," Carlo read. "Until recently, the peninsula's isthmus has been shut off from the European continent by a simple but forbidding green metal gate guarded by Spanish soldiers. Thus, the British colony has to depend upon deliveries from Britain for meat and other staples. Fruits and vegetables are brought in daily from Morocco, some ten miles across the strait."

Once they were apportioned into two taxis, Greg raised his brows and said under his breath, "I thought this was to be one of those self-guided tours."

"Hush, love," Anne admonished him gently.

The taxis took them out to Europa Point, where a lighthouse marked the end of Europe. There, Walter snapped photos of everyone. "That's it, Greg. Put your arms around Eva and Anne. David, you're not smiling."

"That same travel restriction between Gibraltar and Spain is the reason for the colony's unusual lifestyle," Carlo went on, once they were in the taxi again, "where thirty-two thousand Gibraltarians inhabit the 2.2-square-mile fortress colony."

No one asked him to quit, but Diana suspected everyone was relieved when they were let off back in the central square.

David didn't take her hand as they ambled along the streets, following traces of the market alleys built during the nearly eight hundred years the North African Moors held the Rock.

"It is called the Rock," Carlo said, trailing along behind, still quoting from his guide book, "after the Moorish leader, Tarik, who captured it and named it for himself, Mount Tarik or Jabal al-Tarik—later corrupted in English into Gibraltar."

David winked at her, a conspiratorial grin twitching on his lips.

Ahead of them, Eva walked a little straighter, smiled a little more, as if she were at last relaxing and enjoying the trip. Walter, who didn't look quite so athletic in Bermuda shorts, walked stiffly beside her, apparently perturbed.

At the base of the limestone Rock, they all boarded a cable car to the summit. During the rattling six-minute ride, Murad managed to wedge her away from the others. "*Chérie*, I will not push myself on you, but I want you to know I'm here if . . ." his large, velvet-brown eyes flicked over to David, who was chatting amiably with Greg, ". . . if things don't work out for you."

So, instead of his normal temper tantrum, the prince was taking another tack. It made her sigh. "What can I say, Murad? We must be star-crossed. I'm Roman Catholic and you're Buddhist—"

"Hindu, Hindu," he whispered into her ear. "But I told you that my religion will not interfere with my love for you."

Frustration finally overtook her. "I will not join that endless lineup of fresh, new women each designed to outdo her predecessor, Murad."

"Look, isn't the view lovely!" Eva bubbled.

Murad grimaced at her bonhomie but out of politeness was forced to acknowledge that the snowcapped Spanish Sierra Nevadas in the background and the blue Mediterranean *were* lovely. In the far distance the Atlas and Rif Mountains of Africa were bluish bumps on the horizon.

During the descent, the cable car paused at the Ape's Den so they could see the famous Barbary apes. "They're the only tailless monkeys native to Europe," Carlos told the group. "There's a legend that the British will never lose control of the Rock while they protect the monkeys."

"But I may well lose control of my temper if Carlo keeps this up," Greg told Diana in an undertone.

By the time they reached the base, everyone was weary of Carlo as their self-appointed guide. David took over, suggesting lunch in the marketplace. The police who patrolled there wore blue British bobby uniforms, but spoke Spanish. The girls who kept the shop waited on foreigners in flawless English but chatted among themselves in Castilian. Moroccan women in ankle-length robes, the lower half of their faces covered with a white cloth and their feet painted in intricate henna designs, strolled along the cobbled streets with schoolgirls wearing Scottish tartans and punks in mohawk strip haircuts and black leather and gold earrings.

Ahead of David and Diana, Walter berated Eva, and whatever confidence the chunky woman had momentarily acquired seemed to desert her. "The next time you want to play magical flute, let me . . ."

At one cluttered stall, David stopped and pointed to a thin gold chain from which was suspended a gold nugget in the shape of a monkey. "I'd like to see that, please," he said in English to the old proprietor.

"Here," he told Diana, "turn around and let me put this necklace on you."

"As a good-luck charm?" she asked, lifting her hair so he could fasten the clasp.

"Only if you believe so," he teased.

Murad sniffed contemptuously. His brown fingers lifted a scarf, a marvelous thing of lace ribboned with gold filigree. "This is what a beautiful lady like yourself should wear, Diana."

Before she could dissuade him, he paid for the article and handed it to her with all the embarrassing homage of an earnest suitor.

She was cornered, unless she wanted to make everyone uncomfortable by refusing the gift and thereby evoke petulant behavior from the prince. "Why, thank you, Murad." She folded the scarf and tucked it into her shoulder bag.

It was late afternoon when David led his yacht's guests to an unpretentious Moorish cafe, its ceiling and walls draped with bolts of billowing, brilliantly colored cloth. An off-key Spanish soprano sang Gypsy laments, while a guitarist strummed, and the polyglot tourists clapped, cheered, and toasted one another.

David ordered Arabic bread, *kibbe*—a baked ground lamb and wheat dish—and some iced Russian vodka, on which Anne and Greg proceeded to get tipsy quickly. Even Carlo, Diana noticed, seemed less stuffy. The outing was good for everyone. Well, maybe not for Eva and Walter. What was going on between them? Walter seemed bored by the drinking and only picked at his *kibbe* meatballs.

"Personally," Carlo said, "I really would like to tour the fortress. It's supposed to have quite a collection of artifacts."

"This day is all yours, *amico mio*," David told him. "The speedboat returns to the yacht at dusk, so try not to be late getting back to the harbor."

"Eva and I'll go with you," Walter said.

"I—I really don't feel like doing any more walking, Walter," Eva said, guilt forcing her voice into a little-girl register.

Once stolid Walter left, the mood of the whole group seemed to brighten. Greg told the other five at the table about an amusing incident: "About three years ago, a kept woman of a friend of mine was shot by his outraged wife—at no less a public place than the Arc de Triomphe—and *Le Monde* reported the woman was shot in the pubic arch!"

"Now you're being positively Wasp-like, Greg," Anne told him, "punning in English." But she giggled anyway.

He really was witty, Diana thought, but in a way that reminded her more of Noel Coward than John Wayne. Besides, his voice didn't have the slow drawl that complemented macho body language.

Anne proceeded to tell a bawdy joke, then everyone was vying for center stage, laughing and talking at once. Amid the cacophony of clinking glasses, laughter, and music, David poured a glass of local red wine for Diana and himself, then raised his in a toast. "*L'chaim*—to life! And to our relationship."

She didn't think the other four heard him. "Which is?" she asked evenly.

He stared at her for what seemed a long time, and while he did, the laughter and music and clink of glasses and tableware faded. "I haven't quite decided yet."

You're going to get more than you're bargaining for, she thought comfortably, as she took a sip of rather ghastly tasting wine.

When she set her glass down, David rose and nodded toward a staircase that could be seen through a doorway curtained by multicolored strands of beads. "Rooms are to be had here, Diana. Come to bed with me—now."

Sudden anger prickled her. Did he think she was waiting for him like an unsigned traveler's check? She glanced at the others, who were giddily tipsy and oblivious to it all. A hundred thoughts flitted through her troubled mind, all overridden by the bitter knowledge that she wanted him. His unexpected invitation had ignited a triangular clot of pure heat that was even now dampening her upper thighs.

She met the steady blue eyes and, wordlessly, grasped her purse, placing her hand in his to let him draw her toward the beaded curtain. Behind a counter, a man in a soiled white apron looked up and returned David's brief nod.

In the subdued afternoon sunlight, the low-ceilinged room was spartan. Nothing about its furnishings—a bare bed beneath an *oeil de boeuf* window—could distract Diana and David from their frenzied need. The room's airless heat surrounded them and they stood looking at each other, prolonging that first moment, each knowing that once wasted hurriedly, it would be beyond recall.

David released her hand to cup her face with gentle hands. He stared at her intently, his searching gaze shifting from her eyes to her lips to her hairline and then to her eyes again.

When his lips at last claimed hers, she tried to control the excitement lurking just beneath the surface of her skin. She had never experienced the effects of sensual attraction that surpassed her coolly rational examination. For a woman who considered herself sexually sophisticated, she realized she was, in fact, naïve— mentally a virgin who had never really been touched by love or even by passion.

Momentarily, his lips released hers, and she felt as she did when she had been swimming too many laps. The overpowering maleness of him stunned her. Looking up into his face, she saw that the kiss had affected him, too. Raw urgency burned in his eyes.

Without too much introspection, she knew that David's aura of all-powerfulness fulfilled the long-neglected but unappeased child in her. She had had adulation and attention from all but her father, and the timid little girl in her craved such a male to take care of her.

Yet, nagging conditioned responses reminded her he possessed as much a criminal mind as did her stepfather. She repressed a sudden panicky urge to flee. David must have sensed her recoiling, because all at once escape was impossible as he took her hand and placed it against his chest. "Feel the pounding?" he asked with a wry smile. "I'm as nervous as you."

Struck dumb with longing, she couldn't remove her splayed hand from his chest. She stared at him, moistened her lips, nodded.

He gathered her against him and gentled her with caresses until her hands went to the back of his neck. With a feverish need, she returned caress for caress, kiss for kiss. His hands were skilled and expert, masterful enough to prevent rebellion, not rough enough to panic her as he cupped her breasts and rotated their weight against his palms.

A man's hands were so maddeningly good! Her mind rejected the whispered warnings of who and what he was and what her mission was, and her body willingly submitted to his erotic subjugation. Frantically, with clumsy, fumbling hands, they pulled at each other's clothing until it was gone. He threw her onto the bed and drew her hard against him, pressing her open palm to his aroused flesh. Her fingers closed around him and guided him toward her. God! She was so wet and ready.

His rhythmic possession of her was the most thrilling excitement she had ever known. Helplessly, blindly, she turned her mouth to his. Then, she felt him exploding too soon, leaving her still craving the pummeling of him deep inside her.

"Oh, God, Diana, don't move. Give me just a moment."

It didn't matter. She lay there, melting beneath the rain of his tender kisses on her lips and cheeks and brow, feeling his fingers sliding sensuously through her tousled hair and stroking the line of her spine.

It was then, up close, that she noted the inside of his left forearm. With her forefinger, she tracked the small, rectangular patch of rough skin, starkly white against his tan.

"How did you come by that scar?"

"At a plastic surgeon's office in Rome." His voice was harsh. "The doctor removed the serial number a Nazi soldier tattooed there when I was five."

She didn't know what prompted her to do it, but she bent her head and kissed the puckered whitish patch. As she did, the gold Barbary ape on her necklace swung back and forth entrancingly.

David captured it and drew her back to him. "With your

eyes half closed like that," he teased, "and your mouth half open—you look as if you're halfway to orgasm."

"I am."

He reclaimed her lips and rolled atop her. His fingers dug into her shoulders, and his body plunged into her swiftly, thrusting and pulling. She breathed shallowly, concentrating wholly on the marvelous, marvelous feeling taking over her body. Suddenly, she was riding the crest of the wildest, most drenching flood of passion . . . adrift in a sensual minefield, while climactic explosions wracked her body.

Afterwards, they lay on the bed, their ragged breathing slowing, their heated bodies cooling. Their perspiration lay on them like dew, and David raised up on one elbow to wipe the sheen from her upper lip with his blunt fingertip. "Want a cigarette?"

"How did you know?" she asked, a bemused expression lingering at the ends of her lips.

"I've watched you." He reached for her purse on the floor and withdrew her cigarette case. "You invariably seem to light a cigarette whenever you and I come together," he said, grinning as he lit one for her.

The Gitanes's potent taste cleared out the tannin aftertaste of the wine she had drunk earlier, but was hardly what she needed to slow her racing heart and still the pulse pounding in her ears.

Her past encounters had always ended with the anticipated little frictional bursts. This time . . . this time there was a mysterious merger of sexual-emotional patterns that rocked her senses. In the contentment that followed she realized a far more significant climax of mind and soul. Yet, she sensed that she had yielded something, an intrinsic part of her that she could not identify.

He watched her with sleepy blue eyes. "I just feel as

if my intellect, which I have always counted on, has been overruled by more primitive emotions.''

Whatever torpor she felt evaporated instantly. ''Somehow that sounds like a backhanded compliment.''

''You're a dangerous lady, Diana. My intellect told me that from the start, from that moment in Vacheron-Constantin. It said, 'David, my man, here is someone who will get in your blood, who will weaken you like malaria fever.' ''

She saw that he was teasing and relaxed against him once more. ''Be forewarned,'' she said with a light-hearted smile, raising on one elbow to ground out her cigarette in a broken shell of an ashtray that rocked precariously on the sill of the oval window.

He drew her back down beside him, saying, ''There are still two or three hours left before we have to leave the room. Get some rest.''

His fingers barely touched her lids, closing them. She dozed off almost at once, cradled in his arms. When she awakened, maybe an hour later, he was gone. She sat up, pushing back the hair that had fallen across her forehead. Her mouth felt like a cat litter box.

She realized someone was knocking on the door, that it was the knocking that had aroused her. Gathering the rumpled sheet about her, she went to the door. ''Who is it?''

''Eva. May I come in?'' Her voice was hesitant, apologetic. Diana let her in. ''Herr Mendel asked me to awaken you at this hour. In time to leave for the boat.''

Diana went back to the bed and shook a cigarette out of its silver case. She dipped her head to her lighter flame. ''I suppose I am embarrassed, Eva,'' she mumbled.

Behind her, Eva said. "Please . . . do not be. Your friend, Anne . . . and the Greek—"

"Greg?" Diana exhaled the first soothing puff.

"*Ja.* They are in another room."

"I see. And Murad?"

Eva's dumpling cheeks blushed apple red. Her big hands fidgeted with each other. "I know I am no Miss Universe. I have never even tried to make the best of myself. Chin up, tummy in, you know how that goes. Mainly, because I didn't have to. I suppose it is some kind of signal I emit—that I like sex. A lot. Men feel this. Herr Mendel has probably picked up on it. He knew to find me in one of these rooms with Murad this afternoon."

With Murad!

So that was where the explanation was going. "We seem to be quite a prurient little group."

"Anyway, Herr Mendel said he had some business to attend to and asked that I awaken you in an hour. He said to tell you that he would meet you aboard *The Star of David* later this evening."

After Eva left, Diana dressed. Her pride was bruised. Was it business he had to attend to? Setting up the final arrangements for the fencing operation? Never, in any way, had he admitted that he was guilty of the crime she was trying to pin on him.

She strapped on her flimsy sandals. A purse brush whipped her hair into place. She knew he felt something for her. She simply could not be wrong about that.

She took a last glimpse at the disheveled bed. Could Tom be right? Was she letting her intense attraction to David cloud her judgment?

28

June 25th

Perspiration poured down the bony chest of the middle-aged, hippie-looking Frenchman, saturating his scruffy graying beard. He and the man next to him were the only occupants of the Moorish baths underneath the Gibraltar Museum. A fourteenth-century Moroccan structure, its sixteen-sided vaulted roof sheltered hot and cold baths and a steam room, whose heated haze shimmered around the two men, all but obliterating them.

"Yashiv Yadan is concerned about Operation Wrath of God," Bernard Gaillard said, wiping the back of his hand across his sweaty cheek. For the sake of secrecy, he spoke in Hebrew, a language in which most of the sounds were made at the back of the throat, like gargling.

"There is no need for concern," Hamemuneh replied.

"You have surrounded yourself with too many enemies. What about the American narcotics agent?"

Absently, Hamemuneh brushed at the beads of sweat trickling down his stomach into the coarse patch of golden fur at his loins. "He will serve our purpose. St. Giles's death will be seen as part of the American's drug investigation."

189

"And St. Giles?"

"What about him?"

"Hamemuneh, Sciolla reported to him that you were a Jew, a very influential Jew."

"We expected as much. That was part of the bait, that and the paintings."

"Yashiv wants to bring in a squad at Sardinia."

"No."

"For your own protection."

"No. St. Giles is too clever. He'd detect a trap."

Uneasily, Bernard Gaillard shifted his buttocks on the slick tiled bench. "There is more."

"What?"

"The *shiksa* you brought to the pub . . ."

"Yes?" Was Diana still sleeping from the doctored wine? What would she think when she awoke and found him gone? He had brought her along on the yacht merely because he was passionately attracted to her, but now, after this afternoon, she was truly under his skin. She was sensitive and warm, while he had always felt separated from other people because of his responsibilities. He had not realized how lonely he had been until he met her.

Bernard pushed himself off the bench and, hands clasped behind his back, paced before Hamemuneh. Eerily, his body wove in and out of the drifting curtains of steam.

"Well?" Hamemuneh prompted impatiently. Sweat was flooding his eyes, and he brushed it away with the heels of his hands.

Bernard planted his hirsute body in front of Hamemuneh. "She's an undercover agent. For a high-level international insurance firm."

Hamemuneh stared hard at the other agent. "How can you be . . . of course, you're sure," he said wearily. "With the information network Mossad has at its fingertips . . ."

Steam enveloped Bernard, but his voice reached Hamemuneh, clearly plaintive and pleading. "Your infatuation for this woman is dangerous."

There it was . . . the warning of her as a dangerous woman . . . twice in one day. He should have heeded his vague instincts earlier this afternoon.

Against the misty background Hamemuneh saw her. There was so much more complexity in her expressions than in other women's. The way in which she used her eyes to convey inner feelings fascinated him. She had succeeded in intriguing him despite her beauty, purely by dint of her extraordinary personality and patrician subtlety.

Despite that passionate attraction they had shared, was she going to be his friend or his enemy?

"I am not blind to the danger, but I will deal carefully with it in my own way."

"No," Bernard said quietly, reluctantly. "No. That cannot be."

The ensuing silence between them was interrupted only by the hiss of escaping steam.

After some time had passed, he said, "I see. Then this comes from the senior officers?"

"It is an order direct from Yashiv, Hamemuneh. The problem with the narcotics agent will solve itself, but we must deal with the *shiksa*. She must be taken out. That is one of the reasons I was sent."

The hot humid air Hamemuneh sucked in singed his nasal passages. He bowed his head. After a moment, he looked up. Sweat blinded him, so the bearded man was barely visible through the mist. "I have never failed Mossad. If she must die, her death will be my responsibility. I will take care of it—in my way and in my own time."

29

June 25th

An extraordinary man, Diana acknowledged. There was
a vitality in him, an eager restlessness that drew her
relentlessly. Despite his apparent calmness, his eyes
were constantly in motion, scanning his world like ra-
dar, missing nothing. Yet they were never furtive. They
were really one of his most astonishing features.

Diana was in the bedroom of her Emerald and Diamond Suite, tinkling with the mirrored piano, which
resembled a refugee out of a Liberace program. Her
overlooked aptitude for playing was a disgrace, as her
grandmother had often bemoaned, but she really wasn't
ready to face the other guests over the dinner table.
Cocktails had been uncomfortable enough, feigning an
insouciance around the others she didn't feel at all.

A knock at her door seemed about to put an end to
her self-imposed exile. When she opened it, Tom was
filling her doorway, his craggy face crooked in a cyni-
cal grin as his eyes assayed her. She was wearing one
of her favorite dinner dresses, a silver lamé with tam-
bour beading, its uneven hemline well above her knees.

"What do you want?"

Right arm akimbo, he leaned his left shoulder negligently against the door frame, clearly out of sorts in the ill-fitting *haut monde* uniform: black tie and evening clothes. "Just checking."

"Same rented evening clothes you wore to the *bal masque*, aren't they?" she jeered.

"On an expense account," he grinned sourly, "these duds are called a disguise. You know, Miss de Revillon, I was watching you and Mendel at cocktails this evening. Have you looked in the mirror lately? It's all over your face—you've fallen for the guy."

A torrid flush stole up her neck and crimsoned her cheeks. She felt as if she'd been caught *flagrante delicto*. She jammed a fist on her own hip. "That all you have to say, Agent Estevez? If so, I've got better things to do than waste—"

"No, I'm also telling you that when the time comes to take him down, you won't come through because you can't distinguish right from wrong now." His glance lowered pointedly to the gold necklace with the monkey pendant. "Apparently, it doesn't take much to buy you," he sneered.

Moving away from the doorway, before Diana could respond, he ambled off down the corridor, whistling, and she slammed her door. Back against it, she stood shaking, her professional pride stung to its core. Silently, angrily, she renewed her determination to locate the stolen paintings. Estevez had finally succeeded in goading her into besting him at his own game.

Which meant a stop-off at the stewards' quarters while they were still busy with the evening's entertainment chores. The tour of the bridge with David had paid off— she had spotted the crew cabin assignment. A man by the name of Sciolla bunked in 3-G, not a likely coincidence and one she certainly meant to check out.

The corridor that housed the crew was narrower than that of the other decks, darker, and here the gnashing of the engine room machinery seemed to vibrate the walls. She glanced quickly up and down the hallway; then, with the hope that the door lock would be one of those inexpensive ones, she tried one of her credit cards.

Presto! Quickly, she stepped inside. The small room smelled like a man's gym locker and was just as messy. A bathing suit poster of the French teenage singing star Minette and one of the Grateful Dead graced one wall. Dirty clothing was strewn over the floor, and the bunks were unmade. She started there, looking under the mattresses. She searched through doorwide closets and bathroom medicine compartments.

She didn't know, really, just what she was searching for, but she had been in the cabin too long. After a last look through the built-in drawers, she had to abandon her hunt— and none too soon. No sooner had she started down the corridor, than Ahmed came around the corner. He slowed down, stared hard at her. She offered no explanation, only smiled coolly, and continued on past him.

All during dinner that night, her eyes kept drifting back to David, who was seated across from her. Handsome, brilliant, generous . . . and a thief. Could she be wrong? Could he be innocent of the crime she was trying to pin on him?

Or was David cleverly turning the tables on her, playing her own seduction game? He *did* have a reputation as an international playboy. Was the entire chapter only a farce for him?

He looked up from a conversation with Greg and caught her glance. His lips curved in a smile of amusement, as if he knew what she was thinking, yet in his vivid blue eyes she could detect a hint of wistfulness, too. He excused himself from Greg and came around the table to her side. "Dance with me, Diana?"

From the corner of her eye, she saw Tom Estevez, who was busily charming the charming Joan, glance her

way with a lifted brow of derision. A triangle, Diana
thought irritably. Tom, David, and I form a dangerous
triangle of attraction, suspicion and, yes, mutual respect for each other's talents.

"I'd like that," she said, laying aside her napkin.

The orchestra, on a dais in one corner of the salon, was
playing smooth renditions of Cole Porter and Rodgers and
Hammerstein, all the old favorites that she liked so well,
and she melded with David, feeling the oneness she had
only felt in his arms. It seemed they twirled endlessly to the
faint and faraway melody of *Blue Champagne*.

He looked down at her and said, "I'm lonely for you . . .
and I need you, Diana. Move into my suite tonight."

Jesus, she was so tempted. She shook her head. "Not
tonight. Not yet. What has happened—"

"Diana, my suite has two bedrooms. I actually prefer
sleeping alone. By moving in, you are not committing
yourself to anything."

"I . . . I have to think, David."

Tenderly, he kissed her forehead. "I am a patient man."

A man of his multiple talents would be, she thought
gloomily. When he returned her to the table, he asked
Maja politely to dance.

Anne said, "Good lord, what's wrong, Diana?"

"I think I am falling in love."

"That, my dear, is a bloody first for you. Let's cel-
ebrate."

"I'm not at all certain celebration is called for." She
fished a cigarette from her beaded bag.

"I see," Anne said, eyes going to the dance floor.
"Could your love possibly be unrequited?"

When she didn't answer Anne, her dearest friend said,
"All men are bastards."

Listlessly, Diana plucked at her napkin, rearranging

the bright magenta Souleiado linen into pleats. "Does that sweeping indictment include Tom Estevez, Anne?"

"All of them. Especially Tom. I refuse to be the object of his pity or his compassion."

"Is that why you've taken up with Greg?"

"Tom more or less lost interest. You must admit Greg and I are more compatible. We're from the same stratum of society, have the same values. Neither is shocked by the antics of the other."

Diana looked up at her. "Then you've found out?" she asked cautiously.

Anne grinned. "That Greg is bisexual? Oh, darling, it was so obvious. But I *was* surprised to find that he's into *ménages à trois*."

Diana realized she was gaping stupidly, as Anne said, "With Murad and Eva, this trip. Why do you suppose Murad invited the Vachs and Roumeys along? For diversity. Even if that dusky shit had conquered your heart, he soon would have grown bored. Murad's sort always does."

Ye gods! Diana really felt positively naïve. Her stomach roiled, and she quickly lowered her head. A sleek curtain of her tawny hair hid her face as she swallowed the nausea.

Anne rested her hand comfortingly on Diana's. "Here, darling, let me offer you one of my special powders." She winked and rifled through her purse till she found a cellophane packet.

Diana's brow shot up involuntarily. "Heroin?" Her question was more gasp than word.

"Greg and I picked it up yesterday in one of those seedy Moroccan stalls."

"Why do you do this, Anne? I know you're intelligent enough to realize how dangerous this junk is."

Anne smiled wryly. "Well, darling, it does have all the advantages of death . . . without its permanence."

🐾 30 🐾

June 26th

With only anemic determination, Diana donned the khaki jumpsuit she was wearing the day she had boarded the yacht. In the dark, the outfit could pass for a mechanic's coveralls. She might be taken for one of the forty-member crew.

She stuffed her hair under Tom's Chicago Bears cap, which he had left on a poolside table. A purse flashlight was the only object she had with her. It was four in the morning, but the recessed lighting in the yacht's corridors was on, albeit dimly.

If the paintings weren't in David's office or suite, then the other likely place had to be the hold—a vast space to search. For all *The Star of David*'s modern ventilation, the hold retained a musty smell that wrinkled her nostrils as she descended the belowdecks storage stairway. Despite the bluish fluorescent lighting in the narrow companionway, she felt she was descending into Hades itself.

An open-mesh steel catwalk carried her past the crew quarters to a wine cellar, whose doors were locked, as were those marked "Freight Room" and "Gymnasium." Damn! Why hadn't she thought of that? She would have to locate a master key later that day.

When she tried the door marked "Launderette and Linen Room," she expected it to be locked, too, but it wasn't. She eased it open, beamed the flashlight into the darkness, and almost smothered a gasp.

Catherine and Maja, both naked, were lying on piled linens spread across a wall-length counter where laundry was folded. Their limbs were entwined, their russet and ebony hair enmeshed, their hands and mouths groping and slurping feverishly.

As the betraying shaft of light struck them, Maja arched up like a black cat, hissing. "*Merde alors!* Get out!"

Catherine's soft laughter was a mocking purr. "Why, it's dear Diana in drag. Want to join us, love?"

Jesus Christ! "Sorry, you're not my type," she managed to get out.

She backed away, closing the door on the scene. Why hadn't she guessed the obvious? The clues had all been there. Some investigator she was! She never did understand lesbian relationships. How absolutely blah the idea of sex was without a man's hot, wondrously throbbing penis.

She moved on, drawn by the muted drone of the engines. A steel-grate ladder off the catwalk led her to the engine room door. She peered inside. No one. More tense after her last discovery, she ventured in. She was out of her element here, and she suspected her usual finesse at bluffing her way out of uncomfortable situations wouldn't work here if she were caught snooping.

Overhead, green and white shafts, pipes, and ductwork made a surrealistic spider web. She meandered down one aisle separated by alien machinery and back up another one, satisfying herself that the engine room was an unlikely place to hide art.

Then she saw an open door leading to a darkened anteroom. Rather than risk turning on the room light, she used her flashlight to explore its recesses, occupied mostly by bins of spare parts, tools, and nuts, bolts, and screws.

Then her flashlight beam flicked across the bridge telephone box. Now she was back in her own element. One thing her work had taught her was wiretapping. With her flashlight, she followed a set of wires from the metal box to a concealed miniature tape recorder. Tom Estevez's work, no doubt.

Perhaps she would beat him this time. She would monitor the tape herself, then replace it. Deftly, one hand holding the flashlight, she began to release the wires from the recorder with the other.

Suddenly the door closed, leaving her in Stygian darkness except for the flashlight's narrow beam. Someone was moving in the room! She could hear breathing. Whirling, she flashed the light back and forth wildly.

A hand clamped over her wrist, and her flashlight clattered to the floor, its wedged beam of light playing on worn sneakers. "Who is—"

"Diana! I should have known."

The explosive grunt of her name belonged to Tom. The whining roar of the engines had deafened his approach. She tried to yank her wrist away but his big hand refused to give. Frustration with her laxity of vigilance—this made the second damned time he had sneaked up on her—caused her to space her words in a hissing demand: "Do you mind releasing me?"

At once he let her go, but there was a tinge of impatience behind his usually good-natured drawl. "Not at all. Do you mind telling me what you are doing messing with my wiretap. Not trying to beat me to Mendel, are you now?''

In the dark, her pupils were beginning to bring into focus his roughcut face. She sugar-coated her voice. "Now, Tom dear, why would I want to upstage the supreme male chauvinist?''

With a sigh, he reached down and collected her flashlight, passing it to her. "Look, lady. Why can't we become partners for this operation?''

"You mean sort of like the good guys teaming up?''

He ignored her mimicry of his tough-guy slang. "Albeit unwilling ones, obviously. We could trade information and work together to end this to our mutual benefit. You get the paintings, I get the drugs.''

"Who gets Mendel?''

"We'll worry about that particular problem when we get to it.''

"Well,'' she began reluctantly, "I suppose you have a point, but I'd insist on—''

His kiss smothered all further words, as he enveloped her in his bear hug. She had never been kissed against her will, and his kiss was almost punishing. As if he was making a point. A damned good point, she thought grudgingly, as she found herself enjoying the domination of his very thorough kiss.

Too quickly, his arms set her free. "Just sealing a bargain.''

She could almost see him grinning. No doubt a smug, triumphantly male grin. Her response was with the clipped tone of the British. "You seem to dally with every female aboard this yacht.''

"For your information that wasn't dallying. And, if your friend hasn't told you, I'm no longer sleeping with her. It wasn't a steady thing, anyway. Come on, I'll walk you back to your room.''

"Thank you, sir," she said with elaborate politeness, "but I do think I'm a big enough girl to find my way back on my own."

Back in her room, she braced her hands on the bathroom counter and stared into the mirror. Tom's beard-stubbled face had rasped her cheeks. Her skin was as pink as a peach and just as tender.

She wrestled with her feelings about Tom, one of those "good guys" with whom she should be in love . . . and which was totally impossible simply because there was David. Even though he was dangerous and maybe even corrupt, if what Tom said about David was true, she knew she had fallen head over heels in love with him.

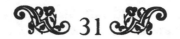

31

"A beer," Tom told the flat-nosed man behind the counter. Tom was heartily sick of wine and awfully curious about just how much of a part Sciolla played in the total picture of the crime. "Lowenbrau."

At 1:30 in the morning the yacht's disco was still going strong; the twenty-by-sixty-foot room, walled with mirrors, was as tightly packed as the Afruidisiaque had been and almost as hot. The programmed soft rock music, at least, was less ear-shattering. The colored strobe lights lent a surrealistic, slow-motion movie effect to the gyrating dancers out on the parquet floor. From his stool in a corner of the disco, he watched David and Diana circle each other with sensuous motions. A mating dance, Tom thought.

"Hey, why the glum look, old chap," Anne asked, sliding onto the padded leather stool next to him. She wore a short, red dress, spangled all over with swishing long fringe, a sort of twentiesish getup.

Before answering, he took a swallow of the frosty beer, letting it slide down his gullet. "Just thinking about my former wife." Which was true in a way. With a sinking sense of self-disgust, he had realized that he

202

was more intensely attracted to Diana de Revillon than he had been to anyone since Natalie left him.

"You should know better than to dwell on a past spouse when you're in a pub," she said. He could tell she had had a few; her speech had the slightest of slurs.

Sciolla approached and she glanced at what Tom was drinking and ordered the same. "Ugly creature, isn't he?" she commented after Sciolla went away.

"I thought you were a champagne gal."

"At the moment, I'd really prefer an English bitter, but I suppose a German lager will have to suffice. Now, what were we talking about? I haven't the foggiest—oh yes, former spouses, wasn't it? God rot them in hell," she said cheerfully.

He grinned. He sincerely liked the Englishwoman and her irreverence for everything that everyone else took seriously. "Shall we drink to that?"

She poured some of her beer into the glass she held tilted, then with a grin raised it aloft. "Here's to dear old Spencer. May I never see him again. May he get a terminal case of the clap. May his prick rot off."

"My, my. You are bloodthirsty."

"Vindictive, Di says." She took a sip of the beer. "What about your spouse?"

"What about her?"

"I understand, old chap. You don't want to talk about her. Then I'll talk about mine. Do you know dear Spencer hasn't kissed me on the lips for the last two years? Shit, he hasn't eaten me for the last seven."

Tom gulped the beer in his mouth.

"Any kids?" she asked.

"Three." He'd talk, the subject was safer. "Two daughters and a son. They're obnoxious as hell, but they mean everything in the world to me."

"I have a daughter and a son. My daughter's sleeping

with a black supremacist who is approaching middle-aged crisis and premature ejaculation. My son's screwing everything but girls. If there's a way my children could pry the silver out of my teeth while I'm asleep, they would."

"Charming children."

"I once told you I didn't want to know about the present lady in your life. I've changed my mind. Is she the one responsible for your . . . er, dwindling interest . . . in the two of us."

Tom cleared his throat, and she said, "Oh, do be honest, Tom. I'm a big girl."

He wondered if anyone had ever figured out a gentle way of telling a woman you simply weren't interested sexually. "Her name is Wendy. She's a lobbyist. You might also say she's a passionate friend."

The thought of Wendy led him back to Diana again and how merely kissing her had made him realize what little real feeling he had for Wendy. If he were totally honest with himself, he'd face up to the debilitating fact that he was falling more and more in love with Diana, because of both her beauty *and* her professionalism.

"I'd like to be your *passionate friend*," Anne said softly.

"Why me?"

"Because there are not many men like you left: steady, virile, wise. You are on the endangered species list, in case you haven't heard. Besides, I'm a very chic cocksucker, as you've already indicated to me several times now."

He chuckled. "I'm truly flattered."

She pushed the empty glass from her. "Beer and champagne don't mix too well, do they? I think I'll go back to my room and pass out on the bed." She picked up her sequined bag. "So much more ladylike than on the dance floor."

"I'll walk you back."

"You know," she said, once they reached the hallway outside the disco, "I didn't sleep well last night. I never do, when I am overhappy, underhappy, or in bed with a strange man."

He chuckled. "Well, which was it last night?"

She tossed him a mischievous look. "You guess."

On the way down the corridor to her room, she grabbed at her stomach and leaned up against the wall. Sweat sheened her powdered cheeks. She made the gasping sound of the dry heaves. He swung her up into his arms and carried her the rest of the way.

Behind him, Diana called out, "What's wrong, Tom?"

He half turned, waiting for her to catch up with him. She was dressed in some sort of tiered black organza, the kind of material you could almost see through. Talk about premature ejaculation. "Anne's stomach has wisely rebelled against her combination of drinks. Can you open her door for me?"

"Sure."

Once they were inside, he laid Anne on her bed and started removing her pumps.

"I'll finish undressing her," Diana said. "You get a cold wet washcloth."

The opulent bath suite carried out the cabin's sapphire theme, with a lapis lazuli Jacuzzi and lavatory. Like his own, the place had enough stuff to run a hair salon. The two thousand little white mirror lights revealed that his five o'clock shadow had sprouted into a two-day-old beard.

When he returned with a damp washcloth, Anne had already passed out. The sapphire brocaded coverlet was pulled halfway up over her slip-clad body, and Diana was zipping Anne's fringed red dress over a satin-padded hanger.

He sat down on the bed next to Anne and gently laid the folded washcloth on her forehead. She groaned, and Diana snapped, "You shouldn't have let her drink so much."

"You know, lady, you remind me of a Doberman. One false move and you bare your teeth."

She sighed and ran her hand through her bountiful blonde hair. "I'm sorry." She crossed to an overstuffed chair and slid into it. Beneath her lashes, she flicked him a sideways glance. "Why is it, Tom, that I don't think you like me?"

"Make that past tense." He strained to be honest. "Actually, I was put off by your beauty. And a certain caustic intelligence."

She smiled, but he could tell she was wary. "I thought we were partners."

"We are. Which reminds me . . ." he paused and nodded toward the bathroom.

She caught the message and followed him inside. He turned on the water faucet, then continued in a lower voice. "Diana, your private life is none of my business . . . I'm just asking you to be careful."

"What are you not saying?"

"David is a consummate con artist. He is an accomplished and dangerous criminal. Just keep that in mind."

Her body language, the way her supple muscles stiffened, imperceptible though it was, betrayed her defensive attitude. "Anything else?" she asked levelly.

"Yes. I've sifted through the latest telephone tape. Very little going on of interest except what may or may not be a coded call put through by one of Mendel's employees on the yacht, an Algerian *pieds noirs*, whom I'm pretty certain is involved some way in the art heist."

"Ali Ahmed Sciolla."

"How did you find out?"

She affected a shudder. "That one would make even his mother cringe. A hunch set me onto him."

He couldn't help but grin. "I should have known it. Feminine instinct."

"Coincidence would be a better word." Relaxing now, she leaned back against the counter, bracing her hands on the hand-painted tiles. "I remembered that the day of the heist one of Marmottan's employees had a record as a petty jewel thief. My memory usually serves me quite well, and I also recalled he had an Arabic given name and Italian surname—as did, I observed, Sciolla."

"I've checked the twenty-odd employee cabins," he said. "Nothing turned up in the one Sciolla shares with another steward."

"So did I," she laughed. "Sciolla almost caught me coming out of his room. We ran into each other in the corridor."

"You deserve your claim to being a professional. You're quite thorough."

"Thank you." He suspected she was habitually deft at handling compliments, but he didn't miss the flush of pleasure that crept up over her model's slanted cheekbones.

"We could have saved ourselves a lot of trouble if we had split up our investigative tasks to begin with."

Amusement curved the ends of her luscious wide mouth. "Why Mr. Estevez, I had the impression you didn't like working with women."

He turned off the water faucet. "What can I say? I have a weakness for dizzy dames."

She made a move at him. "You can say 'good night' and leave now while I am still in a good humor."

He winked. "Good night, Gracie."

"Gracie?"

"An old American joke," he said, heading for the door. "Too old for your tender years."

Just as he was too old for her. He felt it in every bone and muscle in his body. He'd take the three weeks coming to him as soon as he wound up the investigation and got back to Washington.

🎭 32 🎭

Once safely into the balmier Mediterranean, the wind that had swept the turbulent Atlantic abated to a tempering breeze. Marseilles's appearance off the port bow signaled the beginning of the beautiful and sophisticated *Côte d'Azur* and its leisure sun spots: St.-Tropez, Cannes, Nice, Antibes, and wedding-cake Monte Carlo.

The breathtaking Notre Dame de la Garde, topped by a gilded statue of the Virgin, overlooked Marseilles's port, populated those days mainly by North African immigrants. *The Star of David* would bypass the harbor, David explained at a poolside brunch, "because the Algerian areas around the port are no longer safe for pedestrians."

"Then let's visit that island out there," Joan, at his side, suggested. Even with the table parasol in place, she still hid from any stray sunbeams under a large straw hat and dark sunglasses.

Diana, stretched out next to the pool with a hand trailing in the cool water, wore large sunglasses, too— not so much to deflect the sun as to covertly observe the others. Outside of Anne and Tom, she thought, any of them might be in league with David, though she

208

doubted this. David was a lone wolf, not the type to work with others unless a specific purpose was served.

The poolside was a cruise-ship travel poster of serenity. Eva and Carlo and Greg and the mundane Dr. Corneille were playing four-handed gin at one table. Anne was stretched out on a chaise longue, reading *Tropic of Cancer* for the third or fourth time. Her conical breasts, perfected by Dr. Kord, were bared to the inimical sunlight.

Walter was doing laps in the pool. Nearby, Tanya and Noël, his black flesh set off by a white net Speedo and white silk scarf, were playing shuffleboard with Murad, Maja, and Catherine.

"Diana," Catherine called out, her voice as playful and as sharp as a kitten's claws, "are you interested in playing a game with Maja and me? Shuffleboard—or something else, maybe?"

"I'm not much for games, Catherine. I prefer the real thing."

Tom Estevez strolled over from the hutlike bar. In each hand he held a flute of mimosas, champagne mixed with orange juice. "Could have fooled me, Miss de Revillon," he said, passing one glass to Anne. His grin was infectious, but his thick brows were drawn together in a thoughtful scowl.

"Well, Diana, would you like to go with us?" David was asking her.

Her head swiveled toward him. She hadn't heard him. "Where?"

"To the Isle d'If. You can see it from here."

She glanced in the direction he had nodded. The island, crowned by a magnificent castle, rose mysteriously from the afternoon haze drifting over the lazy Mediterranean. She knew the edifice, really a fortress, was where the Man in the Iron Mask, Petain, and other luminaries had once been imprisoned, and from which Dumas's Count of Monte Cristo had escaped. Like the native New Yorker who's never been to the Statue of Liberty, she rarely visited what was in her own back-yard. "Sure, *pourquoi pas?*"

Within the hour, by David's order, the black Rivas were winched into the water. The speedboats filled quickly with the afternoon's sightseers—everyone, in fact, but Eva and Carlo, who elected to stay behind and play gin rummy. "Cells are not my passion," Eva had explained.

The two sleek speedboats sliced through the water, spraying everyone with a fine mist. Diana wore the scarf Murad had given her, causing the ends of his mustache to lift in a triumphant smile. She noted that he and Maja had managed to sit together. A case of two of a kind seeking one another?

As the island loomed larger, the water cleared to al-most transparent aquamarine. Close up, the turreted Chateau d'If, which occupied the entire island, looked supernaturally beautiful. A ferry from the mainland was disgorging tourists festooned with obligatory cameras.

David sprang onto a rocky ledge that was a natural outcrop and took Diana's hand, helping her from the bobbing craft. After she was safely ashore, he led her up the steep stone steps, leaving the rest strung out behind.

The gloomy fortress's immense outer courtyard was indented with lookouts, and David drew her up a flight of worn-smooth limestone steps into one of the se-cluded niches. Far below, the surf pounded against the island's rocky barrier.

When she shuddered, he asked solicitously, "Chilly— on a warm day like this?"

She shook her head. "No." But recalling Tom's

warning about David she wrapped her arms around her sides.

Backing her against the opening, he braced his hands on the sill at either side of her hips, pinioning her. "What is it, Diana? Tell me."

"Nothing. Really."

"Take off your sunglasses, so I can see your eyes. They tell me the truth, you know, even when your mouth doesn't." He took them off himself and smiled down at her. She couldn't help but think how arrogantly male he was, how self-sufficient he was. "I think I like the sunglasses better," he said. "They protect me from the danger of your bewitching eyes."

Either he was one hell of an actor, she thought, or she and Tom were on a wild goose chase. The con artist who had absconded with the Antwerp diamonds—ice worth 125,000 Belgian francs—and the Pierluigi gold bars had to have been an exquisite actor. She opted for flippancy. "Now why is it that I feel you are the last person on earth to need protection?"

"It's you I would like to protect," he said in a low, beguiling voice. "Please move in with me tonight for the duration of the cruise."

Looking into his magnetic eyes, she didn't know what to think. All her powers of judgment failed her when dealing with this extraordinary man. When she opened her mouth to reply, he put a finger on her lips and pressed her against the half wall behind them. The last of her saliva disappeared from her mouth, leaving cotton in its place. It was a sheer one-hundred-foot drop to the jagged rocks. "My deflated ego can't suffer too many more of your rejections," he smiled, almost tauntingly. "Argue with me anymore, my love, and I'll see to—"

"So there you two are," Tom interrupted. "Sorry to

spoil a tryst, but the last tour of the day begins in less than two minutes.''

She could have blessed the husky narc.

The chateau-fortress consisted of a main inner courtyard bounded by three floors, all honeycombed by small, cavelike cells. Over each door was a plaque identifying its famous or infamous occupants, usually some political prisoner, and giving the dates of incarceration. Some prisoners had survived in these cells as long as forty years, which truly staggered Diana's imagination. Over one windowless cell she read:

CACHOT DIT EDMOND DANTES
COMTE DE MONTECRISTO

The cells were dank and cold and depressing. David's teasing mood was noticeably subdued by the chateau. On the return trip to the yacht, he sat silently, listening in a detached way to the others chatting about the tour.

"Imagine the guide claiming the Count of Monte Cristo escaped from that hole in the wall!" Greg said. "A total figment of Dumas's imagination, but leave it to the French to capitalize on a prison."

"Some say Dumas modeled the Count after a real person," Joan said. "God, aging's bad enough, but to grow old like that . . . !"

"Positively morbid," Tom contributed with a wry grin.

"I can't imagine how anyone endured even one day," Diana said, "much less forty years locked away in that place."

At dinner that evening, David made no further mention of the afternoon's sightseeing—nor of his desire for Diana to move into his suite.

Perhaps that was why she went to him that night after

the others had drifted off to their own rooms, at nearly one in the morning. Or perhaps she was simply feeling reckless. Whatever, she was starkly aware that she was desperate for his touch.

When he opened the door, his tawny hair was rumpled and his upper torso was bare. Coarse curls the color of old gold whorled down his chest to jeans that he was in the act of zipping. She had on the same shimmering lacquered red caftan she had donned for dinner.

"Were you asleep?" She felt terribly awkward.

"No, I wasn't able to sleep. I was just getting dressed to go for a stroll on deck."

"I've . . . I . . . may I come in?"

He took her hand and drew her into his suite, all done in the brown and gold shades of topaz. His very touch set her off, creating a blazing excitement screaming for release. His hands aligned along her jawbones. "Actually, Diana, I was about to storm your door and drag you over here."

His fingers strolled up her cheeks, gripping her head and bringing her mouth to his with urgent insistence. He found the zipper on her gown and as it dropped about her ankles, her braless breasts tilted free into his hands. "Oh God, David," she gasped.

Then he was kissing her lips again and she thrilled to the crushing pressure of her desire-tender breasts against his chest. Desire swept through her body with the force of a wild fire, and like the forest she was unprepared for it. "Take me, David," she demanded in a feverish whisper against his mouth. "Take me."

Somehow, they moved into the bed in one of his vast bedrooms and in a frenzy discarded their clothing. He pushed her beneath him, thrusting himself on her and into her. She kissed his muscle-corded neck, pressed her fingers into the hollows beneath his shoulder blades.

She could sense his deliberate restraint behind her wildness. His teeth nipped her throat. "Is this what you wanted?" he asked. "Do you honestly think this will satisfy either you or me?

A fiery heat burst through her. She was lost. Futilely she attempted to hold on to that moment, but then there was a tremendous humming in her ears and she was coming and coming. Her arms wrapped around him tightly, holding him against her as his hips undulated with pounding thrusts. When he exploded within her, she realized quite suddenly, quite sadly, that that metaphysical melding of flesh was the only answer to life's pain . . . and that the fusion was too quickly spent.

Afterward, he stroked her hair softly, testing it between his fingers with what seemed exquisite enjoyment, his voice low and musing. "That afternoon at Deauville, I knew I wanted you—and that I would find you again, somehow. At night, I would lay in my bed, imagining your hair spread across my pillow, and I couldn't sleep thinking of you, how you would feel, how you would taste, how it would be to make love to you. I was certain that after I had possessed you . . . that, like all my possessions, I would tire of you."

Her eyes plumbed the clear blue of his. "Have you?"

Tenderly, he kissed her. "I feel for the first time I've come home, that all the years of wandering across the face of Europe . . ."

"The Wandering Jew curse," she said, trying to hide the sorrow in her soul.

"Exactly."

At that, she slid her face down across the broad, taut plane of his stomach, burying her face in his groin. She craved the taste and the smell of him. In her need for reestablishing that frightful combination of pain and pleasure that became true intimacy, her tongue explored him, detecting the soft wiry hairs, his goose-pimpled flesh, his saltiness, and his musky odor.

He groaned. "Diana, you are all woman."

Could she possibly ice a man whom she was beginning to love? The question nagged at her, long after he fell asleep—a sleep that soon turned restless with mumbled, incoherent words and a thrashing of his arms. Sweat beaded his face and chest. She leaned over him and prodded his shoulder gently. "David, wake up."

With a groan that was almost a shout, he sprang upright, looking at her as if surprised she was in his bed, then he tunneled his fingers through his damp, tousled hair. "I'm all right," he murmured, looking somewhat abashed. "It's an old dream, one I haven't had in years."

"Tell me about it."

With a muttered oath, he rolled out of bed and strode naked to the bathroom, where she heard him splashing water on his face. When he came back, she sat up in his bed, watching him. "I should have let you sleep in the other bedroom," he growled.

"But you didn't and I'm here. So tell me about your dream."

His mouth flattened, and it was as if the tender intimacy had never existed between them. "You *are* persistent." Defiance steeled his voice and he began to prowl the room, his physique superb, that of a once-caged animal, now fiercely resistant to fetters of any kind. "I dream I'm a child again, back at Dachau."

She ached to go to him, to comfort him, but cautiously held her tongue.

"The chateau today . . . it reminded me of Dachau. You know, I remember, while we were waiting in the station at Linz to be taken by train to Dachau, I gobbled a strip of bacon a Gentile teenager had discarded as fat.

I was breaking our Jewish dietary law, but I didn't worry until I had finished about God's wrath. When I wasn't immediately turned to a pillar of salt, I experienced my first pangs of spirtual cynicism.

"My disillusionment deepened at the camps, when I saw what God had obviously chosen to ignore. The German soldiers at the desks examined our naked bodies then announced *'Gesund'*—'healthy'—for those of us who looked as if we could work. Then they turned thumbs up, sending us off to the right. The ones who looked too old or too young to work were directed by the downturn of thumbs, and they joined the group on the left.

"Not just Jews, but Gypsies, Communists, homosexuals—all the undesirables in that group were told they were going to be deloused and were marched away to 'showers.' They received, instead, cyanide gas.

"For some reason I was spared—my appearance and my general health, perhaps . . . perhaps I appealed to the paternal sentiments of that German soldier in some way . . . I don't know.

"Those of us on the right were sent out to various labor camps. I was trucked with others every day to an underground munitions factory nearby. I soon learned that those who dwelt on the past and speculated on the future and the horror of their existence were the ones who despaired, and they were the first to die. So I became absorbed in even the most minute details of merely staying alive.

"You see, Diana, when it comes to a matter of simple survival," he said testily, "there is little a human won't do. Ethical values and moral standards are luxuries that accompany full stomachs; they are simply absent in those who have been degraded to the status of curs. Over the next two years, I adapted myself to that depraved world.''

She was afraid to say anything, to make any sympathetic gesture or statement, because he might stop talking. His speech was the longest of a personal nature he had ever made to her. Somewhere among his bitter words she might find a clue to the real man behind the disguise of international playboy.

''I learned to steal for scraps of food . . . and to please certain guards in unspeakable ways for other amenities, like ends of soap. The luxury of cleanliness . . .'' There was such misery in his eyes, she couldn't stand it.

''The heat . . . stench . . . vermin . . . filth . . . freezing cold . . . and always the hopelessness. Until a person reached the point that he didn't care about eating, didn't care that he was dying. Skeletal bodies too weak to do anything but lie on the ground, longing to die.''

He paused, his features frozen as with rictus, then went on. ''When Dachau was liberated, I joined the endless columns of the displaced who were apportioned out to various refugee camps. The struggle for survival continued even there. In some ways it was worse, because the homeless and displaced were receiving better rations, were stronger, and fought savagely over such a little thing as a scrap of blanket. They took out their terrible frustration and anger on the smaller, the more feeble. At last, after almost a year of working those frightening, dark mines, a family friend found me and took me away.''

Until she felt the tears splashing on her arms, Diana didn't realize that she was crying.

33

July 1st

The Star of David cruised leisurely past the French Riviera's oases, by day following the deeply indented coastline whose rocks seemed too red to Tom, its trees too green, and its sea too blue. It was all too perfect.

Each night, the yacht put into one of the Côte d'Azur's quaint and charmingly picturesque ports, the favorite retreats of the *beau monde*, where David Mendel and his guests cavorted well past midnight. They always returned for cocktails in the wee hours of the morning, then sought their beds just before sunrise, disappearing like vampires with the dawn.

How the hell did David Mendel, who was a good five years older than he, ever maintain the pace?

Because he's in a hell of a lot better condition than I am. And a hell of a lot richer. At every sunspot Mendel's yacht put into, he gave several thousand to the port's government officials, who were asked to distribute it among musicians, waiters, and other service personnel who might make his guests' visit more comfortable. Mendel repeated his phenomenal largess every time he and his entourage entered a restaurant.

Tom stood at the rail on the upper deck, the midday

sun hot on his back, watching the two Rivas darting around the Gulf of St. Tropez, each with a skier in tow. As far as the yacht was from shore, he thought he caught the scent of sea pines and flower-strewn hills, or maybe what he sensed was the expensive aroma of Joan's personal perfume, drifting over from the striped awning, where she lounged in a lemony lace tank top over matching slacks.

"Tom, you've ignored me," she pouted, coming up beside him.

He tempered his ugly mood of that morning with a warm smile. "You have enough admirers, Miss Rodgers, without me getting in your way."

"Flatterers is a better word."

The caustic edge in her voice caused him to look at her, really look at her. Up close, in the brutally honest sunlight, her skin was crisscrossed with minute lines that would have been wrinkles without the aid of a face-lift or two.

"Please," she murmured, turning her head away, "don't stare. It's terribly rude."

"You're a very pretty woman, Miss Rodgers, and that's not flattery. Those lines you're so worried about—well, I like them. Makes you seem more real to me."

She kept her eyes on the water-skiers. "Unfortunately, moviegoers don't want real people. They want escape, fantasy, illusion."

"Give it to them, then, but don't let their fantasies play so much havoc with your life."

She looked at him now. "Thank you. And my name is Joan, please." She laughed then. "Well, actually, it's Jobina."

"Good old American name?"

"Beats me. You know, Tom, we're the only two

Americans on this ship of fools—which gives us something in common for a start.''

"You're counting out Diana de Revillon."

"Are you counting *on* her? If so, you're out of luck, darling. David's keeping her under wraps."

"That's what I'm afraid of," he muttered, propping his arms on the sun-heated teak rail.

"What are you talking about?"

"Oh, nothing important." He didn't need to look at her to know that his reticence was miffing her. "Listen, Joan, you're too classy a lady for the likes of me. I'm just one of those opportunistic bastards who hang around the scent of money."

Her fragile self-esteem regained, she let out a glissando laugh. "So, you really are an ass-kissing sponger."

"All the way." He flipped his cigar butt into the sparkling sea. Maybe Mendel even categorized him as a sponger, inviting him along to fill the ever-present need for an extra male aboard, because he rarely discussed any more the sale of his yacht. On the other hand, maybe Mendel had broken through his boat-broker cover. He knew better than to underestimate the man's considerable talents, for which he had a healthy respect. He also knew that the financier's interest was caught up with Diana de Revillon.

Tom had to give the golden girl credit, she was smooth and captivating—and sharp. No wonder she had a one hundred percent success record.

Tom's thick brows drew together, blocking out some of the midday glare, and he picked out the two Rivas, startling black against the white sails of boats scuttling across the bay toward clusters of red and ochre tiled roofs—the shoreline of St.-Raphael, Ste.-Maxime, and St.-Tropez. David was skiing behind one of the Rivas;

behind the other was Diana, expertly cutting and leaving a high rooster tail of water in her wake.

Did her libido burn as hotly as her ambitions or was she like one of those fancy baked Alaskas—hot on the outside, arctic in the middle?

The two speedboats wove in and out of each other's wakes, so that the golden couple's paths continually crossed with hairbreadth precision. As the Rivas neared the yacht, Tom made out one of the drivers, Sciolla, at the same time that he cut in too close to the other boat's wake. Diana was forced to go down, and David automatically dropped his tow rope. The two lovers were maybe twenty yards away, and Tom could see their laughing faces, glistening with sun-prismed droplets.

Idly he watched as the boats circled slowly to bring the ropes within reach of their skiers. Then the hair on his neck prickled as he saw the boat piloted by Sciolla pick up speed, hurtling toward Diana. The bastard was trying to run her down! She and Mendel were in the trough of speedboat wake and couldn't see what was happening.

"Diana!" Tom bellowed through cupped hands.

Her head swerved rapidly from side to side, indicating she had heard the shout but didn't know where it came from. Foolishly, for there really wasn't time, he kicked off his tennis shoes. Even as he was hoisting onto the railing, he spotted Walter diving in to swim rapidly toward Diana.

Lungs empty, Tom froze. The next few seconds ticked off for him at a glacial rate. Walter reached the unsuspecting girl and shoved her under, but she surfaced swinging at him. He dodged and back-paddled away.

Then the racing speedboat was upon them. At that moment, David surfaced close by and coldcocked Diana with a battering right. As the Riva flashed by, all three disappeared from Tom's view.

For an anxious moment, he stared. No froth of blood speckled the spume of water left by the boat's passage. Recovering from his shock, Tom drew a ragged breath and dove in. He hit the cold water hard. *Black* was the only impression he had. Beneath the surface, the water was black, not blue. From the spectral depths, he spotted just beyond and above him Diana and David's thrashing legs and, further away, Walter's jean-clad ones. With his shirt and jeans dragging on him, Tom propelled himself toward the surface and gasped revitalizing air.

Walter was no more than an arm's length away, and he looked shaken as he treaded water. David was struggling with an unconscious Diana in tow. Her dead weight was too much even for David's supremely conditioned body. Tom lent a hand, grabbing her beneath one armpit and tugging her toward the nearest speedboat.

Walter climbed rapidly aboard and, between him and Greg, they fished the inert woman from the sea, then helped Mendel into the boat. Breathing hard, Tom hauled himself up over the gunwale next. The boat rocked perilously with so many passengers aboard, all shouting wildly, asking questions.

Diana's hair clung to her face and neck like a fishing net. Her body was as white and wracked as a medieval saint's, and she was gagging. Instantly, Mendel knelt beside her and began to apply a rhythmic pressure on her rib cage. She started hiccoughing, and water flushed from her mouth. Weighted by her thick, wet lashes, her lids fluttered open.

Everyone aboard the one Riva let out a communal sigh and started talking at the same time. "Diana, darling,'' Anne coaxed her anxiously, ''say something. Say you'll never do this bloody sport again!''

''She's chilled,'' Murad said. ''We need a blanket, a sweater. Anything aboard?''

''My poor *liebling*,'' Eva said to Walter, wrapping her big arms around his shivering frame.

Tom's eyes left Diana's bruised face, sweeping the area. The other speedboat was finishing a large arc, heading back toward them. It drew near, and Sciolla cut the throttle. His battered boxer's face was as white as the girl's. ''I'm so sorry,'' he babbled to Mendel. ''I didn't see until it was almost too late. The waves—''

''We'll talk later,'' Mendel snapped, losing his usual self-restraint.

Tom's mind was icy with thoughts that gave him goose bumps. Delayed shock hit him so hard he took a deep breath. After a minute or two, the reaction passed.

When Mendel carried Diana into his own suite, Tom tagged along. ''I'll rouse the doc for you,'' he told Mendel.

Mendel seemed not to have heard him. He was peeling the rubber wet suit from the girl's perfect body. Tom forced himself to turn away and dial the doctor. Behind him, he could hear Diana, teeth chattering, words stuttering. ''Cold . . . so cold . . . did you . . . have to hit me?''

Just then Dr. Corneille answered, and Tom relayed the details of the accident—or maybe incident was the better word.

''Doc is on the way,'' he told Mendel, feeling it safe to turn back to the pair behind him. Mendel had wrapped Diana in blankets and was rubbing her hands and arms.

''*Merci,*'' he muttered absently to Tom.

In a few minutes, Dr. Corneille arrived and both Tom

and Mendel withdrew tactfully to the living room. Moments later, the slender medic came out of the bedroom. "She will be fine. Nothing that twelve hours' sleep will not improve. I gave her an injection—just a mild sedative. I'll check on her later."

Mendel looked relieved. He seemed unaware of Tom's presence, and Tom watched from the bedroom doorway as Mendel crossed to the bed and solicitiously smoothed back the damp hair plastered above one of Diana's sculptured cheekbones, where a net of blue veins pulsed. He mumbled something, and Tom moved closer. "What?"

"I said she takes chances she shouldn't."

"Chances?"

Mendel looked up at him with his ice-blue eyes. "Chances—you know, Estevez—skiing."

Against Mendel's pillow, Diana's hair formed a pool of champagne. Tom noticed that her eyes, irises dilated abnormally, were clamped on Mendel. Her perfectly delineated mouth reminded him of a child's, so trusting.

She had the marvelous features of a model, he thought abstractedly, not the bland, nondescript features of a good detective. Maybe the boating experience would change her mind about her chosen field of work. He doubted seriously if her work had ever before exposed her to mortal danger.

Her murmured "Thank you," came out slurred, as her lids slid shut. The intramuscular dose of sedative Corneille had injected was taking effect. Lying there asleep, she seemed unbelievably young, her flawless skin smoother than whipped egg whites.

Tom stared at his hands. He wondered at the power stirring in them. He wondered if he could control them, so he jammed them into his trouser pockets and left Mendel's suite.

He didn't sleep well that night, and he got up at six-thirty the next morning to get that walloping dose of caffeine the French paraded as coffee. After two cups of the potent brew, he decided to find Sciolla and do some roundabout interrogating.

Long ago, he had learned that an interrogator had to impress his subject, not through any use of authority but through sheer force of his personality. The best interrogators inspired total confidence in their subjects, the power of their personalities tempered by a credibly understanding and sympathetic nature. The subject had to believe implicitly that he was just talking man-to-man with someone who was interested in his opinions and problems.

Tom's ability to observe and interpret, as well as his skill at maintaining control of himself at all times, despite his boiling Latin temper, had made him one of the most proficient interrogators in his unit.

He found himself, however, thwarted that morning. Carlo, the only one at breakfast at such an ungodly hour, pored over a legal journal. "How's Walter?" Tom asked him.

"Oh, fine. But now the other Riva is missing. They say the steward made off with it."

"Who's 'they'?" Tom pressed.

Carlo took a swallow of his fresh-squeezed orange juice and waggled his hand. "Oh, just some of the crew members. They think the guy felt so terrible about what happened, he just took off." Carlo dug his serrated spoon into a broiled grapefruit half. "David's going ashore soon to report the missing boat to the authorities."

Tom caught up with Mendel at the end of the corridor. David kept on walking, and Tom fell into step with him. "If you don't mind, I'd like to come along."

Mendel flicked a glance at him. "What makes you think I'm going anywhere?"

Without looking at him, Tom drew from his shirt pocket a well-chomped cigar stub and jammed it between his teeth. "You've got a missing boat, Mendel, and a missing employee. You don't seem like the type to let something like that get by you."

"You're sharp, my friend—and you have sharp ears. So the news of the missing boat has already spread all over the yacht?"

"Just about."

"Well, you're right, I intend to do something. The man driving the boat was probably scared shitless and took off for the mainland, where he no doubt ditched the Riva. I'm going to report the accident."

Again, accident—not incident. Tom's hands knotted in his pockets. Just how far was Mendel involved in the attempted murder? Tom was willing to bet he was up to his neck in it.

"At this moment my steward is probably drinking away his fear in one of the waterfront's seedier bistros," Mendel said wryly.

Tom doubted that. Sciolla was no doubt well on his way to some isolated paradise—somewhere like Martinique—with a couple of hundred thousand francs in his pocket to ease his change of address. "Great. I'll just go along for the trip then. The police can always use another witness."

Mendel could have told him to mind his own business. Most likely, though, he reasoned the wiser course would be to pay the obligatory call on the local police.

Though it was not yet nine, the sun worshippers were already out, and the waterfront was a tropical version of a fashionable Paris boulevard. The missing Riva wasn't among the colorful fleet of fishing boats and yachts that crowded the rectangular basin of the Vieux Port.

Along the quayside, the ground floors of pink and yellow four-story houses had been converted into sidewalk cafés, quaint restaurants, luxury boutiques, galleries, and antique shops, all overlooked by a hexagonal citadel on a hillock east of the village.

Away from the quay, they followed a street that wound uphill until it became a stairway. Then it plunged into a tunnel that emerged again onto a tiny, shady square with a burbling fountain before finally opening onto a cobbled surface that led to the police station, flanked on either side by a hole-in-the-wall pipemaker and a rug weaver.

The duty sergeant was officious, pompous, and curt until Mendel informed him that *The Star of David* was the big yacht out in the bay, then the man turned unctuously obsequious. Carefully, he jotted down the information Mendel gave him.

When the sergeant asked for a description, Mendel deferred to Tom. "What would you say, Estevez? Maybe one hundred and eighty-five centimeters or so?"

Tom shrugged his shoulders. "Probably. Flat nose. Curly black hair." He wasn't about to give himself away with any trained observations.

They waited while the sergeant left to run a name check. The walls of the small anteroom were papered with wanted posters that reminded Tom of an American B gangster movie. Behind the counter was a black woman who never looked up from whatever she was typing laboriously on an old manual Olivetti.

The sergeant came back with a computer printout. "The fugitive has been hauled in several times on suspicion of theft, prostitution, and drugs, monsieur, and convicted once for larceny. We can put out an alert for him."

Mendel and Tom signed the complaint, then made their way back to the Vieux Port. "This hasn't exactly been the quiet cruise I had in mind," David grumbled.

Tom tried a sympathetic "good ol' buddy" grin. "Think I'll go fishing in Norway next time."

They had barely reached the quay, when a police Citroën with a whooping klaxon skidded to a screeching halt beside them. "We've found your steward," its uniformed driver reported in French.

David glanced at Tom, perplexity at the speed of the arrest written on his face.

"A fisherman just reported pulling him from the sea," the patrolman explained. "The missing speedboat was recovered not far from the site."

Sciolla had drowned? Tom was certain the man had been wearing a life jacket the day before. Why not this morning?

"You will need to attempt an identification," the policeman continued. "Apparently, the fugitive banked the stolen Riva steeply, panicked and fell in the water, then somehow was run over by the speedboat. It has happened before that way."

When Tom saw Sciolla's body laid out on a dilapidated dock, he understood what the policeman had meant by an "attempt at identification." Bone and cloth seemed to have been passed through a food processor set on high.

"That appears to be one of the Riva's life jackets," David managed to say.

Tom had seen a lot of grisly bodies, but he had never become inured to them. His stomach curdled.

34

July 2nd

Diana was soaking up the restorative mid-morning sunlight, her feet propped on the navy blue deck chair opposite her. She was badly rattled by the accident the day before and wanted to be alone to sort out exactly what had happened. He brain was still groggy from the sedative.

Noël and Tanya came giggling around the corner, and she opened her eyes, tucking her sunglasses atop her head. "Hi, kids. What's up?"

The exotic couple sat down at her table. "We're waiting for the captain to lower the speedboat for us," Tanya announced in her Down Under whine. She had a leprechaun face with a sprinkling of wee gold coins across her nose and cheeks. "We're spending the day in Cannes."

"I thought I'd show Tanya the Palais des Festivals," Noël informed Diana. His attire that morning consisted of cowboy boots topped by casino-pink Bermuda shorts and a fawn leather vest, sans shirt, and, of course, his trademark bandana, this one of purple silk. "You all right—I mean after that close call yesterday?"

Gingerly, she fingered her jaw. "Great. Just great!"

Which was true in a way. After such a close brush with death, she supposed certain aspects of life were put in their proper perspective. Like getting caught up in the rat race, like fretting about what a guest would think about the damned color of the drapes.

In the minidramas she enacted daily, she had always moved about life's stage untouched by harm, because no one had ever suspected a feckless playgirl could be capable of leading such a peculiar double life. Now, not only did someone suspect her, he obviously meant to kill her.

When this operation for Security International was finished, she meant to implement some changes in her life. Slow down. Stop and smell the flowers, as the saying went. But first, she had to consider what exactly she would do about Sciolla.

About David . . . well, her mind kept backing away.

"I got my start in photography in Cannes a couple of years ago," Noël was saying. "Snapping photos for *Life*'s Paris bureau at the Film Festival at ungodly hours—while the established photographers slept."

"I thought news photographers never slept," Diana teased.

Noël's perfect teeth gleamed against his shiny ebony skin. "During the festival there are six hundred films whirring away nonstop at all hours of the day and night in the Palais and at dozens of screening rooms around town, so you never know when some celebrity or actor might decide to sneak in and see his or his competitor's film. That first year, I subsisted at Cannes for ten days simply by bumming canapés at various bashes where producers, distributors, theater-chain owners, and studio execs get together at exhibition booths to haggle and make deals."

"And that's where I met him," Tanya said, taking

Noël's hand in hers. "I was there with my parents. My father's a director for an Australian studio—Outback."

"Of course," Diana said, making the name connection. "Darren Gordon."

"Too right." Tanya looked terribly pleased that Diana had heard of her father. "Say, want to go ashore with us? We could make a day of it and—"

"Thanks, anyway, Tanya, but I've seen enough of the Palais at past festivals."

The girl shrugged her narrow shoulders. "Right. Well, enjoy the day." She tugged Noël out of his chair, and the couple strolled off, still giggling—over what this time, Diana couldn't imagine. Ahh, the joy of youth, she thought, readjusting her sunglasses on the bridge of her nose.

"Feeling better?" Tom asked.

Startled, she glanced over her shoulder at him. He was wearing beat-up, faded tennis shoes, his hands shoved into his jean pockets. She lifted her feet from the deck chair they were propped on and said, "Have a seat—if you promise not to light up one of those obnoxious cigars."

"In deference to a convalescent—I promise." He glanced around the empty poolside. "Up early, aren't you? It's not even ten."

"Never can sleep past nine. Sleeping in always gives me a headache. Besides, I slept almost all day yesterday and then all night."

"Mendel?"

"I think he's showering." She paused. "It seems I owe you a 'thank you.' I understand you were one of the ones instrumental in my rescue."

"Aw, shucks, it was nothing, ma'am. Just a little ol' good deed I do every day. All in the line of my work." He tossed her a casual two-fingered Boy Scout salute.

She chuckled. "I just bet. With a dive like you made, you should give up—boat brokering, isn't it?—and join the cliff divers in Acapulco." For all his laid-back indolence, she realized the narc was a muscular, quick-moving man. Sobering, she said, "Tom, I'm sincere—thank you. It's nice to know someone cares."

The almost rigid line of his mouth curled into a self-deprecatory, unexpectedly chauvinistic smirk. "I have to admit I surprised myself. Normally, I make it a rule not to give aid and comfort to any radical females."

She grinned. "Glad you cleared that up. I was beginning to wonder what came over you. We're anchoring off Cannes today, in case you want to go in and have that thick skull of yours X-rayed." She hesitated, then decided to ask anyway, "Tom, was your marriage that rough?"

"Not when I consider I have three kids to show for it, two daughters and a son."

"Is your wife, your former wife, a radical female?"

"In some ways, she's a bit like you. Natalie is French and she possesses the kind of cool that isn't artifice . . . it's that innate and terribly polite sort of cool that you all learn so thoroughly at your boarding and convent schools that it becomes automatic."

"It sounds as if you still love her."

He stared hard at her, eyes narrowing warily. "Tell me, if you truly love someone, Diana, in spite of their faults and everything, can you ever really stop? I don't think so. Or else, it was never love to begin with, right?"

"I hadn't thought about it like that."

"Natalie was fascinated with me because I was unusual, different from anyone she was used to—I suppose it was a combination of my street-wise, Hispanic background and my hard-ass cop image. Her fascination with me lasted right up until the unusualness was eroded by too little money, prejudice, whatever you want to call it.''

She didn't know what to say, how to allay the pain in his smoky pale brown eyes. Then, she put her warm hand over his swarthy one where it lay on the arm of the deck chair. He looked up from their overlapped hands into her eyes. She didn't know what he found there, but he growled, ''I think I could use a cigar.''

She smiled. ''You have my grateful permission to smoke this once. You've earned it.'' Fascinated, she watched him suck in on the cigar, reminding her of Sam.

After he exhaled a blue whorl of smoke, he asked, ''You aren't smoking?''

''Should I be?''

''Yes. Because I have something to tell you that is not very pleasant.''

She leveled her gaze on him. ''That Sciolla tried to kill me?''

''No. Worse. Sciolla is dead.''

Her hands started trembling, and she gripped the chair arms to stop the trembling.

''He fled with the boat—somehow fell out . . . and the boat ran over him. At least, that's the version of the local police.''

Chill bumps surfaced on her skin the way they did when she sometimes got too much sun. ''Sciolla failed to murder me and . . .''

She was unable to finish and Tom finished for her in a cement-mixer voice. '' . . . and he was silenced. Just like the good old Mafia films.''

Her heart was double-timing. ''Tom, cover for me, please. I'm going ashore.''

''The hell you are!'' he growled.

She stood up. Her legs were wobbly. "Listen. Someone has to keep an eye on David, remember? I want the
paintings, you want the drugs. I'll be back by dusk."

He stood also. His brown eyes were almost black
with his inner frustration. "I got this feeling it wouldn't
do me any good to argue with you or you can bet your
great ass I would."

With exaggerated slowness, she turned her head, her
mouth open with feigned indignation. "Tom!"

She left him and went directly to Noël and Tanya's
cabin. "Hey, I've changed my mind," she told Noël,
who opened the door. "I think I'll go ashore with you
two lovebirds. But I'll leave you on your own while I
look after some other things."

"Sure thing, man. We're leaving in fifteen minutes."

She hurried to her room, changed into a lacy white
sundress and sandaled thong heels and jammed her
horn-rimmed glasses into her shoulder bag.

On the way out, she bumped into Carlo, excused herself, and stepped around him. "Diana? . . . "

"Yes?" She looked over her shoulder, hoping whatever it was he wanted wouldn't take long. She didn't
want to have to make excuses to David in person.

Carlo caught up and walked alongside her. "There's
something I wanted to tell you. It's about Catherine."
Nervously, his hands jingled the coins in his pockets.
"I know how spiteful she can be, and . . . well, I just
want to apologize for her, if she's given you any problem."

She managed to smile. "That's all right, Carlo. I can
handle Catherine. We go back a long ways."

He let out a sigh of relief. "So do she and I. I know
what a boring fellow I can be."

She began to say something ameliorating when he
held up his hand. "Oh, please, *cara mia*, don't try to

be nice. I am aware of what I am and that's why I need Catherine in my life. She has what we Italians call *grinta*."

"*Grinta* has many definitions, Carlo."

"Yes, but in Catherine's case, it's the combination of gutsy vitality and magnetic aggressiveness. I love her, Diana."

Watching Carlo plod heavily away, she remembered what Tom had told her earlier, about loving in spite of faults. True love was indeed blind. Well, if so, she didn't intend to be one of those blind lovers, if she could help it. But who could? Certainly not Carlo, nor Tom, nor Anne, who, Diana was sure, still loved her Spencer.

On the boat ride into Cannes, Noël talked about making a living as a child backgammon hustler at the posh Hôtel du Cap d'Antibes. By the time the Riva docked, the Rolex Beach Crowd was already spread out elbow-to-elbow on the imported sand like so many frying fish. Diana bade her companions adieu and went directly to the nearest car rental office on Boulevard de la Croisette.

From there, the reliable little green Renault she'd picked up took an hour to climb the winding road that led up through Grasse, the home of the world's finest perfumes, and north through Provençal olive groves and rugged hills rampant with wild rosemary and tall sunflowers, their enormous heads turned in perfect unison toward the brilliant sun. Provence possessed a quality of light, the suffused pure light that bewitched Van Gogh and Cezanne.

Her eyes flickered frequently toward the rearview mirror. She wasn't certain if she was being followed but at Castellane, a tourist center predicated on its famous bauxite canyon, she turned abruptly off the *cour* onto a narrow side road.

Two cigarettes later, she pulled up at the cypress-lined drive leading to her grandmother's horse farm, five hundred acres of manicured rolling meadows and neat whitewashed rail fences. The restored *mas* was in reality a chateau, whose rough terra-cotta walls surrounded interiors hung with Picassos and accented with the tapestries of Jean Lurçat. With its stables, chapel, and other outbuildings reflected in the adjacent Verdon River, the chateau resembled a slightly scaled-down Disneyland castle.

An old cast-iron tethering ring had been put to work as a door clapper on the ancient nail-studded oak door. A downstairs maid let her in. "The Comtesse is in her office, Mademoiselle Diana."

Quietly, Diana opened the office door into a room crowded with trophies, ribbons, photographs, and other equine memorabilia. A huge fieldstone fireplace filled one entire wall. *"Bon jour, grandmère."*

The old woman looked up from a ledger in which she was jotting figures. She was still wearing the wide-brim black felt over a black silk scarf that she wore out-of-doors, yet looked every inch a French aristocrat of distinguished lineage. "Diana! You couldn't have come at a better time. I'm buried under paperwork and I need a week's break, at least."

"I'm just here for the day, *grandmère.*"

"Then have lunch with me." She closed the ledger with a slap and rose stiffly from her chair. "Used to be, breeding and racing horses was a hobby of those born to serious money. Now taxes demand that one run it as a business. Thoroughbreds were never a mere commodity, they were a hobby for rich people."

Lunch was served on a stone balcony, whose hoary

griffins overlooked the jade-green river. Freshly picked wild lavender in a slender cut-glass Baccarat vase graced the glass tabletop. Both *Le Provençal* and a day-old edition of the widely read afternoon daily, *France Soir*, which had come in the mail, were already laid next to her grandmother's place setting. One of the maids hurriedly set another place for Diana.

Over refreshing tomato-juice cocktails and succulent melon balls, her grandmother related the latest happenings. "Roue Rouge refuses to mount and Savoir Faire has a respiratory problem, the veterinarian says."

"You could always sell out."

"Never. Still, it's not like it was in the old days. I wouldn't have imagined a horse farm would ever go public or that Merrill Lynch would float a company just to get some brood mares."

"Weren't you the one who advised me to take up this *hobby* of horse breeding?" Diana teased.

In the languorous, shimmering summer sunlight, Diana relaxed, basking in the surroundings as her grandmother talked. The chateau was far more than a place to live. It was a lifestyle all its own, imbued with a timeless heritage and with memories of her childhood.

She recalled life there as uncomplicated, peaceful, and serene. In those long-ago childhood days, it had seemed to her that everything important was a long way off. Then, as the years went by, she realized it was the accumulation of many pleasant, though insignificant, experiences that really made life worthwhile.

"It's men like Sangster and Mendel," sniffed the old lady, "who have turned horse breeding into an industry."

Diana laid down her fork. Her grandmother would no doubt hear about the cruise eventually through the news media, if not from her coterie of socialites. "I've been cruising the Riviera on David Mendel's yacht, *grand-mère*. It's anchored out in the Golfe de la Napoule now. That's why I was able to drive up."

Her grandmother stopped eating. "I see. Is this something serious?"

"Are you asking if we're going to marry?"

"I'm not that out of touch with the mores of your generation, Diana. I am thoroughly aware that in these times going to bed with a man isn't automatically followed by a trip to the altar."

"May I remind you, *grandmère*, that your generation was the most immoral since Edwardian days."

"At least we were discreet about it."

"Discreet—or furtive?"

"That will be quite enough, Diana!"

She sighed. "I'm sorry, *chèrie*. To allay your suspicions, there is nothing serious between David and me. I think he and I take a sort of perverse delight in tormenting one another."

"A Jew . . . and you," the doyenne murmured. "I never would have thought it."

"*Grandmère*, his heritage is as important to him as the crucifix is to us." She leaned over the table and kissed the old lady's forehead. "I have to be getting back to Cannes. I'll call you after I return to Paris."

Diana didn't drive straight through to Cannes. When she reached Grasse, she stopped at the arcades along the Place aux Aires and went into the nearest store, a *papeterie*. The stationery store manager let her use his phone. She probably could have used her grandmother's telephone, but she didn't want to risk implicating her grandmother in any way.

She dialed a number she knew by heart and waited anxiously for the phone to be answered.

At last, Sam's voice came on the line, grouchy as

ever and so good to hear. People were wandering in and out of the store, so she lowered her voice. "Sam, it's your favorite goddaughter."

"Who?" he joked back.

"La Comtesse de Revillon's granddaughter, you old crook. I just drove up to visit her. *The Star of David* is docked off Cannes for the day, so I took time off to lunch with her." There, he now knew she was with David.

"Been having a good time?"

"Wonderful! Went skiing yesterday. Almost got run over by the boat, but its driver, a man by the name of Sciolla, apologized profusely."

"You probably deserved the scare. You take too many chances."

"You may be right there. Bad part of it is, Sciolla later was run over by the boat in a freak accident. I understand he was killed instantly."

"*Mon Dieu*, what a gruesome way to die!"

"Yeah. Well, sorry, Sam, but I've got to run."

"As you wish. I'll check on you later."

What he would do immediately would be to check on Sciolla—in detail. His whole life up to his death the day before would be gone over with a microscopic precision.

She felt relieved now that she had talked to Sam. Regardless, she had to return to *The Star of David* to take up her painful vigilance once more.

35

Berthed at the port of La Condamine's, *The Star of David* vied for superyacht status with those on either side of it—the *Nabilia*, owned by the Arab speculator, Adnan Khashoggi; the *Atlantis II*, Stavros Niarchos's play toy; and the famous *Creole*, recently acquired by the Gucci clan. Most of the yachts were crewed by onetime German or British naval personnel.

The guests of the *Nabilia, Atlantis II*, and *Creole*, along with the transients from the flotilla of other pleasure boats, had already gone ashore to enjoy the mystique of Monte Carlo—that golden ghetto whose citizens were rarely there longer than it took them to establish income-tax-free residence.

Those pleasure seekers camped out at the Hôtel de Paris or the Hermitage, two Belle Epoque gems, the former with an employee for every guest, then they made for the Place du Casino, which opened at ten in the morning, or for the boutiques that sparkled with the prerequisites of luxury.

"Would you like to go ashore?" David asked her.

They were alone in his bedroom, and she lay among the disordered satin sheets. Surprisingly, he insisted she

240

sleep the entire night with him. Why? Watching him, trying to anticipate what he might do next was like waiting for the pain to begin in the dentist chair. "Where to?"

He turned back to the bath mirror and finished shaving. He crooked his jaw, stretching his skin taut to create a smooth path for his razor. "Oh, explore the art galleries, then some lunch, and after that, we—"

"Are you buying?"

He grinned wickedly at her odalisque reflection in his mirror. "If I must."

"Then you've got a date. After lunch, what?"

"A trip into the interior for anyone who cares to go— a health trip."

"What is the destination of this health trip?"

In the mirror, his eyes twinkled. He patted dry his jaw. "You'll have to wait and see. Then, tomorrow night we all have reservations for a party at the Monte Carlo Sporting Club. It's American Night—in honor of their Independence Day. Your Independence Day," he amended, underscoring her half-American heritage.

Her curiosity about the "health trip" was aroused, as was that of the other *Star of David* passengers. After a week of boutiques and casinos, they were manifestly bored, and apparently David was delighted to furnish some diversity for their amusement.

They all agreed to meet at one that afternoon in the lush landscaped square in front of the Casino. "We leave from there by chartered van," he told them, advising everyone to dress comfortably in slacks or jeans.

"In Monte Carlo?" Joan asked. "What if the paparazzi snap a photo of me like that? I'll stick to heels and hose, thank you."

His plans for the day sounded so mysterious, but then so was he. Normally, Diana wasn't one to overreact.

She had never felt so alive as when she was in danger, but this time . . . maybe she should get out, now.

And yet. And yet. Her pride—and a passionate fascination that amounted to an obsession with David Mendel, and which she didn't want to acknowledge as love—enticed her to continue the cruise and her investigation.

The principality's palm-lined boulevards teemed with six-figure handcrafted sports cars and taxis. Hand in hand with David, who had dressed in a casual white cotton jacket over a black T-shirt and blue jeans, she browsed along the fashionable yellow, white, and ochre maze of streets. *Carabinieres*, named for the guns they carried, patroled outside the exclusive establishments, ever alert for terrorists.

At an antique shop on Boulevard des Moulins, she spotted a miniature Dutch sterling wine caddy in the form of a nineteenth-century ship, and thought what a marvelous gift it would make for David.

How morbidly absurd! Selecting a gift for someone you intend to put in a prison cell.

Next, they stopped in Centre du Tapis, an Iranian carpet shop, then wandered into a branch of Sotheby's. A diamond and ruby necklace estimated by the auctioneers to be worth nearly $14 million caught her eye. The piece had once belonged to Josephine Bonaparte. Diana glanced at David, wondering if his mind was locked into the calculation of a master thief.

"You know, David," she murmured, "what would be worse than to have an ancient work of art like this necklace stolen would be to discover it had been melted down and broken apart for its far smaller value in metal and stones."

"And thus lost forever to art lovers," he said. "A true tragedy. Shall we eat?"

The Hôtel de Paris's Salle Empire was one of the world's most elegant dining rooms, and the chic local residents flocked to it, but he opted for a more casual lunch on the hotel terrace.

She leaned back in her cane-framed chair and absorbed herself in people-watching. Or at least she pretended to. The aristocrats, financiers, artists, intellectuals, and the social elite of the world who were summer fixtures at the hotel held no interest for her.

What did get her attention were the priceless vases, clocks, paintings, and tapestries, one of them a Gobelin, that carelessly adorned the Hôtel de Paris.

"Diana."

Guiltily, she looked across the table at David. He was openly studying her over his champagne glass. "Yes?"

"You're staring," he chided her gently, "as if you expect a sneak thief to make off with the *objets d'art* displayed here."

She twirled a silver fruit knife between her thumb and finger, as the sunlight glittered off it like a strobe. "I don't have to tell you that hot art can fetch a better price than jewelry or sterling flatware."

"*Vraiment?*" he drawled.

"*Vraiment.*"

The way he stared at her, she felt impelled to meet his eyes. "I know, Diana. I know all about you."

Her breath rasped in. She didn't have to ask what he was talking about. "How? Why haven't you said anything?"

"How I know is not important. I suppose I haven't said anything because you have amused me by your various ploys to entrap me—and, too, I feel a sort of grudging admiration. You are a damned good undercover agent."

"David . . ." she cleared her throat, feeling terribly sick at her stomach. "David, did you do it? Did you steal the Marmottan paintings?"

"If I am the thief you're seeking, you don't seriously think I'd admit such a thing to you?" He stared straight at her. "Besides, if I am . . . mind you, I said 'if' . . . you might consider that I might have done it for a good cause."

She was so confused. She didn't know what to believe. Especially since Tom was so certain David was an archcriminal who was behind the attempt on her life.

"Then again," he said, accepting a menu from the captain, "I freely admit to thievery, though the items I've stolen have been on a somewhat less munificent scale."

She was so startled, she knocked over the water glass. A busboy was there at once, dabbing at the spilt Perrier with a linen napkin. When he left, she glanced at David. "You knew you would take me by surprise."

"I assumed you might have guessed."

"Guessed?"

He turned his attention to his menu, offering mildly, "When I was at Dachau, I adapted myself to the business of surviving. Besides other languages, I mastered some unusual skills."

"What are you talking about?"

"In the camp, I began to acquire other languages. I grew up in Vienna with German. I already knew some Hebrew, which made Yiddish a snap. Then over the next two years I learned Polish at the munitions plant. Three Gypsy circus magicians took a liking to me and taught me Rumanian and Hungarian. The Rumanian made Italian and Spanish a cinch. French I learned in the Lorraine coal mines. But besides the languages, the Gypsies taught me other things."

"What, for instance?"

"Oh, the tricks of their trade—how to deceive the eye, how to hide objects, even quite large ones, behind my palm or up my sleeve. I learned the art of substitution and how to distract a victim for a mere instant at the crucial stage of a trick. As I told you before, I became an artist at hustling—for a crust of bread, a tiny bit of soap, a remnant of blanket.

"The veal sounds tasty, doesn't it?" He closed his menu and laid it aside.

"Then what happened?" she pressed.

"Well, after the Americans released us, I continued to hone my valuable skills in the relocation camps. By the time the family friend I told you about found me and took me back to Vienna, the pleasures of petty crime were too tempting. I took particular pleasure in lifting watches and items of jewelry from the Viennese, since their jewelry had quite often belonged originally to Jews who had entrusted their valuables into neighbors' hands for safekeeping—even as they were being herded off to death camps. I never felt any qualms about relieving those self-satisfied Viennese of their ill-gotten gains.

"Have you decided what you would like?" he asked, facilely changing the subject.

Her eyes held his in a stand-off. "Something light, I think. I seem to have lost my appetite."

By 1:15, *The Star of David* passengers had all assembled—Anne, Greg, and Joan, the last to arrive, Joan toting two elegant boxes of designer clothing she had just purchased. "I couldn't help myself," she apologized breathlessly. "I found all sorts of little shops on Avenue Princesse Grace . . . . a lovely black leather suit at the Rive Gauche and a Thierry Mugler silk blouse at Adonis."

Greg rolled his eyes. "Spare me any more shopping excursions, David. Joan and Anne exhausted me."

The rented Volkswagen Vanwagon left Monte Carlo along one of the three routes leading out of Monaco, a tortuous road that climbed toward the snowy Alpes Maritimes. The narrow blacktop passed charming alpine villages, their hillsides dotted with wild olives, pines, and ancient twisted fig trees.

"Some people have a talent for traveling," Tom drawled, glancing pointedly around the van at the club seating, the small refrigerator, and the television set.

"Traveling is indeed a fine art," Murad said. He was reclining on a flame-stitched berth, his head cradled on Maja's lap.

"David, aren't you going to give us a hint as to where we're going?" Catherine asked petulantly. She and Carlo were holding hands like two lovers, and Diana found it difficult to believe that earlier in the cruise Catherine had been in the arms of a woman lover.

"Patience," David counseled with an enigmatic smile. He sat next to Diana, his arm draped around her shoulder in what could be construed by anyone as an affectionate gesture.

The landscape they were passing now was pitted with ravines and there was almost no vegetation. At intervals, the road shadowed a river that was turbulent with runoff from melting snow. From their position on the hillside above it, the river was a thin line running along through the stones and then cascading down to become a larger stream.

"I ate too much lunch," Anne groaned. "Next week I check into a Marbella starvation camp."

"I'd sooner submit to a root canal," Greg said.

"Look," Tanya said, pointing toward a cliff where three ibex were poised like statues, watching them pass.

Everyone craned to see, and Noël moaned, "*Merde,* I knew I should have brought my camera."

"Some photographer," Catherine purred.

"Catherine!" Carlo warned in an authorative tone.

Tactfully, Eva turned the discussion to art, " . . . she received a medal with honors from the Leonardo da Vinci Academy in Rome."

Diana stared out the van window, giving only half her attention to the conversation. Below, the clear and fast-running river separated pastures dotted with wooden-roofed chalets. In some places, the river swirled toward gigantic slashes in the mountainsides that created gorges. Once she spotted a teenager trying to body-surf down one of the less dangerous rapids.

Four days left, she thought. *July 7th. Four days.*

The road climbed nearly three thousand feet, passing a picturesque hamlet, before it dwindled into mere wagon ruts. "We walk from here, my friends," David said, instructing the uniformed chauffeur to park the van and wait with it.

"In these heels?" Joan asked, her jaw gaping in astonishment.

"I warned you to dress casually. Besides, it's worth it."

"How far do we have to walk?" asked Tanya.

"Perhaps three kilometers," he said. His hands spanned Diana's waist as he lifted her from the van. "I've never been there. Some friends told me about it."

The trail tapered even more as it skirted a bluff, becoming a narrow footpath. A lot of good-natured grumbling began about their impromptu, vigorous hike. The path wound upward over reddish slopes and past savage gashes in the mountain that created wonderful rock formations. Although it was cool at that altitude, everyone began to perspire. David took off his jacket and slung it over his shoulder. Walter had dark stains splotching the armpits of his light blue denim jacket.

"Well, there goes forty francs worth of hosiery," Joan said, when a thorn bush snagged her stocking. Her tone was lighthearted, but she wasn't at all happy about the tightrope act they were all performing.

David grinned. At least he seemed to be enjoying himself. "Sorry, I wasn't informed the hike would be so rigorous. When we get back to Monte Carlo, you are all treated to an outfit at the shop of your choice."

There was something about his reckless giving, Diana thought, that implied he would just as easily give away his life.

To her relief—as well as the others'—she was sure—the trail began a gradual descent. There were bushes and pine saplings alongside for hand holds. They passed several lovely little waterfalls, with Noël still bemoaning his missing camera.

"We're here," David said.

"We are? Where?" Eva asked, looking around, puzzled.

The trail had opened onto a wide, smoothly worn rock ledge where the rushing river had formed a large pool of whirling, Jacuzzi-like water. The plateau of ledge continued on around a promontory of the mountain.

"At the mud baths."

"Mud baths!" Anne groaned. "I walked this far when I can get one in my local spa!"

Tom knelt at the poolside and scooped up a handful of mud, letting it dribble between his spatulate fingers. "Sulphur mud," he said, wrinkling his nose.

To Diana, standing next to him, the stuff looked extremely fine, smooth, and an unappealing baby-poop green.

"This is very special mud," David said. "Excellent for the skin and body and even the hair."

Catherine's cat's eyes danced. "Does that mean we all strip naked?"

"Now just a minute . . ." Joan said.

Without a hesitation, Noël was already yanking off his bright chartreuse raw silk shirt.

Tom rinsed off his hands and looked around. "For the more inhibited, it looks like there are plenty of nooks and alcoves for privacy." He pointed. "Further up the river. Around that bend."

Diana was fascinated to discover who stayed and stripped and who sought the subtle privacy afforded by jutting rocks. As she would have guessed, Catherine and Carlo stayed right where they were, along with Tanya, Noël, Eva, and Murad. Walter, Maja, Greg, and Anne elected to follow the trail around the river bend.

Tom wasn't much interested in the mud treatment. "I'd rather fish. Think I'll scout around."

"May I go with you," Joan asked. "Lying in the sun—special mud or no—is not beneficial for *my* skin."

After that, everyone seemed to scatter to his or her own personal spot in the sun.

David had already tugged his T-shirt out of his jeans when he took Diana's elbow. "Come on. I want you to myself."

He started in the opposite direction, downriver from the pool. After trekking about a hundred yards, they had to climb a pebbly slope that dropped off precipitously to the jagged rocks bordering a narrow wedge of river.

Pushing through several yards of thick undergrowth, they scrambled down to a ledge almost concealed by low-lying bushes—scrub pine and fragrant alpine flowers. The stony plateau wasn't quite as wide nor the mud as plentiful. There was less chance of intrusion, though, and the burble of the waterfalls along the river muted the laughter and shouts of the others.

Oddly, she felt unaccountably shy as she stripped in front of him. Perhaps it was the primitiveness of their surroundings. On either side sheer rock faces rose to disappear into lush undergrowth near their summits.

He sensed her reluctance. "Those bikini swimsuits you wear aren't much more concealing than your all-in-the-buff."

"I realize you may find it a strain on my credibility," she said, her fingers lingering timorously at her unzipped jeans fly, "but I'm not used to disrobing before men."

"Now that I find extremely pleasing to my male ego." He dropped his jacket and shirt on a rock and went to her. Above the band of his jeans, his stomach was flat with hair arrowing up it to whorl around his nipples.

"Ihr ge-felt mir," he said softly, his fingers working nimbly at the buttons of her white silk blouse.

Her breath became shallow and rapid, just like the river. "That's Yiddish, isn't it? What does it mean?"

"Like most Yiddish expressions, it's difficult to translate precisely. More or less, 'I find *you* pleasing.' "

After they were both naked, he drew her toward the mudhole. "Lie on your stomach, and I'll cover your back with the mud, then you can do mine."

Reluctantly, she stretched out on the smooth warm stone next to the mudhole and rested her head on a bent arm. David hunkered over her, plopping the fine-grain mud onto her body.

She turned her head away, closing her eyes against the much-too-provocative sway of his genitals. Almost unwillingly, she reveled in the sensual pleasure of his hands grazing her shoulder blades, sliding down her spine to lather her buttocks, then following her thighs and calves to the tapering of her ankles and the arches of her feet.

"David," she said, her eyes closed, "if you know all about me, then you must know I've had some experience in tracking down stolen art. For instance, three years ago thieves crawled beneath infrared detectors in the Pacific Asia Museum in Pasadena, California, and swiped 171 ancient Japanese netsuke figures. They made the mistake of trying to unload the stolen works at an auction—the worst place because firms like Sotheby's and Christie's publish in advance descriptions of the items they offer. Last year, those quaint Japanese figurines turned up in Christie's January catalog, and I spotted them."

"Congratulations," he said, his tone dry and faintly mocking. His hands continued their erotic play on her flesh.

"Oh, it's not always that easy for me. Guarded galleries are rarer than reasonably priced restaurants in Monte Carlo. Once fenced, a stolen work may be sold repeatedly to good-faith buyers and later laundered by a top auction gallery. Art theft in most cases, however, is high profit, low risk—wouldn't you say?"

Did he understand she was warning him—that despite the incendiary nights she had shared his bed, despite what she might feel for him, she would not neglect her duty. If he knew all about her undercover work, then he also knew that she was a professional at her job, the best.

"I would say that you and I must trust each other, despite all outward appearances." His hands ceased their ministrations. "After all, wasn't it your job to seduce me?"

She rolled over and looked up into those blue eyes that would strip her down to her soul itself. "That was before . . ."

"Before what? Wasn't love created to maximize both pleasure and pain?"

He kissed her hard then, and though she strove to keep a part of her inner self separate and remote, she had to acknowledge bitterly that he was able to arouse her with words and looks as well as with the touch of his mouth and fingers on her flesh.

When he released her, she levered herself upright. "It's my turn now to cover you with mud. Lie down."

He stared at her for a moment, then nodded, his golden head haloed by the brassy sunlight. "All right, Diana, we'll keep it light and easy."

Unself-consciously, he dropped prone, his bronzed body spread like the points of a compass. Kneeling, she dabbed a glob of mud across his shoulders. She took advantage of the rare moment when he was relaxed and unguarded to marvel at his male beauty, to touch his heated flesh where it sheathed those mighty muscles and tendons. Most unsettling impulses swirled and eddied in her blood.

"Ummm," he said.

"Finished," she said and smudged the rest of the mud in her hand over her own face.

He chuckled. "Not bad camouflage."

"Uggh." She rubbed goo into her scalp.

Modestly, she turned away to finish covering her breasts. By the time she and David were completely covered, their gender was still patently obvious, but their identities were debatable. They lay side by side in the hot sun, letting its rays bake the mud dry. Eyes closed, she could hear David next to her, breathing evenly, shallowly, asleep—or, she thought so, until he suddenly bolted upright.

"What is it?" she asked.

"Nothing. I'll be back in a moment."

She watched him stride away, his gorgeous body so fit. Lowering her head onto her forearm again, she dismissed his departure as a call of nature. After what seemed at least twenty minutes had passed, she reached for her purse and a cigarette. She heard a clatter of pebbles and glanced up from lighting her cigarette, expecting to see David.

Catherine, looking like a African warrior in her mud pack, slip-stepped down the slope toward her, then she paused midway. "Oh, Diana! I was looking for David."

"Why?"

Catherine feigned a look of distress. "Don't tell me you're jealous? You shouldn't be. You and I are old friends, Diana. You shouldn't be selfish about sharing him."

"I'm afraid I have a few hang-ups, Catherine. For example: I prefer men of discrimination."

Catherine laughed. "You really have become priggish. Well, when I do locate David, I'll be sure to tell him you're waiting for him—after me." She turned to go and threw over her shoulder, "Don't overbake, darling."

When she was gone, Diana expelled a long, deep breath of mock irritation. Hardly had she stubbed out her cigarette in the mud, when she thought she heard a scream. It was difficult to be sure, with the cascading of water drowning out normal-level sounds.

Puzzled, she pushed to her feet and stood for a moment, like an ibex gaining its bearings. With her hide encased in mud, she felt stiff as a marionette. Then some visceral force prompted her to move—suddenly she didn't feel safe standing there so exposed.

Her faltering steps of uncertainty quickened to a lope at the sound of the next scream, which was cut short. She reached the slope and began the rugged ascent. Near the top, she paused, her breathing ragged. Her glance was caught by something below the lacework of green shrubbery, something white. Cautiously, she moved several steps down, off the path, holding to willowy switches for balance.

Then, she saw the object quite clearly. Catherine's body lay sprawled awkwardly on the rocks projecting from the river. Her eyes were wide, staring sightlessly out of a bloody, shapeless mass that had been her face. The current sloughed mud off her body, mixing the mud with her blood in the pink eddy of water about her.

36

July 4th

That evening, in celebration of American Independence Day, the United States Sixth Fleet stationed its honor guard, dressed in splendid navy whites, in a double row leading to the doors of the Monte Carlo Sporting Club. The Grand Public Ball brought out the local expatriates as well as the rich, beautiful, and famous, who had jetted in from all over for the party.

Inside, red, white, and blue were the dominating colors—from the tablecloths and napkins to the floral centerpieces and the balloons and streamers on the ceiling. *The Star of David*'s passengers occupied one long banquet table near the dance floor. Claude Melter and his San Francisco Orchestra provided the music.

Although the Fourth of July gala, hosted by His Serene Highness the Prince of Monaco, was the highlight of the July social season, *The Star of David* passengers were watching a cabaret entertainment with somber faces. They had spent most of that morning being interviewed by the principality's police. Diana, since she was the last to talk to Catherine and the first to find Catherine's body, was still being interrogated.

David wondered just how much Diana would tell the

255

police. Probably not much if she hoped to close the case on her own—and, knowing her, she hoped to. He glanced across the table at Estevez's unfathomable face. How far, if any, was the narc agent mixed up with Diana?

David asked the question that he had asked over and over again of himself. Would she be his love or his enemy—or both? He was on fire for her. When he was with her, his head hammered with his need for her. His blood rushed through his body like the Paris–Lyon Express. The urge to throw her on the ground beneath him and take her, dominate her, until she submitted, was overwhelming. But that wasn't how he wanted her. He wanted her to come to him freely, trusting him wholly. It would have to be that way.

"I saw her body," Walter muttered, taking a fortifying gulp of gin and tonic. "Horrible . . . horrible. Her beautiful face smashed on a rock . . . her leg twisted up at the knee . . . the way it shouldn't go."

David excused himself to the two women on either side of him, Tanya and Joan. On the stage, a kettledrum introduction was reverberating through the darkened room and no one else really noticed his departure.

The taxi ride took no more than five minutes. From the inside of his black tux jacket, he took out a skull cap and entered the synagogue. With the *kippah* covering his golden hair, he became just one of perhaps a dozen inside at that hour of the evening. The lights were turned low, so that the perpetually burning lamp was the focus of the evening worshippers.

He took a seat on a darkened pew in a far corner, next to a bearded man who, like many of the worshippers, wore a *tallith*, a tasselled shawl of woven wool. "*Shalom aleichem*, Hamemuneh," Bernard Gaillard said in a lowered voice.

"And peace be upon you," David responded, keeping his gaze fixed on the ark of the covenant against the eastern wall.

"Hear, O Israel, the Lord our God, the Lord is one . . ." Gaillard intoned.

"That was you I saw by the river yesterday?"

"Your eyesight is excellent," Gaillard said.

"I told you I would take care of her myself," David murmured.

"*Oi*, Hamemuneh! She was our *faind*!"

"*My* enemy—not Mossad's."

"Hamemuneh, she telephoned her employer, Samuel Breckon, the day before yesterday from a public booth in Grasse. Did you know that? And that she implicated you with Sciolla?"

"Sciolla took it upon himself to try and get rid of her. He's dead now. I took care of that myself."

Gaillard's lips compressed, becoming lost in the midst of his beard. "And so she is dead. I took care of *that* myself—on Rabin's order."

"Like hell you did! You made a mistake. The same kind that Mossad agents made in Norway in retribution for the Munich Massacre. You killed the wrong woman!"

"*Oi!*" Gaillard gasped. "How can that be?"

"You shoved another woman with the same build onto the rocks. The mud concealed her hair coloring."

"But I saw her come from the spot where you two had been lying. She even mistook me for you for a second, so, naturally, I . . ." His words of rationalization trailed off, and his shoulders slumped.

"Nevertheless, the wrong woman is dead. Between the botches you and Sciolla have made, now we have really attracted the notice of the police. I want you to report what has happened to Yashiv. Tell him either he and Rabin trust me or I abandon the Wrath of God Operation.''

Gaillard straightened his back resolutely. ''They trust you.''

''Then I will take care of the girl. There will be no more interferences.'' For a moment, he could see Catherine's broken and bleeding body.

Two escapes from death. Could Diana escape again?

His appreciation of her was sharper, honed by the storm clouds on the horizon. The time of plenty made more poignant by the drought of the years coming.

Wearily, he rose from the pew. ''*Shalom*, my friend.''

37

July 6th

The Star of David was due in Porto Rotondo the next
day. As the yacht drew nearer to Sardinia, David became more and more occupied with planning the festivities for the grand opening of his hotel, the Relais la
Citadelle, the latest addition to his string of luxury
properties.

Diana was dressing for dinner, fastening a lacy bra
that revealed more than it hid. David sat on his bed,
holding one of his ship-to-shore conversations with the
hotel manager.

"You seem particularly pleased," she told him, after
he hung up.

"Monsieur Clerc tells me that the Italian prime minister will be flying in for the opening. Craxi's presence
should generate a great deal of publicity."

"Strange you should be concerned with publicity
when it seems you go out of your way to avoid it."

"Diana—how much does your Samuel Breckon
know?"

She glanced up and saw glittering in his eyes a fever,
burning low like a pilot light, ready to ignite. "What?"
she asked breathlessly.

259

He crossed to her, palming her breasts in his supple hands. "You understood me."

Even suspecting what she did about him, he still had that power to make her go weak-kneed at his slightest touch: the scarcely veiled danger of him, his brilliance, his flaming strength. "Nothing." She gave a reckless little laugh. "I work on my own. We communicate rarely."

"I see," he said, and she knew he didn't believe her. Beneath the whisper of her blood, she had heard another sound—an inner voice telling her David must be stopped.

Do you love me? she wanted to plead, like a child.

She said nothing but watched him with empty eyes as he strode from the suite. In Sardinia would be a contest of two strong wills and for the first time in her life she was unsure of her abilities.

At dinner, the guests were still in a sober mood, appalled by Catherine's death in what they believed was an accident. Carlo, his face twisted in on itself like a crumpled photograph, had accompanied her body by plane from Nice–Côte d'Azur International to Rome. Eva had left Walter for good and had gone home with Carlo to Milano. Maja and Murad had caught the same flight out, planning on motoring on to Murad's palazzo in St. Moritz.

"I still can't believe it," Anne said to Diana. Her friend had barely even touched her wine that evening. "I didn't like Catherine, but I certainly didn't wish her dead."

"No one did," Diana said, silently amending her statement. Someone did.

She caught Tom watching her and when the music began to play he left Joan in the company of Tanya and

Noël and came around to where she was sitting. "Dance?"

David was discussing with Greg a portfolio his firm could handle. "Of course," she said. "After all, I do owe you my life."

"You know what the Chinese say," he told her, as he led her toward the dance floor.

"I'm almost afraid to ask."

He took her in his arms, his big frame all but dwarfing her slender one, making her feel, as before when with him, that sense of security, of being protected. "They say that once you save someone's life you are forever responsible for that person."

She laughed. "It appears you may have quite a task on your hands."

"You're hopelessly in love with Mendel, aren't you?"

She stiffened. "That's none of your business."

He looked like he could shake her. "Diana, don't you understand either he or someone connected with him wants you dead!"

"You've come to the wrong Judas, Mr. Estevez."

"Let me remind you that whatever your feelings are for him, drugs are involved. You have a duty to stop the cocaine deal from going through."

"Damn it, Tom," she hissed, "don't you think I know that?" Just thinking of drugs and how her stepfather had manipulated her mother with them created a cold rage in her. Jesus Christ, how could she be at such conflict within herself!

"You don't dance any better now than the first time," he said.

Here they went again, like dog and cat, as Anne put it. "Perhaps it's the man leading me."

"Ahh, yes, David Mendel does a good job at leading—leading you astray. Mendel made it look like he helped save you from having a speedboat put a permanent part in your head. Now, you're upside-down-inside-out in love and you're ready to turn a blind eye to such things as ethics and morals and justice and right and wrong.''

"Don't you dare lecture me! Your divorce made you so hard inside, so ruthless, you haven't any feelings left at all. You're the one who's turned a blind eye to compassion, because everything is not either black or white or right or wrong. Don't you see, Tom?''

"So what? Whether you're right about me or not, come tomorrow, your boyfriend is gonna deliver the paintings. You can bet your sweet ass on that, lady.''

"If you don't mind, I—''

"May I cut in?'' David asked coolly.

Tom nodded cordially enough, but she caught the exchange of flinty looks that flashed between them.

Once in David's arms, she tried to steel herself against the peculiar current that invariably short-circuited her sensory system, leaving her short of breath and tongue-tied. Silently, she cursed the feminine side of her that weakened her resolve and made her an emotional cripple.

"The other day . . . on the terrace at the Hôtel de Paris . . .'' God, she was stuttering like a schoolgirl, staring at his black bowtie, ''. . . you told me about the skills you had mastered in order to stay alive.'' She raised her eyes and met his inquiring gaze with a baleful stare. "You were testing me, David.''

He looked down at her with eyes that were clear and were without artifice, eyes that held nothing but love. "No. I love you and trust you, Diana.''

A silence trembled with her whisper. "Don't.''

He put several inches between them the better to see her face, and she knew that that infinitesimal distance would go on forever. "Don't love you," he asked softly, "—or don't trust you."

Blinded by tears, she spun out of his arms and pushed her way through the other couples. Back in his suite, she fondly touched his personal items, like a child seeking reassurance. His hairbrush, sunglasses, a penknife . . . items that had become familiar—no, dear—to her.

Then she threw herself across his bed to await the dawn of their last day together. He came to her later that night. She heard him undressing in the dark, then felt the bed give with his weight. Silently, he gathered her in his arms and merely held her. They both understood that there were no words to bridge the chasm of anguish and mistrust that yawned between them.

Toward dawn, the telephone rang, and he rolled over, turning on the nightlight to answer it. The brief conversation was limited to a few insignificant comments that gave her no clue as to the caller. "Yes, I understand," he said and picked up a pen to scribble something on the nearby notepad. "Nine is fine."

Nine what? Nine thousand dollars? Nine paintings?

After he replaced the receiver, she said nothing, snuggling back into his arms, wanting only to savor the final hours with him. When next she awoke, sunlight shafted through the porthole. Her eyes swept the room, finding him in front of the floor-length closet mirror, knotting his tie.

Covertly, she glanced at the notepad. The top sheet he had written on in the middle of the night was gone, as she expected.

"You might want to go shopping today in Porto Rotondo," he said, his eyes surveying her in the mirror with an affection she would have sworn was genuine. "I'll be busy at the hotel, but I'll have a limo at your convenience for the day. Plan to arrive at the grand opening about seven tonight.''

Lolling in his bed, she accepted his lighthearted kiss, choking back a plea for him to stay with her. After he left, she went to the nightstand. Taking the pen, she performed the old trick of lightly scribbling over the indentations left on the notepad by the previously written message. Only a phone number emerged. She tore off the sheet and took it with her when she joined Anne and Greg for some sightseeing of the Italian port.

Tom declined to join their outing. She knew why, too: He was keeping an eye on the yacht, guarding against a possible transfer of the paintings. Good. That freed her to pursue an avenue of her own.

Outside, the weather was beautiful, the sky a deep sapphire, perfect for sailing buffs at Costa Smeralda. She spotted the Aga Khan's high-speed sailboat, part of the afternoon regatta that led to the San Pellegrino Trophy at summer's end.

Noël and Tanya caught up with Greg, Anne, and Diana at the limo, a dark green Mercedes waiting on the wharf. ''Mind if we hitch a ride to the airport?'' Noël asked cheerfully. ''We've booked an Alisardi flight out to Naples.''

''Not at all,'' she said. ''You two deserting us?''

He grinned and hugged Tanya. ''Oh, I imagine we'll catch up with all of you the next time around.''

Diana wasn't so certain about that. After the chauffeur dropped Noël and Tanya off, he drove on toward Old Town. The crystal water, untouched thus far by pollution, reflected rose-tiled cottages, cafés, and the shops rimming the bay. Farther on, dramatic cliffs plunged onto the widest and whitest beaches in the Mediterranean.

Tucked away in the terraced hills were sparkling white villas and several modern hotels catering to an exclusive clientele. Diana's eyes sought out the majestic pink-stoned Citadelle, nestled on the eucalyptus-covered hilltop.

Though it was still early, townspeople jammed the narrow streets and alleys bounded by stalls set up for market day. At one time the whole island had belonged to the Borgias. Many of the shoppers were shepherds and they and their families had come in from the harsh, mountainous interior for the day to prowl about the resort village, oblivious to the snapping shutters of tourist cameras.

For a while, Diana and Greg and Anne browsed through the maze of stalls piled with gold jewelry, fragrant herbs, brass pots, and clay jars. Every so often, they would run across a chic boutique offering Valentino and Gucci fashions or Bulgari watches and gold jewelry.

"Your mind's not on shopping," Anne said.

"No, I suppose not. I guess I'm still not awake. How about a cup of coffee, you two?"

"Laced with whiskey?" Greg suggested, wrapping his arm around Anne's shoulders. Diana thought he seemed truly fond of her friend.

"Not this early," Anne said.

"Don't tell me you're changing your wicked ways," Diana said.

"Very reluctantly."

In a trattoria, a waiter, who was little more than a boy, found them a table on a tiny upstairs terrace facing the Mediterranean. Diana finished her cup of espresso and then excused herself, while the other two lingered over cigarettes—packed, incredibly for them, with mere Turkish tobacco.

Downstairs, she found the wall phone they had passed when entering. Rapidly she dialed the number that had surfaced on the scribbled sheet. "Shit!" she said beneath her breath when the call didn't go through. That was one more thing she appreciated about the United States—its efficient phone system.

She tried again, and an operator came on the line. Diana gave him the number, and the man said, "I'm sorry, but there is no such number."

"You're certain?"

"Si, *signorina*, I am certain," the operator said, a little testily this time.

Perplexed, she hung up and stood for a moment, thinking. She looked again at the paper in her hand. The numbers had to mean something.

She walked over to a plump woman behind the counter. "Do you recognize this number, *signora*?" she asked and passed her the paper.

The woman, who had a faint mustache, stared at the paper, looked at Diana as if she was mentally retarded, then shook her head. "No."

"Well, *grazie*."

With reluctant steps, Diana climbed the stairs back to the terrace. Greg and Anne were already getting up to leave. "I'm determined to find a shawl at one of the boutiques for this evening," Anne was telling Greg.

She didn't find the shawl, but Diana found the answer to her number problem. In a stall cluttered with crates of Italian wine, she spotted the last three digits of the telephone number—112—stenciled on one of the crates. "Pardon me," she said to the leather-skinned old vendor, "but what does that number mean?"

"That is the warehouse the wine was consigned to at the wharf, *signorina*."

So that was where the transaction would take place! "That's it!" she said and impulsively hugged Anne.

"What's it?" Anne asked, slightly dismayed.

"Why . . . you can borrow my shawl for tonight. The lace one threaded with gold that Murad gave me in Gilbraltar."

"Thanks," Anne said, quite puzzled now by Diana's out-of-character exuberance.

Now that she knew where the exchange of the paintings and drugs would take place, Diana didn't know what she was going to do about it. She could call the local police, she could tell Tom. She could just remain silent, too.

But she knew she wouldn't. She knew that when all this was over, the victory would be a Pyrrhic one.

Forgive me, my love.

38

July 7th

The glittering grand opening was typical of *la dolce vita*. Hibiscus blossoms adorned the Grand Salon's central fountain which was flowing with wine. Arrangements of peonies and lilies tumbled from the crystal chandeliers, the air laden with their scent.

Standing in the receiving line next to David, Diana greeted the prestigious guests of honor: the Marchioness Pia Persichetti of Rome; the Duke and Duchess de Badajoz, she the sister of the King of Spain; King Constantine of Greece and his Queen, Anne-Marie; Princess Dimitri of Yugoslavia.

Then there was Diana's old friend, Bernard Lanvin of the great Paris *maison de couture*; Ann Getty, the beautiful oil billionairess; Prime Minister Craxi and his lovely wife, Anna; the widow of a Swedish newspaper publisher; and, of course, Joan, who represented the Beverly Hills–Bel Air circuit and who had latched onto the prominent owner of an American football club for the evening.

At dinner, the men sat like stuffed penguins in their white ties and tails and all the women were fairly drooping from the weight of their sapphires and emeralds.

Diana wore a simple black velvet dress by Yves Saint Laurent, high-necked and long-sleeved, and with a hint of a bustle—very nineteenth century.

Grapes spilled from Italian terra-cotta centerpieces onto the peach-toned taffeta-covered tables, where guests dined on veal stuffed with apricots and, for dessert, chocolate mousse served in flower pots with yellow roses tucked in the middle. Regional wines were served, the familiar chianti as well as a noble red Brunello di Montalcino and an inexpensive white Pomino.

Photographers fluttered about the tables feverishly, imploring the beautiful people to look their way, and swirls of strobe flashes collided in the opulent room. Diana barely heeded the conversations going on around her.

"Now that the Riviera has become such a sweaty hellhole, we've . . ."

"I want a subscription to the Metropolitan Opera—a parterre box next to theirs . . ."

". . . fast becoming an 'in' enclave among those who can sniff out incipient chic."

She glanced over at a table where Anne and Greg were holding forth with their usual irreverent repartee. Diana could tell just by the slightly shocked and bemused expressions of the other guests around the table that they were far from bored.

At her side, David continued to play the charming, charismatic, and gracious host. He told the Italian prime minister, "Our syndicate of international banks is planning to finance the acquisition of several Italian hotel chains, Signor Craxi, all in the classic palace style like Le Citadelle."

She attempted conversation with the newspaper publisher's widow, who insisted on plying her with questions about David. Diana kept her answers carefully impersonal.

"I understand he's firmly entrenched in the Italian hotel and resort field," the bleached-blond matron said.

"To my knowledge, yes."

"But isn't the Italian government communist these days?" the widow asked.

"It's a coalition." Diana wished she had a cigarette. She didn't feel like making small talk that evening. She was nervous and edgy. "Socialist, communist . . . I don't know."

Across from her, Tom sipped his wine and listened, while a slightly amused smile tugged at his mouth. Tom and Joan, Greg and Anne, they were all who were left of the cruise's original passengers, she thought, rather surprised by the melancholy she felt. Soon, even the four of them would be going their own ways.

"Communist—capitalist," the widow pronounced, "what's the difference."

"The difference," she said tartly, completely out of patience, "is that capitalism exemplifies man's inhumanity to man, and communism is exactly the opposite."

"Ohh." The stately matron didn't know what else to say.

David laid his hand over Diana's, his eyes glittered with amusement. "You're very lovely tonight," he told her, his voice low and intimate.

"Don't do it, David."

"Do what?"

She shrugged her shoulders in a hopeless gesture of dismissal. "All right," she said, her words dull and laggard. "If you don't mind, I think I'll powder my nose."

Gently he squeezed her hand, then rose to pull out

her chair for her. Behind her, his hands clasped her shoulder, and he put his head next to hers. "Don't stay long," he whispered, grazing her neck with his lips. They felt feverishly hot against her chilled flesh. "I haven't seen you all day, and I've missed you wildly."

"David . . ." she turned to him, her voice dropping to a wisp of breath, ". . . did you try to murder me?"

She watched him carefully and his eyes took on that haunted look she had often glimpsed. He was a man under great strain. "No. You must believe that even if you believe nothing else about me, Diana."

In the gilded and mirrored restroom, she seated herself in a Limoges silk chair and lit up a cigarette, ignoring the uniformed woman who sat at the pink marbled table, ready to pass out fluffy monogrammed hand towels. White snapdragons hung in huge wicker baskets suspended at either side of the makeup mirror. Diana stared at her reflection, seeing a beautiful woman with smoldering brown eyes and honeyed hair caught up in curls by a pearl and diamond tiara.

Can I do it? she asked herself between puffs on her Gitanes. *Can I turn David in? He is not only a thief, he may well be a murderer.*

But, Jesus Christ, she loved him!

She wanted to howl in outraged pain. She wanted to do something primitive and childish, like throw an ashtray.

Instead, she smashed out her half-smoked cigarette in the glass ashtray and returned to the dining room. Across the crowded room, David saw her and began making his way toward her, stopping here and there to reply to greetings. He was so handsome, she thought, and smooth.

And conniving?

He put his hand at the small of her back, and his

touch sizzled through her gown. He inclined his head next to hers and said in that voice she found so seductive, "The dancing is beginning and I want you to lead off with me."

Almost apathetically she let him lead her toward the dance floor. At the same time that the orchestra opened with a fanfare, the dining room's ceiling rolled back as if by magic to reveal the star-studded sky, reminding her of diamonds on black velvet. Half a moon hung amid the stars, silver and mysterious. All of a sudden, a fantastic fireworks display erupted overhead. The guests breathed "Oohs" and "Ahhhs" and applauded wildly.

The orchestra fanfare slid into a romantic rendition of "Stardust" and David took her in his arms. For a precious moment, it was only the two of them, alone and somewhere far away. Then other couples began to drift onto the dance floor, destroying her illusion.

"Would you mind if I returned you to your chair, love? I still have to arrange some last-minute details on tomorrow's festivities with the hotel manager." He nodded toward a portly dignified man, who stood in a side doorway.

Before she could protest, he escorted her back to the table and told Tom, "Estevez, I'm going to leave my most valued possession in your keeping for a few moments. Please don't try to steal her from me."

She glanced at her wristwatch. It was ten of nine. *Nine.* So that was what the number represented, the time of the meeting.

His thoughtful gaze on David, who was weaving his way to the side door, Tom said, "I could use a smoke. Let's go outside."

She knew what Tom wanted to know and she still wasn't certain what she would tell him. With reluctant steps she let him lead her from the Grande Salon. At her ear, he said harshly, "You know he's getting ready to turn the paintings? When? Tonight? Tomorrow?"

She flicked a glance at Tom and said calmly, "I don't know anything."

"He's already gone, isn't he?" Above his Hispanic's arched nose, his brows met in a furrowed line that perfectly expressed his disgust. "When will you admit that he tried to kill you?"

At the doorway, she paused and murmured, "I don't think *he* did." She brushed the back of her hand across her forehead. She was so confused. "I don't know who did—or why—but I don't believe it was David."

"Do you really believe anything decent and honorable can come out of your love for him? Don't you realize that one day your love will turn to hate?"

Pushing open the door before he could open it for her, she said, "I'm not like my grandmother or your Natalie, Tom. I won't let prejudice destroy my love."

In the mirrored and palm-potted lobby, they ran into Greg and Anne, who was adjusting the shawl Diana had loaned her over her hair. "I took about all of those stuffy, pompous asses I could," she said. "We're going outside for a breath of fresh air."

The doorman opened the glass door for them, and Anne led the way out onto the broad front terrace, where taxis and limos were arriving and departing.

Then it happened, suddenly and unexpectedly. Diana thought it was the backfiring of a car, but in the same split-second, the white and gold lace shawl over Anne's head was instantly sprayed with bright red blood. Greg caught her as she collapsed. "My God!" he yelled.

At the same moment, Tom shoved Diana back into the shadows of the entrance arch, but not before she saw that Anne's scalp had peeled back from her skull, revealing its contents.

She fought to get through the gaping bystanders who were gathering around Anne's body, but he held her firm, pinning her shoulders against the stone wall. "Listen to me, Diana!" He shook her with gentle impatience. "It's too late to help her. But that shot was meant for you. She was wearing your shawl. Whoever fired it thought you were tailing David. Now where did he go?"

She bit her lip until it hurt, and his stony brown eyes glared at her. "I thought you told me you were a professional."

He turned away, but she grabbed at his tux sleeve. She knew he was right. She had a job to do. With tears in her eyes, she rasped, "Promise you won't harm him."

"You have my word."

She looked deep into his eyes and she believed him. "The wharf . . . warehouse 112."

He released her and loped down the entrance steps, taking two at a time. As she pushed her way through the crowd surrounding Greg, who was weeping over Anne's body, she knew with a sickening horror what she had done. David, his soul marked by the terror of Dachau, would never surrender to be imprisoned. She had delivered him up to his death sentence.

39

July 7th

The night was warm and waiting, seemingly expectant as a new bride. David pressed his arm against the VP70 automatic in his armpit, a reassuring cold metal. In one hand, he held a rolled canvas. Behind him, he heard footsteps, and he melted into the warehouse's shadows. It was Gaillard. He toted an Israeli-made UZI Model B, probably the most respected weapon worldwide and used even by the U.S. Secret Service.

The man was panting. "The de Revillon woman . . . I warned you . . . she was planning on following you . . . she could have blown it all . . . I had to take her out."

Diana . . . dead! A vein pumped furiously in David's throat. He swallowed the salty taste flooding his mouth, feeling on its heels a cold rage rocketing through his body, coiling in his belly and snaking through his veins. He wanted to tear the bearded man into a thousand pieces of bone and tendon and flesh.

"Back me up," he told Gaillard in a controlled voice. Retribution would come later.

He switched on the lights and the overhead fluorescent tubes flickered, then focused a steady blue glare

275

onto the boxes, crates, and cartons stacked in the aisles below. "I'm here, St. Giles."

After a moment, the German drug king stepped out from behind a large crate. He was dapper in a cream-colored three-piece suit. Gold glittered in the open neck of his ruffled shirt and on both wrists and his fingers. Next to him was one of his lieutenants, a tough-looking man with a face badly scarred by acne. In the crook of his arm rested an AK-47.

David inventoried St. Giles. So this was the man who placed no value on human life, only on art master-pieces. He was short, but his smile announced cocky assurance. Besides his obsession with great paintings, David knew the man had another bizarre obsession—Adolf Hitler.

"You have the paintings, Mendel?"

"You have the snow, St. Giles?"

St. Giles jerked his head toward a wooden crate marked "Cheese." "Right there. We've altered the sides of the boxes to provide space for the coke." He nodded toward a crowbar by the crate. "Give the crate a few whacks with that, and it's all yours."

"Clever," David said. "I have Monet's *Sunrise* here." He held up the canvas tube. "The rest are stored behind one of the bulkhead plates of my yacht."

"Clever," St. Giles mocked. "Just in case we didn't come through with the coke?"

David shrugged. "A small enough precaution. Give the plate's bolts a quick wrench," he said, returning St. Giles's mockery, "and it's all yours."

"No, it isn't," Tom said coldly from behind him.

David pivoted. Tom held a .357 magnum in his hand. "You don't give up, do you, Estevez?"

"Nope. You two assholes—" he motioned with his pistol toward St. Giles and his rifle-toting lieutenant,

"—step away very slowly from those boxes. Now, lay down your rifle—gently!"

The lieutenant leaned over to place the AK-47 some feet away. Satisfied, Tom said, "If the three of you would care to come with—"

Before he could finish, his white ruffled tux shirt was instantly dyed crimson. He took two steps backward, fell to his knees and toppled face forward onto the concrete.

At the sound of the rifle shot, coming from a far corner, David dropped the rolled canvas and dove behind an aisle of fifty-kilo flour sacks. So, St. Giles had brought *two* lieutenants with him.

"Your friend should have known better!" St. Giles shouted, his voice manic with triumphant laughter. "A wise man always considers all the possibilities, eh, Mendel, my fine Jew swine!"

That brief instant of taunting allowed David to get off a quick shot—and the man closest to St. Giles went down, clutching a red gash in his stomach. One more to go, and then St. Giles. Unfortunately, Mossad wanted him alive.

David glanced over his shoulder to check on Gaillard and found that the Mossad member had taken a hit square in the face. There was nothing left of it to identify him as Gaillard except for the remnants of beard flecked with flesh. *"Vengeance is mine, I will repay,"* sayeth the Lord.

On hands and knees, David edged toward the light switch. He passed Estevez, lying in the slowly spreading puddle of his blood. David figured he had a chance in the dark, and he had six more shots in the clip against a bolt-action rifle and the AK.

Suddenly, he was down on the floor himself, shot. A bullet had tunneled through his thigh. Not bad, clean through. No bone damage. He was up again, running. The sound of his breathing was loud, too damned loud. He stumbled, losing control of his leg as shock began to hit him. Hardly the expertise he had been taught in the Mossad training camps.

He fired instinctively and was pleased to see out of the corner of his eye the remaining lieutenant crumple. Then a bullet punched a flour sack near him, and the fine powder dusted his hair, momentarily blinding him.

"David!" God, that was Diana's voice! A warning scream that sent him sliding belly first along the concrete. His eyes slashed over to where she crouched, at the same spot where he had been two minutes earlier. Flour splotched her black velvet dress.

"Get out of here, Diana!" he shouted.

She snatched up something, maybe her tiara. As she scrambled for cover behind a stack of desk-size cartons, shots puckered the dust in the wake of her footsteps. Then behind him, St. Giles's cocky, bantam-rooster laughter erupted. "You are a fool, Mendel!"

David looked over his shoulder. At the end of the next aisle, not fifteen meters away, St. Giles stood with his other lieutenant's rifle aimed straight at David's chest.

"Toss that pistol—far away—where I can see it," St. Giles ordered. "And stand up, slowly."

For a fleeting second, David leaned his forehead against the concrete floor. Then, taking a deep steadying breath, he tossed out his VP70, hearing its knell-ringing clatter.

"Don't do it, David!" Diana screamed.

He stood up, raising his hands. Behind him, Diana shouted, "Listen to me! I've got the *Sunrise* with me. You must want it awfully badly to risk all this. Let David go or I rip it to shreds."

Silence. Then, St. Giles yelled, "I don't believe you'll do it!"

She waved it over her head. Then, with some difficulty, she unfurled the painting and struggled to her feet, using the canvas like a shield. St. Giles stood at the end of the next aisle, his rifle still aimed at David. "Watch me," she told St. Giles and positioned her hands on the canvas, as though she were about to rip it down its center.

"No!" the crazed drug king shouted.

That moment of distraction gave David his opportunity, and he sprang at St. Giles. The little man raised the rifle and fired. The shot went wide, and David's shoulder slammed into St. Giles's stomach. Both of them crashed to the ground. St. Giles's fist caught David in the jaw, and he grunted, losing his grip on the man's wrist. St. Giles rolled far enough to get his own hands around David's throat, squeezing, squeezing. David's vision blurred.

Then something roared in his ears, and the pressure lessened at his throat. His vision cleared sufficiently to watch St. Giles's crumple sideways. The man's expression faded like a TV picture. Glacially, he crumpled backward.

For a full sixty seconds, David sat there, trying to get his breath back. Gradually, he became aware of Diana standing over him. Estevez's .357 dangled from her fingers.

Wearily, he looked up. "The man there—St. Giles— is more than a drug dealer. He's the head of a Neo-Nazi organization that assassinates Jews. Mossad—Jewish intelligence—has been after him."

Her eyes widened, and he saw astonished enlightenment reflected there. "You're with Mossad." It was a statement, not a question.

"Yes."

Tears glistened in her eyes. "They killed Anne," she whispered. She wiped her flour-and-dirt-dusted face with the back of her arm, then cried, "Tom?!"

Dropping the pistol, she ran back to where Tom lay. She knelt and, weeping, cradled his head in her arms, "Damn you, Tom, you're too tough to die!"

"What's going on here?"

David looked up to see a blue-uniformed night watchman standing in the doorway. The mustachioed man's gaze fell on the bodies scattered across the floor. *"Dio mio!"* He dropped his flashlight and rapidly genuflected.

"Get an ambulance!" David snapped. "And call the *policia.*"

After the night watchman scurried away, David hauled himself shakily to his feet. His pants leg was blood-soaked. The wounded leg felt like shrapnel was exploding through it with every step he took. He limped over to where Diana knelt sobbing over Tom.

The narc's lids fluttered but did not open. In the vast warehouse, his voice was raspy and faint. "What the hell was Mossad going to do with the paintings and the drugs, anyway, Mendel?"

Cautiously, he hunched down opposite Diana. "See to it that the paintings were discovered stashed somewhere in Paris," he told the narc. He took off his coat and covered Estevez's blood-soaked torso. "You're going to make it, Estevez."

"And the drugs?"

"The local authorities get the drugs. All we want is St. Giles and the names of the men in his organization."

Estevez opened his eyes and managed a wink. "Now

that the drug ring is busted, Mendel, I think I should get the girl.''

Diana bent over him and kissed his beard-shadowed jaw. ''You tough old fart, you'd run off any female who gave the slightest hint of moving in on you.''

''Try me,'' he growled.

In the distance, David heard the screaming of sirens. With a grunt of pain, he rose and went to collect his pistol. Like the night watchman, his gaze took in the corpses strewn over the warehouse. Israeli diplomats were going to have some smoothing over to do there in Sardinia.

''This the place?'' a paramedic shouted from the doorway.

''Holy Mother!'' the paramedic behind him said. ''The place looks like an emergency morgue.''

''Here!'' Diana cried. ''This man's alive!''

With an efficiency astonishing for such an antiquated island, one paramedic took Estevez's blood pressure and pulse while the other started an IV in his hand. Then they began loading him on the stretcher.

David accompanied Diana as she walked beside the stretcher, her hand on Estevez's sleeve. After Estevez was loaded into a World War I–vintage ambulance, she buried her face in her hands. ''Such stupidity!'' she muttered.

David drew her into his arms and pressed her head against his chest. ''It's all over, love,'' he murmured, stroking the strands of hair that had escaped her hairpins.

She lifted her head and fixed him with wounded amber-brown eyes. ''What happens now?''

''I wait for the police. You return to the hotel. There's no need for you to get—''

''That's not what I meant, David.''

He sighed. "I know what you mean, love. It won't work. There's no room in my life for anything but the Jewish struggle for survival."

She was crying. "I don't care. I'll take whatever is left over."

Taking her face between his hands, he kissed her fiercely. Then he released her. "Go back to your father, to the United States. You've always been more of an American than a European. You're Diana Dickinson." He pushed her away. He would learn to live with the pain of her absence. "Go on."

She clung to his hand. "Will I ever see you again?"

"Yes, some day." She looked at him with haggard eyes, as he added, "People change, attitudes change. I'll find you then."

She backed away, one step, then another, tears streaming down her cheeks, her chin quivering. Then she turned and, tawny-gold head held high, walked out of the warehouse.

After she was gone, he went over and almost reverently picked up the Monet canvas. In the fluorescent lighting, the Impressionist's *Rising Sun* sparkled with brilliant promise.

Printed in the United States
by Baker & Taylor Publisher Services